DESERT MAGNOLIA

DEDRA L. STEVENSON

Blue Jinni Media

Desert Magnolia

Blue Jinni Media
https://bluejinnimedia.com

AUTHOR'S NOTE

Writing this book was very personal, and many of its original pages are tear stained. I'm very satisfied, however, to have written something that's dedicated to both sides of my nature, my Southern beginnings and my current life in the Middle East.

As the world becomes more divided, I feel that we all need to take a moment to take stock of our role in it all. We need to sincerely ask ourselves if we are an instrument of hatred and division, or an instrument of good, peace and human solidarity.

Desert Magnolia is, in many ways, a tragic tale, but serves as an example of how fences can be mended and even those who consider themselves mortal enemies can become friends. No matter the color of our skin, our blood is red, and it's the same all over the world. Isn't it time for us to come together as one human family?

This book, as all my books, wouldn't be possible without the help of my partner at Blue Jinni Media, Rodney W. Harper. His friendship and his support is deeply appreciated, as I know that there's no one in the world who would have helped me as he has, and that means the world to me.

Wishing love and light to everyone.

1

PEOPLE ARE THE SAME

Daniella stepped off the plane a few weeks ago. She was new to the Middle East... New anywhere, really. She had recently arrived in Sharjah with her husband and her infant son. The couple were both still in their early twenties, and it was the first time she'd ever been out of the United States, which made Daniella feel more vulnerable than she'd ever felt in her life, but she trusted in her husband very much, and didn't let her thoughts turn negative at all, or at least she tried.

Many of her friends had bombarded her with cautionary tales before her trip. "Haven't you ever seen 'Not Without My Daughter?'" became the question that blurted out of all of their lips, and she had become tired of it. Her husband was a kind man, and in her heart, she knew he would not do anything horrid to her. He simply wasn't capable of it. Of course, in the mind of any reasonable individual, there's this nagging doubt that keeps repeating a single mantra, *what if they're right?* In spite of this fear, there was an even bigger one that had to be addressed first and foremost—the fear of doing nothing. Her greatest fear in life was ending up living in the same town, all of her life, and living the programmed life that everyone expected her to live.

Coming from a small town in Georgia, she had always felt small in the grand scheme of things, as the furthest she'd ever travelled was to Orlando, Florida. Her husband Faisal, and most of his friends had travelled significantly more, but then again, most Americans hadn't travelled internationally, so she wasn't so different from her peers. She often wondered why Americans travelled so little, but thought perhaps it's because most Americans see the United States as being the world in itself, making those who are lucky enough to live there have no need of travelling outside, or perhaps they always felt threatened, or they were simply unable to afford it. Nevertheless, she had always felt like a square peg in a round hole in Georgia and felt fortunate to be on her first international adventure. When the time came to board the plane, she resolved herself to being excited about it, and why not? If she stayed in the USA, she might never go anywhere, so no matter what happened, she was ready for a change.

Indeed a change it was! Struggling to settle into this strange world with her husband wasn't easy at first. There were no American comforts around. The United Arab Emirates was still a young country, so there were no malls or movie theaters, and no English television except for after 5 pm, and even that was only on one channel. Additionally, Faisal's mother, Sofia, wasn't exactly her biggest fan. She was a very traditional woman, so giving up her precious son to another woman was hard for her, and the fact that Daniella was American made it even harder. Daniella found it noteworthy to remember that Sofia had never met any Americans before her, so she was fearful of this marriage and how it may pull Faisal from his native customs. Sophia would have much preferred for him to marry from his own kind.

All in all, the entire acclimation process was hard for everyone, but Daniella managed mostly by finding comfort in the cultural similarities, not the differences. These people were not so different from Georgians. They believed in strong family ties, big homes and big meals. They sipped on their hot tea just as pleasurably as Southerners enjoyed their iced tea. However, dealing with the matriarch of the family was definitely one of the similarities that Daniella struggled with, even though that was also a trait that Emiratis shared with Southerners. Looking back, Daniella wondered what Southern family didn't have a matriarch that was the final word on almost everything?

There was one major advantage, however. Due to the differences in labor arrangements, life in the Middle East afforded Daniella something that she never thought she'd have—a maid. Young ladies from India, Sri Lanka and the Philippines came there to work for a few years as a maid due to the fact that the maid's salary there was higher than what they could earn in their own country. Often, one often found these girls working for a few years, supporting their entire families on their seemingly meager earnings. It wouldn't be long before Daniella was to be blessed with this much-needed help.

Ironically, this help was due to arrive on a day when Daniella was doing a load of laundry under the watchful eye of her mother-in-law, Sofia. Sofia stood there, looking stern in her black Abaya and Sheyla, the traditional clothing of Gulf Arab women. The Abaya is a long cloak-like garment that many Muslim women wear over their clothes, and the Sheyla is loosely worn over the hair. The Abaya's style underwent many changes over the years, going from the stern, plain and strict style to the crystal and embroidery laden elegant fashion statement that it is today. Sofia never went for the stylish and beautiful varieties, always sticking with the strict and plain ultra religious style, always covered in plain black from head to toe, with the Abaya perched on her head, revealing no shape whatsoever. She watched over Daniella separating the colors from the whites and said, "When you get your new girl, you need to buy a new machine you know."

Daniella was very taken back by this. After all, finances were not exactly easy, as they had just paid so much to move there.

"Why should I do that? We're already short of money." Daniella said, in her broken Arabic.

Sofia looked smug and replied, "You don't want your clothes mixing with the clothes of these girls! The new machine is for your new girl. They come from the jungles, you know."

Daniella looked stunned. She couldn't believe her ears. After all, she'd come from a small town in Georgia, where the word, "Nigger" was a household word. Still feeling shocked; she reverted to a tried-and-true method of dealing with the old folks in her hometown. She simply let her feel right and conceded, because that's everything any matriarch wants, to feel that her will is being done.

"Yes Ma'am, you're right. We'll do that right away."

Sofia was satisfied with this and nodded, then turned, whipping her Abaya in the wind, and headed back to her house. Daniella looked back at the sunset and knew that it was almost time for Maghrib, the sunset prayer. Moments later, the Aydan, the Muslim call to prayer, chimed out of the minarets of every Mosque in town. She laughed to herself when she remembered Sofia.

She closed her eyes to really absorb the sound. The beautiful sound of the Aydan was always enchanting, and somehow, no matter how she felt, the sound of it always comforted her. Once it was done, she opened her eyes, with new courage in her heart.

"Ok, here we go." Daniella sighed.

Just then, Faisal approached with their new housemaid, Fahani, who only had the clothes on her back, and smelled a bit strong, as though she hadn't showered. Daniella looked her over, and in her heart she knew that this was one more person in her life that she'd have to look after.

"Welcome home Fahani."

The girl looked up at her and smiled with relief. *Perhaps she had been expecting someone like Sofia*, Daniella thought. Just the thought of that made her smile.

2

THE NEWS

Many years later, Daniella, now a successful publisher throughout the Middle East, made her way to her office to start a new day. The UAE had changed a lot since the early days, and now every comfort of the West was available, the biggest malls, the biggest fun parks, and restaurants of every cuisine imaginable. As she was driven down Sheik Zayed Road, she enjoyed the familiar sights of men and women in business attire, scurrying to work, and the sights of the newest supersized buildings that were being constructed. She had built a comfortable and fulfilling life in this prosperous city, and for the most part, she was very happy.

However, this day was not to be like others; this day that would teach her that skeletons have a way of not wanting to stay in closets. After opening her curtains a little wider and setting down her morning coffee, Daniella fired up her Macbook Pro and checked her email accounts as usual, only to be shocked by the international headline story of the morning, which had been sent to her by many of her friends. Her face became white, and her mouth hung open in shock as she read.

Hate Crime in Georgia

Ross Pierce II, the millionaire entrepreneur, found beaten to death behind a nightclub on the outskirts of Atlanta. Leo Pierce has been arrested for the crime, and the investigation continues.

After shaking her head and recovering her senses, she decided to forget about the office for a little while and go somewhere to think about what she'd read. She hurried back down to her car to find her driver still there.

"Take me to the Jumeirah Beach Park," she said as she entered the back seat.

"Right away Madame." He blurted as he closed the door behind her.

When she reached the park, she walked directly to the beach, took off her shoes, and enjoyed the warm, comforting feeling of the sand between her toes. *Daddy's dead?* She couldn't get the thought out of her head as she walked along the coast, breathing in the gulf air. *How could he be dead?* She thought as she walked along. Ross always seemed invincible to her. After a short while, she knew that it was time to get back to work. The breather had done her good, but she really needed longer to process such shocking news. Processing it all would have to wait.

As her driver stopped in front of her office building, she got out of the car to find a reporter for the Island Channel waiting. A cameraman who was filming everything followed the reporter.

"Ms. Suleiman, I'm Natasha Roman from the Island Channel, and I'd love to get a statement from you about your father's death. Your cousin is being accused of his murder. Do you think that he did it?"

Daniella looked at her, completely appalled, then turned her back and stormed towards her office. Behind her, she heard Ms. Roman shouting,

"Oh come on! Just one statement!"

Daniella's driver forced Ms. Roman away. Keeping his cool at all times, he simply stated,

"Ms. Sulieman has no comment. Leave this area now and don't make me call the police."

"Fine!" barked Natasha as she stamped away. Before she got too far away, she turned back and asked the driver, "Do you think he did it?" The driver said, "Guess we'll have to wait and see. Now go on and get out of here."

Meanwhile in her office, Daniella sat quietly at her desk, peering out the window, watching Natasha get back into the news van. Once she saw the van leave, she stood up to enjoy the view of the Dubai landscape, and it soothed her to see the tall skyscrapers of unique modern designs such as the Burj Khalifa speckled throughout the patches of green parks, grand mosques, date trees, and blue swimming pools with fountains under a blue sky. The sun was strong, and she closed her eyes for a moment, drinking in the warmth on her skin. Her assistant walked in and broke her concentration.

"Do you need anything from me, Ma'am?"

Daniella turned to face her, pointing to the location of the previous spectacle outside. "I don't know if I'll be able to always face *that* when I get to work. Good heavens! It's really something how this has all been blown out of proportion. It's viral."

Her assistant, Mimi, a Philipino, nodded in agreement and added, "Your father was a controversial man. Rich, unscrupulous, one of the South's last plantation owners..."

She sounded as if she was reading that straight off of an article, and in fact, she was quoting one of them verbatim. Daniella looked back to spy the ipad in her hand and realized that she'd been reading from an article on the front page of one of the major search sites.

Daniella laughed sarcastically and replied, "Honey, I wish that's all that he'd ever done wrong. You see, in the Deep South, everything is so hush-hush. No one but family insiders would know the truth."

Mimi felt sympathetic, but Daniella knew that Mimi felt uncomfortable with displays of affection, so she didn't know what to say in this situation. Mimi simply patted her on the back, saying, "Everything will be fine...Well, if that'll be all Ma'am."

Daniella dryly replied, "Yes of course. Please hold my calls. I need to clear my head before the meeting at 12."

Mimi replied, "Yes Ma'am."

After she walked out and closed the door, Daniella tried to center herself. Poor Mimi wasn't very good at dealing with emotional situations. She had always been a great assistant, and very hard working, but she was a little cold and unsure about herself when it came to the drama. Daniella sat in her beautiful office and closed her eyes, breathing deeply. As much as she tried, she could only think of all the demons of the past that she'd left behind in Georgia. There was so much history there—the happy memories of childhood mixed with the horrific memories of her young adult years.

Somehow, as if via a psychic vibe, she could sense that a phone call from someone was coming. Minutes later, the phone rang, as she had predicted. She picked it up with a sense of dread, as she looked down to see that the number was an American number, with a Georgia area code. It was Katie, her step-grandmother, one of the instigators of Daniella's departure from Georgia all those years ago. She reluctantly answered, not sure of what she'd hear after more than a decade of zero contact. On the other end, she heard, " Danny! Is that you Baby?"

Daniella replied, "Grandma?"

Digging her nails into the desk, she asked, "How are you? It's been a long time."

Katie started to explain how the police took Leo away and how sad that made her. She carried on to describe the entire event in great detail, even Ross's murder. Daniella felt her heart beating fast because dealing with all the news, the call, and the reality of what had happened was overwhelming. First, she hadn't heard from Katie in years, and now she was describing one of the most traumatic pieces of news that she'd dealt with since childhood. Daniella stopped her there, "Grandma, I know you're only filling me in, but can I know exactly why you're calling me now? I know you must want something from me. "

Katie became a bit silent, exhaled, then got to the point. "I want you to come home, Danny. Your cousin needs you now. I know he's been a handful, but he's in real trouble! They'll execute him if he gets convicted of this."

Daniella replied, "A handful? That's a laugh! So that's what this is all about?

You want me to come back to a home that kicked me out all those years back, to help you, to help him? What about Brian? Why can't he do it?"

"You know your brother. Brian won't come. He's traveling the world with his family and he ain't returned any of our phone calls in years. Please, Danny. This is no time for grudges. We're still your blood, young lady. I want you to remember that. We're all that boy has." Katie blurted.

"Let me call you back tonight, OK?" Daniella replied.

Katie paused, "OK but please don't take long. The initial

hearing is in two weeks and no one here knows how to help him. It looks bad, really bad."

"I understand Grandma. I'll talk to you later OK. I have to work now." Daniella ended the phone call, still hearing Katie squawking, and looked out the window again.

She thought about the past and the events that had driven her away in the first place. Why has all this happened now? After she was happy and her life was finally in place? Her memory ran deep into the past, to days that she'd hoped she'd never have to think of again, memories that she'd tried desperately to forget. After all, it wasn't everyone who had to witness the terrible things that she had witnessed as a child. People had gone completely crazy over far less.

Her mind wandered...Daniella had been the unfortunate victim of many instances of her mother's increasingly unstable mental behavior, even being forced to witness her sexual misconduct with other men. Carol had made Daniella her accomplice and her confidant, allowing her to witness some of her adultery, often locking her in cheap hotel bathrooms while being forced to hear everything, every nasty detail. Carol never knew it, but Daniella had suffered more than she knew at the hands of these drunken beasts. Sometimes they would try to touch her, a small child, and one had succeeded, and this was the subject of many therapy sessions. Recognizing this destructive thought pattern, Daniella shook her head in disbelief that such gut-wrenching memories were daring to creep up in her head today. *NO! NO! NO! I will not think of that today! I'm happy and I have a family that loves me. That's all that matters. Damn them.* She thought, then hissed through her teeth, "I'm NOT going to be defined by the past. I make my future, only me."

Daniella had many inspirational mantras that she often used to get through the tough days; however, one memory refused to be suppressed, because it was one of the worst, and it had more to do with shaping her destiny than any. Her mind took her back, many years ago, as she heard her parents fighting as they did almost every day.

She was seven years old and Leo was four. Leo was her cousin, but since a tragic car accident had claimed the lives of his parents when he was only 3 years old, Ross and Carol agreed to adopt him.

Leo's father was Ross's brother, Thornton Pierce; so naturally, Ross felt it was his duty to adopt Leo. Leo even called him Daddy and thought of Daniella as his sister. Daniella already had an older half-brother, Brian, but since he wasn't a true born Pierce, as he was Carol's son from a previous marriage, he never felt as though he was a real member of the family, and neither did Ross. When Brian was 9 years old, Ross sent him to a boarding school in England under the pretense that he was doing it for the boy's own good.

Ross was a wealthy man, and with Thornton gone, he was sole heir to the Pierce fortune, and a successful businessman in his own right. He owned a group of companies in town, consisting of a furniture store, petrol stations, restaurants, cotton farms, cattle farms, and peach farms.

His wife, Carol, was a simple country girl who'd never even graduated from high school. When Ross had come into her life, she thought that all of her dreams came true because he had money. Years later, Carol realized the hard way that money wasn't the solution to everything, and life with a selfish and spoiled heir to a family fortune wasn't all it was cracked up to be. Ross married her because she was simple. He thought that controlling her would be easy, and it would be nice to have a woman who would bend to his every whim and never question his reasoning.. Carol thought they had married for love, and never understood his real reasons, so they constantly fought, leaving young Daniella and Leo to raise themselves for the most part.

Their normal fighting had grown commonplace, but this day was particularly violent, and Daniella couldn't help but think of the gun she'd seen her mother put in her purse the night before. She was worried something horrible would happen soon, particularly because her mother's prescription drug addiction mixed with the alcohol, was driving Carol to consider unspeakable actions.

Carol was particularly drunk, wasted in fact, chasing down the booze with a few pills from her pharmaceutical cocktail, and she had a gun. Ross was being extra abusive, emotionally as well as physically. Daniella was keeping Leo from understanding what was going on by encouraging him to swing as high as he could on the swing set. They should have gone inside long ago, but Daniella had spent the entire morning coming up with one game after another for Leo. She was exhausted, and the only thing she wanted to do was go to her room and play like normal little girls played, but Leo would be all alone. "Come on Leo! Let me see how high you can go!"

Leo was laughing and giggling, as he swung higher to please his cousin and adopted sister. Their fun was abruptly interrupted by the crash of a door being flung open, and suddenly, Ross chased Carol out of the door, wearing only his underwear, calling her every foul name he could muster. "Get the Fuck back in the House Bitch! That's all we need, for the whole world to hear about your whoring ways!"

He grabbed her by the arm and forced her back in the

house. By the sound of it, he pushed her down on the floor. Carol was wailing, and Ross was still spewing demoralization.

"Get up Bitch! Or stay down there and open your legs again! Open your legs for every man in the town like you always do! Fuck you! Fuck you Bitch!"

Minutes later, as the kids tried to play and ignore the sounds of the screaming, the gun fired five times. Carol didn't have to be a great shot to hit Ross so many times at such close range. She managed to hit him four times and missed once. When the gunshots went off, Leo fell to the ground and started crying, and both kids looked towards the house in alarm. Daniella couldn't cry because she knew that Leo would cry harder if he saw her lose control, and somehow she knew that if she let herself get scared, Leo would possibly take off running, so she held her emotions inside and let herself go numb.

Daniella said, "Stay right here. Don't you dare move a muscle. I'm gonna see what happened."

Leo sat there in one spot, petrified and not responding to anything Daniella was saying. She snapped her fingers and barked "Leo! Pay attention to me!"

He turned his head to her slowly, and at least she knew he was paying attention now.

"I'm gonna go in and see what's going on, but I need you to be a good boy and stay right here, OK?"

He nodded, still silent, but at least she knew that he was absorbing her words now, so she said, "Ok, good job. I'll be right back. I promise."

Poor Leo, she thought. He was so small, and unfortunately, he had almost never been able to enjoy a normal childhood. First his parents died, and then he had to hear the never-ending fights. The only time he ever got to play and act like a regular kid was with his sister. Now Daniella was right there, looking after him again, being the only real mother figure he'd ever known.

As she made her way inside, she was horrified to see her father crawling on the floor, bloodied from head to toe, looking so bad that Daniella thought for sure that he'd die from this. Ross crawled to the phone and dialed 911. With a feeble voice, he said, "Please help me. I've been shot."

Carol was screaming, with the gun still in her hand. "You son of a bitch! Look what you made me do!!"

She swept around and noticed that Daniella was standing in the doorway, stunned and motionless. Carol threw her own hand around her mouth as she instinctively realized that she'd cursed in front of her daughter.

To smooth it all over, she said, "Baby, he hurt me. You saw the bruises on Mama, didn't you? He hated me and cheated on me Honey, in the worst way. I couldn't let him hurt me anymore, or hurt you or your cousin. You believe me, don't you Baby?"

Ross passed out with the phone still in his hand. Carol's hands were trembling and tears were pouring down her face as she held the gun to her own head. Daniella frowned, her green eyes darkened, and she turned away to walk out the door, grabbing Leo by the hand to quickly take him across the street to the only place she could think of. She'd had enough.

She made her way down the street, and cut around to a dirt road that led to a trailer park. Ross had always told her to stay away from the "trailer park trash" area, but Daniella remembered her Mama being buddies with a woman there and being taken to play there from time to time. She finally reached the pink trailer that she knew. This was the home of the woman Carol had been spending her time with, and not for the cheap cosmetics that she sold, but for her stash of "happy candy", as Carol called it. The woman's name was Stella, a chubby countrywoman, complete with a baby on her hip. She answered the door and said while smacking on a chunk of gum, "Hey kids. What are y'all doing over here by yourself? Where's your Mama?"

Daniella paused and muttered, "Our Mama shot our Daddy just now. Can we stay here until someone comes to get us?"

Stella's jaw dropped. Then, like a good Southern neighbor, she murmured, "Ok babies. Sure you can stay here. Come on in." Leo started crying, with Daniella holding him close.

Daniella's train of thought was interrupted as she heard a knock at the door, snapping her back into the present day. It's Mimi. "Ma'am, your appointment is here."

"I said that I didn't want to see anyone for at least two hours! Please get rid of him. I need to relax and I can't seem to."

Mimi, unnerved, backed up to the door and replied, "Yes Ma'am, right away."

Why did I come in today? Daniella thought. As Mimi left, Daniella felt relieved that she hadn't seen the tears in her eyes. She thought about her father and how he didn't seem to benefit from the second chance at life that he was given. She attempted to silence her mind and tried to relax again, but her thoughts kept wandering. The painful memories of the past refused to be silenced, and finding out that her father had been murdered seemed to have released a floodgate of buried emotion.

She'd tried to bury her emotions deeply throughout the years, with food, cigarettes, or compulsive working habits; and before her conversion to Islam, alcohol, but more recently she'd managed to control this tendency through therapy, good diet and exercise. Many painful childhood memories were due to her belief that she was fat and never good enough to be friends with the popular girls. Ross had contributed tremendously to this condition. She could still hear him say, "No boy is ever gonna like you if you don't lose all that blubber!"

Her thoughts then turned to her mother, Carol. As a child, Daniella never understood what made Carol act so erratically, but years later, events would unfold to reveal that maybe her mother did have reasons for her nervous breakdown.

She remembered the time after the shooting, when her, Leo and Ross were first living in her grandfather's house. Those were the best days of her childhood, the only time she was allowed to be her age.

Her grandfather had left a great legacy in town, as everyone respected Ross Pierce Sr., and even though he'd passed away many years ago, his presence was still felt in their prominent Southern mansion, known to the local residents as Magnolia Manor. Katie was Daniella's step-grandmother, a sweet, well-mannered Southern lady, who always looked well kept, no matter what she was doing or where she went. She could still hear Katie's words. "A lady matches her shoes and bag, and is never caught dead without makeup on! You never know who's gonna be there, even if you're going to the supermarket."

Daniella's blood born grandmother was also a proper lady but had passed away when Daniella was only a year old, so she'd never known her. Katie was the only grandmother on her father's side that she'd ever known, and the short time that she got to live with her was the only time in her childhood that she'd ever felt that she had a mother. Ross was determined to change all that, and her memories brought her to one particular day, the day that seemed to start it all.

Ross had been stomping around the house all that day, yelling about how he needed his own house and how the property across the street would be the perfect spot for it. With his brow furrowed and his eyes darkened, he barked,

"I need my own house! It's just that simple! What do I have to do to get that street cleared?"

Katie explained, "First of all, you don't have the land. Them nigger families have been there for years. Your Daddy has let them rent those shacks as long as I can remember."

Ross looked smug as he maintained, "Well maybe they won't always be living there."

Katie's eyes narrowed, and she asked, "What do you mean by that Ross?"

He shrugged his shoulders and turned his back to her. "Nothing! Just forget it. I need my own house. It's time for us to defend what's ours. It's not just the niggers; it's the Mexicans and anything else that the cat dragged in."

Katie stood there looking at him in a state of shock. She said, "You don't have any idea how crazy you sound right now, do you?"

Ross snapped, "You stay out of my way! That's the end of it!"

"Well, who's gonna do the cooking and cleaning in this fancy new house you wanna build for yourself? I know you won't!" Katie said.

"Danny will," Ross answered.

A devilish smile curled around his lips as he continued, "Yeah. She'll be my chief cook and bottle washer."

"What? She's only a little girl! You can't expect her to do all that!" Katie snapped.

Ross fired back "Yes I can! Get her ready for us. It's gonna take me at least a year to build it, and it's about time she learned womanly duties anyway."

Katie's forehead formed a V shape, and she looked down at her fingers. After a moment's pause, she snapped, "How's she gonna do all that and manage her homework? She's so smart, and she has a real chance to do something with her life. She needs to keep up or she'll never get to college!"

Ross scoffs, "The only thing that girl needs to do is stop getting so fat so she can try to get a husband one day!"

Katie had enough. She turned to walk out, fed up with his nonsense, and said, as she left, "Well I don't think it's right!"

With a scoff, Ross said, "Well, when I want your opinion, I'll give it to you." As she left, Ross put his nose up higher in the air and smirked, feeling very satisfied that he lived to tell Katie what to do.

Little did they know Daniella was around the corner, crouched down, knees pulled up to her chubby chin, and listening to their whole conversation. Tears streamed down her cheek as she held her knees even tighter. Hearing all that made her feel more like one of her father's employees than a daughter. Most little girls were Daddy's special little princess, but not Daniella. She always felt that he resented her.

She snapped out of her remembrance of the past as she heard the Aydan ringing out through the city. Hearing it always made her more centered, as it signified the strength that she'd grown into as a result of embracing a faith that she could believe in strongly, and building a stable family life that looked nothing like her childhood.

Her more relaxed breathing helped realize that she had a lot of work to do and her alone time was over. She looked up to stop any tears from falling, swallowed the bitter sadness, and gathered up her files, keys, phone and bag, then made her way out the door, and down the hall to prepare for prayer before her meeting.

Later that evening, she headed home, and as she opened the door, a sense of emptiness came over her as she realized that she would spend this night alone. Faisal and the kids had already gone to the farm in Al Dhaid, as was their custom when Daniella was faced with a great deal of work. Sometimes, she'd go with them, but this time, they had gone alone to let her work in peace. Faisal hadn't heard yet, so she knew that he'd call as soon as the news got to him. *I could call him and tell him*, she thought, but she didn't want to spoil this trip for her kids. She knew how much they'd been looking forward to it, and tomorrow would always be there.

The apartment was modern and very spacious, and Daniella had worked very hard to fill that space with reminders of how close her family was. Almost every wall had pictures of the kids and locations that they'd visited on their travels. There were flowers everywhere and lovely potted plants near the windows. The space was "breathable", as Daniella put it.

In spite of it all, she felt very lonely, and ever since she'd heard from her grandmother, she'd felt 6 years old again. It was as if all her confidence had been swept out the window. She thought of that as she looked out of her balcony. Then, the solution hit her.

She knew how to cure her loneliness. She called Nay, her best friend in the world. Nay was a tough, confident gal from Chicago, drop dead gorgeous and always very stylishly dressed. She knew something about the South from her aunt that was from Georgia. She even did the funniest imitation of a Southern accent that Danny had ever heard. Every moment spent with Nay was fun, and it wasn't just because she was funny; it was because she was a good, pure-hearted person and a great listener.

Less than an hour after calling her, she heard a knock at the door and her face lit up at the thought of seeing her. As soon as she saw Nay, she grinned and welcomed her inside.

"Hey there Nay Nay! Boy, you are a sight for sore eyes! I'm getting really lonely over here without Faisal and the kids."

Nay chirped, "Well girl, I had to come over here and check on ya, as soon as I heard about your Dad's death. It's all over the net today! Folks are talking about it everywhere."

"Well yeah, it's pretty weird how everyone has blown it out of proportion." Daniella reflected.

She offered Nay something to drink by way of her ever-faithful household help, Fahani.

"Fahani! Fahani!

"Yes Ma'am?" Fahani replies.

"Can you bring Nay and I some coffee and some of those mixed nuts as well?" Daniella asked politely.

Fahani looked squarely at Nay, and with a sarcastic tone, said, "Does Miss Sheenie want some cake too?"

"Girl! Why do you always call me Sheenie?! It's not that hard to pronounce. Shaaa Naayyy Nayyy!" she growled.

Fahani grinned and folded her arms. Daniella laughed and said, "Ok Fahani, go ahead and get some cake too."

Nay furrowed her brow as she caught a glimpse of

Fahani staring at her and said, "Go on now girl! Get out of here. You're gonna make me nervous!"

Fahani left, chuckling to herself.

Nay looked at Daniella squarely in the eye and said, "Ok, now talk to me. Tell me what's on your mind."

Daniella's eyes softened. "I can't stop thinking about him. He never learned from anything. Little Ross and Leo were so close! ... I just can't wrap my brain around it."

She walked over to the window, took a deep breath and told Nay about the time when she saw her father's true nature, a time when she learned just how far Ross was willing to go to get what he wanted. She was eight years old, after the divorce, and after Ross had managed to heal from the gunshot wounds, wounds that had left a "poop" bag on his chest as his intestines healed over a period of four months.

Daniella was 8 years old, and late one evening, she woke to the sound of screaming across the street from her grandparents' home. To her horror, she looked out the window to see four poor shacks on fire and the black families that lived in them in a state of mayhem, screaming and crying. One of the children almost walked in front of a speeding fire truck, but thankfully, her mother pulled her back. The little girl looked at the ground in despair, holding her teddy bear, with tears streaming down her face. Her mother, also crying, tried to be strong and held her close, trying to comfort her the best that she could.

Daniella couldn't believe what was happening. She was grief stricken for the families but was momentarily distracted by the sound of someone bumping a table downstairs. She ran downstairs to see what was going on, to find her father standing in the living room, looking across the street. All the lights were off, and he was sipping on a glass of whiskey.

"Daddy, what's going on? Did all their houses catch on fire?"

Ross replied without even looking back, "Nothing's wrong Danny, go back to bed."

Daniella said, "But Daddy, why did all their houses catch on fire?"

Smugly, Ross looked back at her; his eyes darkened, and then looked towards the window to reply, "Well, you know them niggers and all that oil they use, either in their hair or in their damn food! Hell, they can't get by a day without one of their Kool menthols or a piece of fried chicken. One of them probably lit something on fire by accident."

She peered out the window to see the shocking sight again, the sight of the men crying and screaming for all the belongings that they'd lost and the women silently sobbing and trying to comfort them and the children. Ross took another sip of his whiskey, and to Daniella's horror, she noticed a small smirk creep over his face, and then she knew.

Annoyed by her presence, Ross ordered, "Go on back to bed Danny. There's nothing to see here. You're too young to understand."

"But Daddy!" she objected. "No butts! Get to bed now before I lose my temper!" He said with nostrils flaring.

She knew better than to protest more, so she made her way back upstairs to bed. Once there, she knew it would be impossible to sleep, knowing there were kids her age outside who just lost their whole world, but what could she do? She did what any child would do; she pulled the covers over her head to try to drown it out, but in her mind she knew that this was going to be a long night. Each time she tried to close her eyes, all she saw was the flames burning higher and higher, and all she heard was the screaming children and the wailing women.

As she told Nay about this, Nay's mouth dropped open and her eyes bulged in horror as Daniella had never gone into this much detail with her before. As her forehead crinkled, she shook her head and said, "Oh my God!"

Daniella nodded in full agreement and continued, "Leo slept through the whole thing! He never knew. He and Daddy were always close and Daddy always loved him more than me. Leo could do no wrong. He was Daddy's superstar."

Nay, confused, said, "Well if that's the case, why is Leo on trial for his murder? If anyone had a reason to 'off' him, it's you actually."

Daniella nodded silently at this, and took a deep breath. "Well, there's something I haven't told you... I haven't ever told anyone."

Nay replied, "Oh my God. You're killing me! Do all Southern families have this many secrets?"

Daniella snorted, "Well, I don't think we've got more drama than anyone else. We're just damn good at hiding it."

She went on to explain that her father had hidden a terrible secret all his life. Growing up in a small Southern town made sure of that. No one wanted to tolerate knowing the son of a wealthy Southern gentleman was batting for the other side.

In order to keep the secret, Ross behaved like a typical rich and spoiled Southern boy, showing off his wealth with fancy cars, women, and expensive toys. Women were accessories to him, as he flaunted them in front of the other boys in school. His smokescreen was complete as he fooled everyone in town into believing he was a womanizer, a rich playboy, and not a man who was even remotely interested in other men.

Daniella carried on to explain, "Well, we never knew. No one did. My cousin always looked up to him because he was so powerful and the ladies were so attracted to him. But one day, I guess one of his 'friends' called the house, and there must have been something in his voice. Anyhow, Leo freaked out and attacked him. He chased Daddy down the yard with a baseball bat, threatening to knock his brains out."

Nay paused, then asked, "And, how was your father murdered?"

Daniella looked at her intensely, as it was hard to say the words. "He was beaten to death with a baseball bat. The words 'In God We Trust' was carved into the bat, under an American flag...Well, at least that's what they thought it said."

Nay looked confused and asked, "What do you mean? That's what they thought it said?" Daniella replied, "Well, the police found every piece of the bat on the scene except the word 'Trust'. They looked everywhere they could think of, but no one was able to find it."

Nay shuddered, inhaled deeply, and shook her head. Daniella said, "Honestly, I know my cousin's a redneck, but that doesn't even sound like something he would own! It's a little far-fetched. But, whoever did this, had to have known about the bat incident, so it's gotta be someone who knows us."

Nay replied, "But doesn't everyone in town know ya'll?"

Daniella looked at her with a smirk. "Ha ha, very funny."

Nay said, "Look, here's the thing. I know your family has been horrible to you. They hurt you so much when they kicked you out of their lives, but I think you've got a serious need for closure here. If you don't go back, I'm afraid you'll regret it, won't you?"

Daniella smiled, "There's a reason you're my best friend."

Nay replied, "Damn straight! Life's a potluck baby. You never know what's coming to the table."

3

GOING HOME

As Daniella relaxed on the 14 hour plane ride home, she really tried to forget the past for a little while and just get comfortable. After all, the first-class seat was very luxurious. She stretched out and decided to flip through the selection of movies on board. *Hopefully, they have something funny*, she thought. Before she could start watching movies though, she'd have to switch off her phone, she reckoned, so she reached for it, and was delighted to find a message from Faisal. It read, "Call me as soon as you get there. I love you. Be strong and everything will be alright."

The message made her happy, but it made her feel a momentary tinge of sadness for how much she was going to miss Faisal and her kids. Ahmed, Abdullah, and Leila were surely going to be distraught when they heard about what's really going on. Or so she thought, but then again, they've never even met a single person from Daniella's family, not one. She often felt that her kids must believe she'd dropped out of the air or was adopted, as they'd never seen any evidence that she'd come from anywhere.

Dismissing the thought for now, she got comfortable in

her chair and tried to enjoy the luxury of her surroundings; however, it was difficult. She kept on remembering times in the past, times when Leo seemed like the sweetest little boy in the world. She remembered when she was about 12 years old and in charge of the cooking and cleaning in her Dad's home. He had finally gotten his way and convinced her that a good girl would help her father out with the new house, rather than being a baby about it. There would be no time for playing or hanging out with friends, especially since Ross saw all of her companions as unworthy anyhow.

"All those kids wanna do is party anyway, and they ain't gonna drag *my* daughter into all that mess! You're better off at home where you belong!" He sputtered.

Years later, one fine day, she had just made a nice dinner of roasted chicken, mashed potatoes and green beans, and it was time to eat, so she called Leo to the table.

"Leo! Leo! Supper's ready! You coming?"

She walked into Leo's room to find him crying. He was sitting on the edge of the bed, sobbing, but when he heard Daniella walk in, he quickly wiped his tears and said, "I'm coming."

Daniella turned to walk away but went closer instead. "Are you crying? What's wrong? Is it something at school?"

Leo said, "The boys at school won't play with me. They say I'm weird. They're right. I can't do anything."

Daniella felt very angry at the thought of redneck kids torturing her baby cousin. "Those little assholes! You gotta stand up to those redneck kids Leo, or they'll kick your ass. You want me to teach you some stuff?"

Leo looked shocked. "You? Teach me? You're a girl!"

Daniella said, "Yeah, and how many times have I whipped your butt?"

Leo put his head down slightly and said, "A lot." He

paused to think about it for a minute and said, "Ok, when are we doing this?"

Daniella said, "Right after dinner. But, first you gotta get your wimpy butt up to eat!" Leo laughed, "Shut up!" He smiled widely, as he could always count on his sister to lift his spirits.

Now comfortable in her seat, with a blanket pulled up over her, modern day Daniella smiled as she enjoyed the sweet memory of this time, a time when she and Leo were so close. She tried to get a little sleep, and managed to drift off for a while, wrapped up in such a sweet memory. However, her comfort would not last for long, because as she slept, she dreamt of a not so pleasant memory. She dreamt of the last time she saw Leo.

She had just returned home after her first year in the Middle East, and she was enjoying the sights of the Southern mansions down Main Street made her hometown so special, like living pages out of a novel. She got out of the cab and pulled her suitcase up the walk that led to the back door of Magnolia Manor. Katie was one of the first people she wanted to go visit. Katie had always been such a comfort to her, looking after her all through childhood, especially after her parents divorced, after the shooting.

Immediately after the shooting, Carol had to do a long stint in a local psychiatric hospital, which was much better than prison, but it still removed her from Daniella's life. The gap that left, the need for a mother, was filled by Katie. Daniella was very thrilled to see her, but at the same time she really worried, worried the day will soon come that she'd have to reveal that she was now a Muslim. She knew Katie would never understand. Old folks like them were just so set in their ways, and they only knew their own "limited" little world. Daniella decided that she'd just get on with the visit and just enjoy it this time. She'd worry about telling everyone about her new found faith on another day.

When she walked in the door, Katie hugged her warmly and greeted her with, "There's my grandbaby! Oh, Honey, you've been there far too long! Come on and sit down now so I can get you some tea. I was just making our lunch, but I've got a little cornbread here to snack on."

These words were comforting to Daniella, and it pleased her greatly to sit in the room that had been a source of comfort and strength for her as a child. Katie's kitchen was a sanctuary from the chaos that her parents had created in her life. She enjoyed sitting in the kitchen, sipping on Katie's sweet tea and snacking on corn bread.

Even Lorrie, Katie's old crony sister, seemed to be in a pleasant mood. She was even smiling, which was something highly unusual for her. Usually, she would be the hunchbacked old lady sitting in the corner, snapping and squawking about every little thing that displeased her.

Leo arrived and didn't seem to want to come in at first. Daniella spotted him standing in the doorway and shouted, "Hey, there's my big soldier man! How's my little cousin?"

Leo wasn't moved. He glared at her and said, "There's my uppity bitch cousin who thinks she's too good for Georgia!"

Daniella's mouth dropped. Katie turned around fast and dropped the spatula she'd been turning the chicken with. She grabbed her chest like she might have a heart attack and said, "Young man, you'd better control that tongue of yours! You can't talk to your sister this way! Now, sit down and let me get you some tea. Danny's tired so don't bother her!"

Leo snapped, "I don't want any tea. Not with her!! She hasn't been honest with us!"

Daniella said, "What the hell are you doing? Is this the greeting I get?"

Leo replied, "Hell yeah it is! You're a lying bitch and I'm gonna tell everybody who you really are!"

Katie was gasping and Daniella was shaking her head in disbelief, hoping he wasn't about to reveal the truth about her newfound religious belief. *How did he know? I didn't tell him.* She wondered.

Even though she hoped he wasn't trying to reveal the secret, unfortunately, that's exactly what he planned. He glared as he said, "Her name isn't even Danny anymore! She changed it to sound more like one of those Goddamn greasy rag heads! Ain't that right? Fatima!?"

Daniella started crying and Katie could hardly catch her breath. Leo continued, "She's shacked up with one of them and she's learning their crazy terrorist religion too! Did you know she renounced Christ? Maybe that's why you didn't even come back to pay your respects when Mama died? What kind of religion teaches you to abandon your own blood? I'm glad Mama's dead now so she won't see what a bitch you turned into!"

Katie stumbled backwards as if she'd lose her balance. Lorrie rushed over to brace her up, but she grabbed the kitchen countertop and steadied herself to say, "Oh Honey, is that why you didn't want any Bacon? Dear sweet Jesus! Oh, baby, you're confused...they brainwashed you!! I'm never gonna call you by that crazy name. Your name will always be Daniella. Do you hear me?"

Daniella looked venomously at Leo and shouted, "You shut the Fuck up Leo! Don't you ever talk about them like that! You don't know one Goddamn thing! And I didn't come back when Mama died because I didn't know! None of Y'all even called me! I'm not psychic."

She looked at Katie and saw her shaking her head in total shock. In Katie's case, Daniella was far more forgiving, but the sight of her looking so disappointed ripped her heart out. She'd always thought of Katie as a mother figure, and her "mother" looked as if she would have a coronary because of this fight. Daniella sighed and tried to calm the mood.

"I'm not confused. I'm clear for the first time in my life, and my name can be anything I damn well please. So can we please just calm down?" She spoke calmly, but her attempts at calming the mood were dashed when she spotted the hateful glare in Leo's eyes.

She looked directly into those burning green eyes that matched her own, as though she was searching them for emotions. "Why did you come here? Just to screw with me? What are you gonna do now? String me up like a good ole boy?" Her body was pushing further and further towards his, in a threatening manner. He got angry and walked away. She responded by walking up closer. "What would people around here do if I revealed all of your secrets? Huh? What if I went running down Main Street to tell folks what I know about you?"

Leo turned back with red fury, and it became obvious to Katie, Lorrie, and Daniella that he was holding himself back from physically harming her. As a Southern gentleman, he's been taught his whole life that it's a terrible shame to his honor to put his hands on any woman in anger, especially his own flesh and blood, but Daniella was pushing him to the end of his limits.

"Daniella! Back the fuck off, or you'll be sorry. You're a bitch and you damn well deserve it, but I still don't wanna knock you the fuck out!!!! Get the fuck out of this house! Get your sand nigger loving ass out of this house right now, and never come back!"

The pressure was too much, and Daniella was running on emotional overload by now. She finally broke down and started sobbing as she looked at him, "I've been your sister and the closest thing you ever had to a mother. Doesn't that mean anything to you?"

The coldness in his eyes at this point was something she'd never forget. "If you're not a Christian, you're nothing to me! Now ... I said ... GET OUT!!!"

Daniella was very fearful at this point, certain he would harm her if she stayed, so she left, weeping as one who had just lost her dearest friend. She grabbed her purse and keys, all the while muttering to herself, "I didn't wanna do this now. I'm not gonna sit around here and take this!"

She stormed out the door, and as the screen door swung back to shut, she turned around one more time, to see if anyone cared. Katie was looking out the window crying, muttering, "Lord have mercy..."

Leo peered at her through the screen door and shouted, "Go on! I said get the fuck out! Don't ever come around here again! You Goddamn terrorist!"

Daniella turned back only once, giving both of them one final look, and never looked back at them again, weeping as she left.

As she remembered this, she wrapped up deeper into her cocoon-like plane seat, wiping away the tears. She was exhausted from the stress of it all, but she always had such horrible trouble sleeping on airplanes, so she reached into her bag for some medication she had on hand for "emotional" emergencies. The label read, "Xanax...for the relief of the symptoms of anxiety".

Daniella never liked using this stuff, but felt that if she didn't get a few hours of sleep, she'd be such a wreck when she got to Georgia, and that'd be no good for anyone, so she took a half tablet, just to take the edge off. It didn't take 15 minutes for the pill to start its relaxing effect, and Daniella finally drifted off, cutting off many hours from a cross continental plane ride.

4

FACING THE DEMONS

Daniella arrived at the only hotel in Hadleyville, Georgia, the Western Inn. The hotel was a simple place with simple surroundings. The lobby was basic—a few old sofas with an old TV for guests to watch as they waited. The familiar look of it was strangely comforting, and this familiarity provided a strange rush of contentment as she rang the service bell and checked in.

She had arrived in town without letting any of her relatives know that she was there, but it only took hours for the word to spread to everyone else. Hadleyville only had one small newspaper, with less than a handful of reporters, but by the time she was ready to come out and head to the Georgia State courthouse for Leo's arraignment, they were there, ready to pound her with questions. A miniature man with a very thick Southern accent probed for answers. He blurted,

"Miss Daniella, do you plan to go to the courthouse today? Are you back to see your cousin put down like a rabid dog?"

Daniella looked at this man with such disdain that she

may have barbecued him with her eyes. He felt it and backed off. The others were equally as rude, and unfortunately, they didn't feel a need to hide it. They followed her all the way to her car, bothering her with questions as she vehemently shooed them off.

She drove off, and as she did, more than one of the friendly Southern neighbors looked through their windows and stared from their porches to see whom the "stranger" was in town. One woman was dressed in baggy black shorts with a tank top. She wasn't wearing any makeup and her dull mangled dishwater blonde hair was tied back in a crude ponytail. She crouched down and put her hands over her eyes to shield the sun so she could get a better look. Aside from this one lady who made it painfully obvious that she was staring, and the small barrage of reporters, Daniella was barely noticed as she headed straight for the courthouse.

When she arrived at the courthouse, her nerves suddenly started to get to her. She couldn't imagine what her cousin was going to think of her presence there. She felt fearful of hearing hurtful words like the last time they met, so much so that her hands started to shake. As she approached the big doors of the room, it seemed that everything was in slow motion. For a split second, she felt an overwhelming fear that Leo would bark insults at her, making her wish she'd never gotten on the plane. As she heard the sound of footsteps, she quickly pulled herself back together, however, as she had to speed up her steps to get to the door before the reporters could catch up. She saw them enter from the other side, and they weren't wasting any time getting to her. She managed to reach the doors before them, where she took a deep breath and said "God help me."

As the doors swung open, she found there weren't many people there yet, but the star of the show was there—Leo, who was sitting beside his attorney and only a stone's throw from a burly prison guard. When he heard the doors open, he swung around to see who'd arrived and felt truly surprised to see Daniella standing there. He immediately let go of some of the emotion he'd been holding back all this time as he sat there noticing the look of love and concern on her face. A few tears streamed from his eyes. He seemed totally broken, completely unlike the harsh redneck ass beater than he was a few years ago. At that moment, his eyes were soft, and his look was one of agony and relief, relief that he wasn't alone anymore. Daniella's protective instincts immediately took hold of her and she rushed up to him and sat down on the bench behind.

He reached back and held her hand, then said, "Thank you for coming. I didn't know anyone told you. I'm so sorry Danny. I'm sorry for everything. Daddy had revved me up so much about your living situation, and I just let my foolish mouth say terrible things."

Daniella felt her heart fly at these words. That's all she'd wanted to hear, after all this time. She looked back at him and said, "I'm still your sister, right?"

Leo's heart broke, as he remembered the terrible things he'd said before when she asked him this. He replied, "I didn't do this Danny. I'm not a murderer."

Daniella sighed and said, "I know. You've made a lot of mistakes, but you couldn't have done that."

The courtroom was filling up quickly, and it wasn't long before the bailiff entered the room and announced that all should rise for the honorable Judge Buford Belham. Everyone stood up as this large imposing man made his way to the judge's seat. As he sat down, so did everyone else.

"Will the defendant, Leo Pierce, please rise?" The judge blurted.

Leo and his lawyer stood. The judge then asked, "Leo Pierce, you've been charged with murder in the first degree. How do you plead?"

Leo's attorney, Mr. Hillard, replied, "My client pleads not guilty, your Honor."

The judge nodded and said, "Very well, this court will reconvene at 9 am Monday morning."

His gavel went down. The bailiff called, "All rise!"

Everyone rose from his or her chairs as the judge made his way out of the courtroom. Now, Leo was guaranteed a trial by a jury of his peers. The battle for his life had begun. As everyone began their exit from the courtroom, Leo's prison guard instructed him to get up and put his hands behind his back. As the guard handcuffed Leo, Daniella couldn't stop staring at the spectacle of it all. Leo felt very ashamed and could hardly look at her. She felt so sorry for him that it was difficult to breathe. Her eyes welled up with tears, and right before they took him away, he turned to look at her and said, "I'm glad you're here. Please, Danny. Please try to find out who did this."

"I will. I promise." She said.

She watched helplessly as the guards led her little cousin out. She'd always heard of people saying that when their kids were in trouble, all they could see was the little "child" suffering. That was how it was for Daniella at the moment. She saw the little boy being dragged out of the courtroom, the little boy that she had practically raised herself. She flashed him a reassuring smile and gave him a nod with a wink, hoping he'd be a little stronger now, knowing he wasn't alone.

The room began to empty out and Daniella anticipated

the press would be waiting outside. She made her way to the door, and as predicted, there they were. After all, why not? In a small area such as this, there wasn't ever much going on, so this was the story of the decade.

As soon as she stepped out, the cameras started flashing. The reporters were from all over the region because they were bloodthirsty for something like this, something with controversy and drama to sell newspapers.

"Ms. Sulieman! Did he do it? Did he kill your father? Give us a statement!"

Daniella ran past them, determined to not answer any questions, but here she didn't have the help of her driver to fend them off. They became overwhelming, so she felt obligated to answer. She angrily turned around and snapped, "Yes?!! What do you want to know?"

One reporter asked, "Did your cousin do it?"

"No, he could not have done this." She hissed through gritted teeth.

Another reporter asked, "But the evidence is really compelling! Why do you believe he didn't do it? Don't the two of you have a volatile past? Rumor has it that he really hates you."

Another reporter picked up on that theme and followed up, "Yea! If he hates you so much, why are you here defending him?"

She felt herself getting angrier by the minute. Another reporter, a real country guy, blurted out the question again, but in the form of a declaration. "Maybe she just came back to see him get put to sleep like a dog?"

Daniella felt furious at this remark, but she kept her cool, for Leo's sake. "My cousin and I have had many differences over the years. That's true. But I would never believe he's capable of something like this. I grew up with him, so I know him. That's why I'm here, to be sure he doesn't get punished for something he didn't do."

Another reporter asked, "Is it true that Ross Pierce was murdered because he was a closet homo his whole life? What does this say about the acceptance of their kind in Georgia?"

Daniella replied, "Well I have no idea really. I haven't been living here for more than ten years, so don't expect me to know all that."

The same country reporter commented, "Yea, you've been living in Arabia, haven't you? Maybe we should be asking you if one of you arranged it all somehow? You must have friends who can do this kind of thing."

Daniella looked at him with reddening eyes, but managed to hold in any overly emotional reaction, and politely said, "No comment."

As many people pushed and shoved, she got into her car and drove away. She found the peace and quiet in her rental car to let go of the bottled anger for the redneck reporter and the whole situation. As soon as she was out of earshot, she let out a scream, and just by doing so, she felt enormously relieved. She drove to Katie's house, hoping she'd be well received. After all, it was Katie that told her about everything and asked her to come.

She pulled up into the driveway, past the nameplate of the house, "Magnolia Manor", to a circular driveway, like a roundabout, outside the house. The caretaker's house, now occupied by Katie's nosy old sister Lorrie, was opposite the main house. Daniella didn't even notice Lorrie standing at her window, peering outside to see who'd arrived. She was too busy noticing the huge Magnolia tree on the lawn. The tree had been there forever, as far as Daniella remembered. She and Leo used to play in it when they were kids, forgetting about all their problems, especially problems with their parents. The tree was as big as the house, with branches large enough to hold most adults, and when the big white flowers were in bloom, they radiated a sweet aroma that seemed to make all the stress melt away.

She remembered the day she was in the tree with Leo, shortly after they moved in with Katie and her grandfather, Ross Pierce Sr., after the shooting. While they happily played in the large branches of the tree, their fun was disturbed by the sound of Ross's Cadillac driving up. The second he stepped out of the car, he was yelling, cursing Carol.

"Fucking Bitch! It's not enough to shoot me! She's now gonna marry a damn mental patient, like her?"

As Katie heard him yelling as he was coming through the door, she rushed up to him to find out more. "Marrying? Who is she marrying? I didn't even know she was out of the asylum." Katie asked.

Ross SCOFFED, "Oh she's out all right! She's out and whoring around with one of the lunatics she met inside! I guess she thinks she's gonna get her slimy hands on more of my money! No fucking way! I'm not gonna pay the way for her and her crazy fucking boyfriend to burn through it!"

Daniella didn't want Leo to witness all that talk about their mother, so she convinced him to go play in the barn because sometimes it was just a lot of fun to see the chickens and the cows walking around. She said, "Hey do you wanna go to the barn with me? I heard there's a ghost there, and I wanna look for him."

Leo's eyes got huge as he replied, "A ghost? Who told you that?!"

"It doesn't matter who told me! I know you like ghost stories, so don't you wanna meet a ghost in person?" Daniella blurted as she smiled widely.

Leo nodded. Daniella said, "Ok then come on. Let's go."

As they walked away from the house, Daniella felt sad for her mother. No matter what her mother had done, it cut like a knife to experience her own father damning her.

Daniella's consciousness snapped back into the present day as Katie came to answer the door. After all these years, and ending on such a bad note, Daniella had no idea where Katie's mind would be on seeing her again. Much to her delight, Katie opened the door and flashed a huge smile. She said, "Oh my Lord! Bless your heart! You really came! Oh, Honey, I'm so glad to see you."

Relieved, Daniella hugged her back and came in. Sometimes, she was appreciative of the Southern custom of believing that all the stuff in the past is just water under the bridge, and it's the polite thing to pretend like you don't remember any of it.

Katie directed her to sit down in Big Ross's old chair, in the kitchen, as was the custom of most Southern people. They had always sat in the kitchen, to discuss their day, laugh, and just shoot the breeze, and of course, all this would be done whilst drinking a big glass of sweet iced tea. Shortly after, Lorrie showed up in the doorway, insulted that Daniella hadn't noticed her. She put her hands on her hip and started tapping her foot, like someone who was gearing up to scold a child.

"Well, I don't know where your mind is Darlin'! Didn't you see me out there? I know you must have!"

Daniella realized from experience that this needed a quick save. She rushed up to wrap her arms around Lorrie tightly and enthusiastically, thereby cutting out any justification that the old hen would have to chew her out. Smiling with a warm and sugary sweet grin, she said, "Oh Aunt Lorrie, I'm so sorry! I didn't see you. I swear! If I had, I wouldn't have passed you by without asking you to come over here and have some tea with us."

Lorrie seemed appeased, and it was at this moment she realized why Sofia seemed so familiar. *Sofia would love this woman! Oh my goodness! They would be besties, that's for sure.* The thought amused her greatly, and the corners of her mouth curled up in a delicious private smile as she tried to picture Lorrie in an Abaya and Sheyla.

True to form, Katie brought her a very big glass of tea, right as she was sitting down, and said, "Oh Honey, I'm so glad you're here! Your message didn't tell me the exact time you were arriving, but I was hoping you'd come today, 'cuz I was making us some lunch. To tell you the truth, I know you didn't want me to know you're here today, but I got word from the neighbors. Now, don't be mad that people were talking Honey. We're gonna have your favorite! Fried chicken and cornbread."

Daniella felt annoyed at the realization that indeed nothing stayed private in this town, but overjoyed to hear the invitation. It has been so long since she was welcomed into Katie's famous kitchen. She looked around at how charming the place was, just as she'd remembered it, fully decked out with chickens. The countertops had little glass chickens sitting on them. The curtains had chickens on them. The potholders had chickens on them. The salt and pepper shakers were shaped like chickens. Katie has always loved collecting things with chickens or in the shape of chickens. This brought a warm nostalgic smile to her face, as she took another sip of her iced tea.

She looked up at Katie as she was turning the fried

chicken. It smelled so good, and all at once she felt like a kid again, waiting for lunch. Poor Katie seemed to be overjoyed to have someone to cook for. Ever since Big Ross, her Grandpa, died, and now Ross, she'd not had anyone to cook for in a very long time.

She started taking the chicken pieces out, one by one, placing them on a paper towel to drain the oil off. Daniella thought she looked so cute with her little apron on, almost humming. Katie said, "Oh Honey, it's so good you've come. You know your cousin didn't do this. He may do a lot of things, but he'd never really kill anybody."

Daniella nodded. Deep in her heart she believed this was true. "Yes, I know. That's the first thing that came to my mind when I heard. There's no way he'd do this, but it had to be someone who knew about the bat incident." She looked at Katie, who was nodding along at this point, knowingly.

"Grandma, do you have an idea of who would've known about that? I really hope you can help push me in the right direction. I wanna help Leo, but this isn't gonna be easy. I need proof."

Katie's brow crinkled as she said, "Well, my guess is that it'd have to be someone who hates your cousin and hates people like your Daddy."

Daniella felt a little sorry for Ross at that moment. It must have been hard keeping a secret of this magnitude in a small town for so long, and Katie's reluctance to even say it out loud made her sure that's what made him desperate to hide it. She said, "You can't even say it out loud can you?"

Katie seemed cavalier as she simply replied, "Say what Baby?"

"Say that Daddy wasn't straight. It was his lifelong secret.

I must say, for this town, he did quite well covering it up. God knows, you can't keep a secret around here at all."

Katie's lips pressed into a hard line, as she was obviously uncomfortable to talk about it, then rolled her eyes and said, "Well Baby, we always kinda realized what he was, but we had hoped he'd keep it to himself. I mean, that kind of stuff is really embarrassing around here. But after Leo found out, I guess the whole world found out. I can't hardly walk down the street without someone shaking their head at me."

Daniella smiled and asked, "You mean *I'm* not the talk of the town anymore?"

Katie's mood was a bit relieved as she cracked a small smile and replied, "No Honey, you've been old news lately... well, until now of course. Now that you're back they are bound to start up again. I just can't let myself be bothered about it anymore. I'm too old for all their nonsense now. If they wanna prance around shouting about nigger lovers, we'll have to do what we can to ignore them."

Katie finished putting the food on the table and sat down. Lorrie had been unusually quiet all this time, and Daniella was suddenly curious as to why. It certainly wasn't like her not to force her opinion on everyone, no matter what they'd think of it. Glancing her way, Katie and Daniella understood at once why she was so quiet. She had fallen asleep, and just then she let out a snore that would rival a pig's snort. Katie, as she would put it, normally wouldn't be caught dead laughing at her elder sister, but that snore didn't even let her off the hook so easily. They both broke out into a relieving chuckle over poor old Lorrie.

"Come on over here baby. Sit with me and we'll talk about it while we eat." Katie said, leading her to the table. "Don't worry about Lorrie."

Daniella sat down at the little table and in the corner of

the kitchen. To her, it was the most charming place in the house. This was where she'd sat and done most of her homework as a kid, and in some ways, just sitting there made her believe everything was going to be absolutely fine.

Just before they sat down, the kitchen light bulb burst, leaving tiny shards of glass on the floor. Then they were both startled by a booming sound coming from the basement floor of the house, the area that once was used as a servant's quarters. Daniella looked at Katie with a surprised look on her face when she realized Katie wasn't planning to go see what the noise was.

"Grandma, aren't you gonna check on that? What was that sound?"

Katie shook her head and scoffed, "You wouldn't believe me. Not in a million years. That damn thing makes me as nervous as a fart in a fan factory! Lord, God in Heaven!"

Daniella had to work hard to suppress her urge to laugh out loud at that statement, and asked, "Believe what Grandma? Just tell me."

"It's that damn ghost! He simply won't settle down some days. He's always breaking stuff and stomping around down there! He probably busted that light in the servant's staircase again as well!" Katie inhaled deeply.

"Let's just forget him and eat." She smiled.

"Ok, Grandma. Whatever you like." Daniella said.

She got the impression that Katie really didn't want to talk about it, so she chalked it up to an old woman's imagination. After all, a lot of old Southern women say they've seen ghosts. It was kind of normal actually, at least for them.

They munched away, and for a moment, Daniella got lost in the great Southern cooking. It had been so long since she'd tasted Katie's cooking. No matter how many times she'd tried to duplicate her recipes, she could never get it right. Before she knew it, she'd eaten three pieces of chicken and two ears of corn. The corn bits were stuck in her teeth, so she didn't want to open her mouth very much, feeling embarrassed for how her teeth looked. But her over-full belly was bothering her far more than her corn-filled teeth.

Katie could see that she'd overindulged, so she got up to fetch the Alka-Seltzer. The gentle "plop and fizz" of the soothing concoction provided instant relief as she drank it down. To her surprise, Lorrie had woken up at some point and was staring at her judgmentally. "You're a little bit pudgy to be eating like that, don't you think? You're reminding me of your Daddy." Lorrie blurted.

Daniella didn't want to start any drama with her. She knew that any problems would hinder their ability to focus completely on how to help Leo, so she smiled sweetly and said, "Aww well, who can help it with your sister's delicious cooking?"

She excused herself before anyone could say anything else, so she could go to the bathroom and wash up, and when she came out, she felt ready to talk about suspects. "Ok, let's make a list of some of Leo's worst enemies. Who may have done this? Let's think. As I said before, it's gotta be someone who knew about the bat chasing thing."

Katie started thinking, and it didn't take long for her to remember a name. "Carl! You remember him?"

Daniella replied, "Yes of course I do. But, isn't that his best friend? Why would he be the very first person you suspect?"

"Well, they aren't best friends anymore."

Daniella raised an eyebrow as Katie went on. "Their friendship broke up a very long time ago. Leo hurt him in a really bad way. I'm not sure, but I believe he was messing around with Carl's girlfriend."

Daniella shook her head in complete surprise. "Is there anyone's wife or girlfriend that asshole hasn't been with? You know, come to think of it, all we gotta do is count up the angry husbands or boyfriends that are bound to have a grudge against him!"

Katie said, "I know he is one, but you don't have to use that kind of language Honey. I didn't raise you to talk like that!"

"Yeah!" Lorrie blurted.

She paused, looking down at Daniella the same way she did when she was a child. Daniella felt completely scolded and said, "I'm sorry Grandma."

Katie continued, "Now that being said, Leo sure didn't ever know how to keep a real friend. That's for sure, but this Carl was different. You didn't see his eyes. He was downright mental!"

"Ok," Daniella said. "I'll go pay him a visit, right after I check on that assistant of Daddy's, Mr. Hale. I always thought he was dirty somehow, didn't you?"

Katie said, "Yea, I always did. He was about as crooked as a politician, but I'll give him this. He did love your Daddy. He worked for him for more than 35 years. I can't remember a time Mr. Hale wasn't looking out for your Daddy's interests. He invested for him, hired his lawyers, and kept his name out of the press, even through all the scandals."

Daniella was listening and pondering this. Mr. Hale had always been a real bastard to her and Leo, shooing them out of the store every time he saw them. Daniella was thinking he'd have to be a suspect, if not for anything than the control of Ross's company. Then, a brainstorm hit her.

"Hey, do you reckon Mr. Hale liked Daddy in any other ways that you know of? You know what I'm saying?"

When the idea hit Katie, she could hardly stand the idea of it. Initially, she shrugged it off and adamantly denied it, but after a moment, she reconsidered it. "Well, you know, they always were so chummy, now that I'm thinking of it. Before I knew Ross's secret, I remember your Grand Daddy joking about how Mr. Hale was better than a wife to your father." A smile crept over Katie's face, and when she looked at Daniella with that head tilted to one side look, it made Daniella burst out in laughter.

Lorrie rolled her eyes.

Katie said, "Now the thought of those two as an item would be quite a sight!"

Daniella chuckled and said, "Well, I've gotta pay him a visit anyhow. I'll see what kind of feeling I get from him. After that, I'll see if Carl has anything to hide."

She got up, grabbed her keys and bag, and then grabbed Katie for a big hug. They were never a "touchy feely" kind of family, so it kinda threw Katie off a bit. Daniella was certainly different, changed forever by being in a family of her own, loved and accepted. Hugs were now something she felt more than comfortable with, so she wasn't going to accept any opposition on this. She even hugged old Lorrie, taking her completely by surprise, only to hear a big, "All right now, All right. You go on about your business child."

Daniella released her and said, "It sure was nice to see you, Aunt Lorrie. You haven't changed a bit!"

Lorrie blurted, "Well I can't say the same about you, Honey. You've really put on the pounds since we last saw you. That food in Arabia must be real good."

Daniella's inside joke was burning inside her, and the laughter was about to spill out as she imagined Lorrie saying all this whilst wearing a Shayla. Daniella choked it in, telling herself that she only had a few more moments to get out the door, and then she could laugh her head off.

Katie said, "You sure better be careful Darlin'."

"I will Grandma. I promise. Thanks for lunch. I really loved it." Daniella smiled warmly at her, patted her on the shoulder reassuringly, and then went out the door. She had a sort of sensation of being free, free of the pain her last time in that house had caused. She had successfully replaced a bad memory with a good one. Katie was always such a great mother figure, always caring, nurturing, and Daniella figured it really wasn't her fault that she couldn't stand up to men and their ideas. All her life she'd been taught that men were more important, so by now it was hardwired. Anyone from the South knew the women from Katie's generation were not vocal about their feelings, and the sweet hospitality that she'd just shown Daniella was her way of apologizing.

She drove off downtown to see her old pal, Mr. Hale. As she drove off, she caught the sight of Katie waving at her as she got further and further away.

5

THE BEST FRIEND, THE ONLY FRIEND

Daniella arrived at her father's former office, the place where he had run a successful group of companies. He always had a myriad of things going at once—gas stations, cattle farms, cotton plantations, a few catfish restaurants, peach farms, and a few rental properties. Running the business was a big deal, and unfortunately, Ross had left the whole thing up to his fat and grumpy assistant, Mr. Hale.

This man was grossly overweight, bald, with an almost exaggerated redneck accent. Daniella and Leo had always joked about how Mr. Hale looked more like a Walmart manager than the Vice-President of Pierce Group of Companies.

When Mr. Hale saw Danny coming, he seemed visibly bothered. Daniella could have sworn she saw him roll his eyes, but she was absolutely sure that she saw him tighten his belt strap just before she came through the door. She walked in and he greeted her with an extreme amount of typically fake cordiality. "Well, Howdy!"

Daniella returned the fakeness with exaggerated

fakeness. "Hello, Mr. Hale! Good afternoon to you Sir. It's surely good to see you again."

With a disdainful smile, he replied, "Good afternoon Danny! We haven't seen you around these parts in a coon's age! Been around to visit your grandmother?"

Daniella's lips pressed into a hard line as she said, "Well I think you know why I'm here Mr. Hale. There's no need to beat around the bush. You know my cousin's been accused of killing him, and I know he didn't do this. I'm here to try and help him."

Mr. Hale expected that she would come, and he was ready. His mouth curled into an evil smile and he looked smug; this made Daniella angry. She could see he was ready to play hardball, so she decided to try and toughen up. After all, that old fart had tried to intimidate her for her entire life. *Who does he think he is anyway?* She thought.

Daniella told herself she wasn't that scared and insecure little girl anymore. She was a successful publisher now, married and with a family of her own. Forcefully and confidently, she said,

"Mr. Hale, tell me everything you know. I'm sure there's more to all this than meets the eye. My cousin is in there right now, suffering from something he didn't do. I know there must be a way you can help me understand this."

Mr. Hale looked extremely nervous and irritated, as his face scrunched up as though he'd just tasted a lemon. He said, "I guess you reckon you're gonna come in here and take over now. You may even be thinking that you're gonna get to fire me!"

His nervous reaction made Daniella suspect him even more. Obviously, he was actively thinking about whether or not his position could be threatened. *There's something wrong with this picture*, she thought. She suddenly glared at him, and her thoughts must have been transparent to him.

Mr. Hale cleared his throat and said, "I don't have time for this Danny. I've had a really hard time running this place since your father went and got himself killed." His hands started to shake and his breathing became faster as he barked, "Who do you think you are anyway!"

Daniella was shocked that his words mirrored her own thoughts of him, but she was enjoying his agitation just a bit. He was obviously squirming and uncomfortable, so she decided to push him a little. With a smart look she said, "You know, I'm sure I've inherited at least a small part of this business."

His face suddenly changed from being nervous and jittery to a look of satisfaction, as this is what he was waiting for. This sudden boost of confidence scared her, as she wasn't expecting this sudden change in demeanor. He had something up his sleeve, Daniella feared. With a satisfied grin, he replied, "Oh no Missy. You really don't know, do you?"

Regretfully, Daniella replied, "Know what?"

"That your Daddy cut you out of his will before he died," He said it so fast as if he couldn't hold back his thrilling feeling. Seeing the damaged look on her face from this wasn't enough, so he carried on. "Yeah, not just your Daddy, but your Grandpa and your Great Aunt too! You don't own a single damn cent of anyone's money or even one brick in your Daddy's business! Now, I'd turn my ass around and leave if I'm you."

Daniella struggled to hold back the tears in her eyes. She didn't want to give that prick, Mr. Hale, the satisfaction of witnessing her broken, so she forced her lower lip to stop quivering, sucked it up, and found a burst of inner strength.

"For your information, I already knew that. I just wanted to study your reaction ... Old Man. I don't need anyone's money just so you know! I have plenty of my own that I've made without anyone giving me one Goddamn thing. I wouldn't want a penny of their filthy fortune anyway. I was there, remember? I know how he got all this!"

Mr. Hale, looking smug, said "Yeah right. I bet you're like every other gold digger that comes in here wanting a piece of his fortune. He told me he wasn't gonna leave any money to a sand nigger lover like you."

He grinned, hoping this got a rise out of her. She didn't react, however, and successfully held back the anger. Inside her mind, she was screaming in pain. A lifetime of emotional pain and shame for what her mother did was pounding at the door of her consciousness, but she held it in like a Boss. "You rednecks are so funny ... Ok, Mr. Hale, you can expect to be summoned, so I wouldn't leave town if I'm you."

By the time she said this, his face was turning red with anger. He looked like a giant tomato that was about to explode all over the revolving door. It was almost something you'd watch in a cartoon.

Daniella turned and walked out. She got into her car, backed up, and drove off. As soon as she was out of Mr. Hale's sight, she pulled over. All the grief he'd caused her was bubbling up, and her hands were shaking. She couldn't hold it anymore, so she let herself cry. She didn't just cry, she wept and screamed, "Why did I let myself come back here?"

With tears streaming down her face, she took out her cell phone and called Nay, knowing she'd make her feel better. Nay answered, "Hello?"

Just hearing her voice on the other end of the phone

made her start with the tears again. Daniella's sobbing was making it hard for Nay to even understand her.

Nay was surprised and wanted nothing more than to help Danny feel better. She said, "Ok Honey, slow down. I can hardly understand you, you're crying so hard."

Daniella, sobbing, said, "They're just so horrible! I can't believe I'm back here in this Hellhole! Everyone here hates me."

Nay replied, "Now Honey, I'm sure that's not true."

Daniella sobbed, "Yes it is. I hate them back too! If it wasn't for my cousin needing me right now, I'd buy the first ticket out of here!"

Nay replied, "Now listen to me. I bet you didn't take a second to recover or catch your breath did you? You probably got right off that plane and went to visit Leo. Am I right?"

The silence on the other end was all she needed to hear to know she was right. She carried on, "Uh huh, that's what I thought, so I want you to take a break for the rest of the day. You can pick up your detective duties tomorrow. Isn't there a place where you'd feel comfortable? Someone you can visit who's not an asshole or a bigot? It can't be all bad."

Daniella thought about it for a moment and remembered she had wanted to visit her Uncle Sheldon and Aunt Rosie. They were always so sweet to her and had never judged. A smile suddenly formed, and she said, "You always know just the right thing to say. I've got my Aunt and Uncle nearby. They've always been sweet. You're a genius, Nay!"

"You bet your ass I am! It's good to hear you calmer now. Now go and rest up for the fight. I'll call you in the morning Honey." Nay hung up and Daniella felt a big sense of relief. She sped off to visit her Aunt and Uncle, feeling the anticipation of seeing them again after all these years.

6

REGROUPING

This trip wasn't long, an hour, in fact, and Daniella had called her Aunt and Uncle from the road, worrying that it was really short notice to just show up for a visit, but Aunt Rosie was extremely welcoming and absolutely insistent that she get there as fast as she could. Daniella sped on towards their home, through winding country routes and finally on the little dirt road that led to their driveway.

As she pulled up in Uncle Sheldon's flower-laden driveway, she was immediately struck by how beautiful the place was. Aunt Rosie had planted the most charming Azaleas and Magnolia Trees. The pink and white colors of them were so bright and welcoming, and as soon as she got out of the car, the sweet aroma permeated the air. The tiny bird houses were all around, so the air was further sweetened with the sound of chirping Cardinals and Blue Jays and the tapping of a woodpecker.

As she walked closer, the smell improved a hundredfold, as she smelled the homemade pecan pie the Aunt Rosie had prepared especially for the visit. Pecan pie had been her favorite dessert since childhood, and Aunt Rosie undoubtedly remembered that. She warmly smiled at what a welcoming feeling she was having, even before stepping through the door, and her mouth watered for the delicious pie, especially if it's coming with a piping hot cup of freshly brewed coffee.

She knocked at the door and Aunt Rosie quickly opened it, as if she'd been waiting beside it. She beamed at Daniella. From the foyer, they both heard Uncle Sheldon cried, "Is that my Darlin' niece? Tell her to get in here and give me some Sugar!"

Both Rosie and Daniella snickered, and Daniella replied, "Ok, Uncle Sheldon! Here I come!"

She rushed in and there he was, holding his arms out, smiling from ear to ear. He was a big imposing looking old Southern gentleman. In spite of his age, he was a very spry old guy, full of energy and a positive outlook.

He hugged Daniella tight and his eyes watered a bit. He hadn't seen her since she left for the Middle East and had often commented to Rosie that he feared he'd never see her again when he heard how badly her father and cousin had reacted to the news of her marrying a Muslim and converting to Islam. Rosie had water in her eyes, as she witnessed the happy reunion.

"We thought we'd never see you again Honey. We're so glad that you're back. I'm just so sorry that it took something this bad to get you back over here."

Daniella nodded, "Yes, that's for sure. But I guess that tragedy sometimes does just that, doesn't it?"

Uncle Sheldon nodded, and Aunt Rosie said, "Amen to that Darlin."

Daniella added, "Tragedy often brings families together,

to be even stronger than they were before. Well, at least that's what I hope."

Aunt Rosie remarked, "Well we sure do hope so too! Now come out and see this new deck we've put up."

They walked out onto the deck where Daniella could see the beautiful backyard garden that Aunt Rosie had planted. It was a gorgeous sight. She even had Banana trees and giant Sunflower plants about, a vegetable garden and birdhouses. The grass was lush and green and Daniella let the intoxicating smell of fresh cut grass fill her nose. That, combined with the smell of the lovely flowers and fruits, made a wonderful bouquet of aroma.

"Aunt Rosie, you've got a little slice of paradise out here. Gosh, I should bring you to Dubai with me so you can help me decide what to do with my garden." Daniella said.

Rosie adorably blushed to almost match the color of her roses and admitted, "Well, the truth is that I can't take all the credit for it. Sheldon helped me a little bit."

Uncle Sheldon blurted, "A little bit! Is that what my wife is over there saying?" Rosie shooed him away and smiled to show her lovely dimples, and said, "Y'all stop messing around now and sit down. We can talk after we eat. I hope you brought your appetite girl!"

Shortly thereafter, Rosie brought a lovely dinner for them—casserole, tossed salad, and cornbread with plenty of sweet tea. In the South, cornbread goes with everything, and try as she might, Daniella had never been able to get the cornbread recipe to taste just right. Her mouth watered as she saw and smelled the beautiful home cooked meal. *If I stay here too long, I'm gonna get fat*, she thought.

They enjoyed a lovely time together, biting into the delicious food and chatting about everything under the sun. After dinner, Rosie came out of the kitchen with a tray of pecan pie slices and hot coffee. Daniella was in heaven because there was no better way to finish a meal. Of course, in the South, though, this also meant that the "serious" talk needed to begin. The time for idle chit chat was done.

Sheldon looked sternly at Daniella and asked, "You saw your cousin? What do you think, Honey? Do you think he could have done this?"

Daniella took a sip of coffee and replied, "No. I really don't believe that. I saw him yesterday and I looked in his eyes. He didn't do it. I think someone who really hates him did it, and I'm gonna find out who." Rosie and Sheldon looked at each other with intrigue, as she seemed so confident about it.

Daniella took a bite of pie and Rosie said, "How can you be so sure Baby? Leo does have a really violent side. I won't ever forget when he found out about your Daddy. Everybody told me about how he'd lost his mind."

"That doesn't matter Aunt Rosie. I know him. He is the type to freak out initially when he finds out something shocking, but he wouldn't plan a cold-blooded murder like this, no matter how rotten he is to people." Daniella thought for a moment and continued. "And besides, he's got more enemies than anyone I know! Any of those jealous husbands or boyfriends could have done it. That boy slept with more women than anyone here seems to realize. It didn't seem to matter to him if they were married or not."

Rosie and Sheldon sat for a brief comedic moment with their mouths open in shock. Daniella had to resist the urge to laugh when she saw them. They were both so cute in their innocence because it was obvious that they didn't know anything about Leo's many indiscretions.

Sheldon shook it off, cleared his throat, and asked, "Do

you know anyone in particular who may have been so hateful towards him, someone who would do this?"

Daniella replied, "Well, I'm gonna go visit Carl after a while. Do y'all remember him? He was Leo's best friend in school."

Rosie huffed in disgust. "Yeah, I remember that vile little boy! He was so ill mannered that I almost turned him over my knee! I swear if there weren't such things as child abuse laws, I could've shown that boy some manners! He came here once with your cousin and all he could say was F this and F that! I never heard the F word so much in all my natural born life!"

Again Daniella had to actively stop herself from snickering. Rosie just didn't know how cute she was, even when she was mad. "Well, I guess that was before Leo had an 'indiscretion' with his girl. As I understand it, Debbie and Carl finally got married and had a few kids, but Leo kept on sneaking around with her for years. I'd be willing to bet that one or more of those kids aren't even his!"

Rosie looked like she'd pass out from the shock. She started fanning herself and Sheldon held her from her back and squeezed her shoulders. That was par for the course for how old Southern women handled the shocking news. There are no more dramatic females on Earth, except for possibly Arab women, but at least Southern women snapped back from it with more strength than ever, hence the Scarlett O'Hara effect.

Sheldon said, "Well, do you think you'll be ok talking to this Carl fella all by yourself? I can go with you if you want me to. Lord, I can't believe that Leo's hurt that boy so much! What's gotten into him?"

"The Devil's done got into him!" Rosie cried, still recovering from the shock. Uncle Sheldon was the one who snickered this time. "You're right Baby. That boy's done gone down a sinful path, that's for sure...but look who his Daddy was! It's no wonder."

Daniella carried on eating to finish up her pie, and with the last sip of coffee, she said, "Well Y'all, I better take off before it gets much later. I have a long drive to where Carl lives and I don't wanna be out in those boondocks after dark! God knows who or what would be out there."

"You got that right!" Sheldon boomed. "It sure was nice to spend some time with you, Honey. Please don't let it be 10 years before you come back to see us."

"Not a chance Uncle Sheldon, I promise you that. I'm so sorry that I was away so long. I promise to bring my kids next time, and I bet Faisal would even make the trip...God, I can't believe none of y'all have ever met! That's all my fault, and I'll make it right, just as soon as this trial business is over." She reached around Sheldon to give him a big hug.

Sheldon said, "Next time we'll get your cousins Ricky and Linda over here with their kids! It's about time for a family reunion, once this mess is over." He looked up at her with his older and wiser eyes, and she felt so protective of him, definitely never wanting to disappoint him again, not after all he'd done for her and Leo, and even for her father.

"I promise Uncle Sheldon. I miss Ricky and Linda so much! I keep up with them on Facebook, but I really wanna see them face to face before I leave."

Rosie blurted, "How's your Grandma? Lord, I haven't seen her in ages!"

Daniella said, "Aw she's fine." She thought for a moment and continued, "Well, she's saying that there's a ghost in her house, but other than that, she's good."

Daniella had a sneaky smile on her face, as she certainly

didn't take the ghost thing seriously, but her grin started fading as she saw the pale look on Rosie's face.

"Is the light still blowing up in the servant's quarters?" Rosie blinked, her voice quivering.

"You know about that?" Daniella snapped.

Sheldon said, "We stayed over there for a spell when your Grandpa died. I'm surprised no one told you...Well, that was a long time ago... Rosie and I saw the ghost of a man with a beard and really white eyes there. Katie put us in the spare bedroom in the basement, what used to be the servant's quarters. One night, we woke up to the sound of boots stomping down those slave stairs. I went over there to see what was going on. I thought maybe there was an intruder. That's when I saw him. He looked almost like you could see right through him. Then, the light on the stairs, right above him, blew up."

Daniella listened and felt the cold sweat breaking out on her skin. Is this real? She thought.

Rosie blurted, "We both decided we'd never stay there again, but we never said anything to Katie. Lord, God in Heaven, I hope she'll be all right.

"Well, you better get on that road Honey," Sheldon said.

Daniella didn't know how to react to that story, so she simply filed it away as something to deal with later. She muttered, "Yeah, Ok, You're right. I better get going."

They all made their way out to Daniella's car for their goodbyes, but it wasn't a sad occasion. They made their plans to meet again, right before Daniella's departure, just as soon as Leo was cleared of all charges. This kind of positive thinking was what she needed, and after her time with them, she felt recharged and totally relaxed.

As she pulled out of their driveway, she saw them both waving from the rear view mirror. They were charming, like a scene from a movie, a sweet family movie. She knew it would be too late to go see Carl today, but she didn't regret the time she'd spent with her Aunt and Uncle at all. So far, that was by far the best afternoon she'd spent in a very long time. When she arrived back at the hotel, she fell asleep. She needed that rest, and she had a deep and restful sleep, without nightmares.

7

ANOTHER LINK IN THE CHAIN

Daniella woke the next morning rested and refreshed, but late, too late to eat the continental breakfast. She got ready in a hurry, grabbed a cup of coffee and a donut, jumped into the car and headed toward Atlanta. Carl's farm was an hour outside the city limits, so when Daniella spotted a diner just outside the city, she took her last chance for food before getting there. After all, Carl was unlikely to invite her for a meal, she thought.

She got a call from her editor as she got out of the car, and the more she heard from him, the more annoyed she became. She really thought she'd had all the loose ends on her company's latest publication wrapped up before she left. She thought to herself that there's nothing more bothersome than loose ends, especially as she's trying to focus on other things.

"Look, Ahmed, I desperately need this book wrapped up this week so we can choose a cover design by next week! I will be on Skype with you guys Sunday night at 9pm here ok? I want the final edit done and a couple of choices of book jackets done by then. I'm really busy over here, and I need you guys to be up to speed at all times, OK?"

She walked into the diner, and just after hanging up with Ahmed, she noticed all the customers checking her out. In small town Georgia, she wasn't exactly fitting in, dressed this way, a bit too posh. Most Americans in small towns felt most comfortable in jeans and tee shirts, with flip-flops or sneakers. Women in Dubai always dressed up, whether they wore the Abaya or not. In Dubai, Daniella would always be in the latest fashion of Abaya and Shayla, but for the trip to the U.S., she opted for a smart, loose-fitting pantsuit.

She smiled friendly at all the people as she made her way to the table, and just as she passed the kitchen, she noticed a familiar face. The sight of Luwanda Jenkins stopped her in her tracks. Known as one of the most attractive girls that ever attended her high school, Luwanda left an impression on everyone she met, especially boys. Her good looks were almost legendary, so when she saw the way Luwanda looked now, she was aghast. The poor gal looked positively beaten up by life and very overworked, with her hair back in a net, and she'd obviously put on a lot of pounds over the years. Not exactly obese, but she'd put on at least 20-30 pounds, Daniella speculated. In spite of all this, however, she was still quite attractive, but tired and drained.

Daniella shook her head in disbelief and sat down at the table. The waitress came up and gave her a menu, then said with the thickest Southern accent ever, "I'll be back in a minute to take your order."

The choices were the biggest array of fried foods she'd ever seen. This made Daniella smile. She found a lovely Barbeque Chicken Salad on the menu and ordered it with some iced tea. When the waitress left, Daniella couldn't wait to get up and speak to Luwanda. She'd always been curious as to why she'd dropped out of school in the 11th grade, especially since her grades were always good. *Gosh, she was even on the student council and had won the local beauty pageant.* Daniella thought.

She caught sight of her in the kitchen and said, "Luwanda Jenkins, oh my God? Do you remember me?"

Luwanda looked up, and at first didn't recognize Daniella, but after a moment, a look of recognition washed over her and she smiled broadly. "Oh my God! Danny? I? Oh, child! I haven't seen you in a dog's age!" She took off her apron and put it down, then made her way over to Daniella. "Let's go sit down and catch up! It's time for my break anyway."

The pair went back to Daniella's table and sat down. Daniella smiled and asked, "So, Wanda, tell me, girl! What have you been up to? How long have you been working here?"

Luwanda suddenly looked a little sad to answer this question, and looked down at her hands for a somber moment. Daniella felt extremely guilty she'd asked her.

"I guess I've been working here for a lot of years now, guess about 16 years since my first girl was born. I had to quit school when I got pregnant with her."

Daniella replied, "I really wondered about that many times...why you left school. You always got such good grades. I heard you say one time you wanted to be a lawyer."

Luwanda said, "Yea girl, I got good grades, but I was dumb in some ways, especially with men. I thought we were in love, but he left me when he found out I was pregnant. I should have known because everyone told me what a player he was. But with me, he was as sweet as pie, and he really loved me, or at least I thought he did. I think his damn daddy didn't want him to marry me."

She winced as she said these things, looking more uncomfortable by the minute, and then said, "Enough about me now. Tell me about you Honey! I heard you moved up to New York or someplace like that to make your fortune."

Daniella laughed, "No! Not New York, but in the Middle East. I live in Dubai. Have you heard of it?"

Luwanda reacted with a great deal of alarm, "Oh No Honey! You moved to Arabia? You aren't afraid? I'd be afraid of them A-rabs. They don't like something, they just blow it up!" Daniella smiled at the misconception. Hearing this from Luwanda made it impossible to be angry because she didn't know how innocent she was.

Daniella simply replied, "Na! They're nice actually, well, most of them are. Dubai is a great city. You'd so love it there. Maybe when I go back, you can come visit me?"

Luwanda burst out into a hearty laugh, and affirmed, "Honey, I can't afford to go to Atlanta Georgia! And you want me to go to Arabia?"

She could barely contain her laughter. "You are a funny girl!"

Luwanda explained that her break was now over and it was time to get back to work. Daniella followed her back to her work station. She asked Danny if she'd be there for a while because it would be nice to catch up more during her next break. Daniella agreed and walked back to her table to wait for her food.

Precisely as the waitress brought her salad to the table, two lovely girls walked into the diner. They waved at Luwanda, so it was obvious to Daniella that these were Wanda's girls. They sat down and another waitress brought them over a couple sandwiches and two iced teas.

Daniella carried on observing them while she ate her lunch, occasionally looking down at her IPhone to check for messages. The barbecue chicken was actually quite delicious, so she took a moment to simply enjoy the succulent flavor whilst sipping on her iced tea. Being back in the South definitely meant she'd be eating far more than what she had been used to in the Middle East.

When she was done, she paid her check and decided to greet the girls. She walked over to the table and noticed that they were chatting and the older one seemed to have very motherly instincts towards the younger one. She tapped the older girl on the shoulder and when the young woman turned around, Daniella noticed the most striking green eyes, and it felt like looking in a mirror, as Daniella's eyes were the same color. She thought of how incredibly unusual this was to see on an African American girl. She had just been discussing how Luwanda's "Baby Daddy" had left her with two kids to look after. It never occurred to Daniella to ask if he was white.

"Hi, there! I know you don't know me, but I'm a friend of your Mama. We went to high school together, and when I saw you, I just thought I'd come over and introduce myself...My name is Daniella. What's your name?" The girls looked very apprehensive, especially the older one.

"I'm Lizzie and this is Sadie." Lizzie turned back towards her sister, then Daniella said, "Wanda didn't tell me what beautiful girls she has. She's a sweet lady, but I'm sure Y'all know that already. Your mom was one of the coolest gals in school, and certainly one of the prettiest."

Lizzie rolled her eyes, obviously annoyed, then turned to Daniella and said, "Ma'am you'll excuse me if I don't feel like reminiscing with any white folks from my Mama's past!

You people made my Mama's life a living Hell when she was young, so I'll just say good day to you."

Daniella was floored, as she never expected such boldness from this striking young lady. She could see Lizzie tracking her from the corner of her eye, as though she was waiting for her to leave. Not wishing to scold Luwanda's children right in front of her, she simply exhaled audibly and moved near the kitchen to say goodbye to Luwanda.

"Hey Wanda, it's been so nice seeing you again! I'm sorry I can't stay. Maybe I'll drop by again before I go home? Maybe we can meet up for dinner, somewhere nice."

Luwanda looked thrilled at the possibility and replied, "Oh, it was nice seeing you too Honey! I'd sure like to see you again. You know where to find me now if you wanna get together."

She smiled so genuinely at Daniella that it warmed her heart. Luwanda obviously didn't notice the scowl on Lizzie's face. Daniella did, but instead of scowling back, she simply let her face drop, still unable to understand the hostility of this moment. Those piercing green eyes followed her all the way out the door.

She got in the car and decided that now she needed to forget everything else except Carl. Refueled by the food and the encounter with Luwanda, she sped off to Carl's ranch.

8

BLAST FROM THE PAST

As she drove to Carl's place, she remembered a day in Katie's kitchen long ago. She was about 14 years old, and Leo and Carl were 11. Carl just walked into the kitchen and Leo said, "Hey Dude! How are you? Why weren't you in school today?" Carl stood in the middle of the kitchen, looking as though he felt quite sorry for himself and said in a thick hillbilly accent, "Oh man! My mama let me stay home cuz I was so tired. I was in my Grand daddy's field yesterday picking cotton all day!"

He stood there after this revelation with his hands on his hips and posing with his hips poked forward, which almost made him look S-shaped. Daniella found it hilarious. She burst out laughing, much to Carl's dismay. He snapped back, "What the fuck are you laughing at?!"

Daniella, still giggling, said, "Well, if it ain't little Cottontail, who's been picking cotton all day! I think I'm gonna call you Cottontail from now on! Hahahaha!"

Carl got furious and snapped back, "Stop laughing Bitch!"

Leo snapped, "Don't call my sister a Bitch, Carl!"

Carl couldn't believe Leo was taking her side, but everyone who truly knew him understood that Leo followed the rules of a Southern gentleman—Fun was fun, but no outsider was gonna insult family.

Leo just laughed it off saying, "Oh come on! That was funny and you're too sensitive. Let's go outside."

Daniella, knowing he'd been silenced, waved and added, "Bye Cottontail."

She smiled slyly and he furiously flipped her off. Remembering this day made her smile, but it also raised a red flag. There was always something off about Leo and Carl's relationship. He had always hung out with Leo, but Carl never really felt like Leo's equal, and after that day, everyone in school started calling him "Cottontail." Being called a funny name made him act differently. Everyone thought he was, at least, amiable before, but after his nickname had caught on, Carl was a much meaner person, according to what Daniella heard through the grapevine.

Seeing the two of them together always made no sense at all. Leo was drop dead handsome, and he had a smile that sparkled. It was electric, and the girls flocked to him, not just for the smile, but the swag in his demeanor. He held himself like a man who knew he was valuable and didn't have to brag about it. Carl, on the other hand, was short and lanky—way too skinny, and unlike Leo, he felt the need to brag loudly about everything, as if he were announcing to the world that he was special and more than worthy to be around Leo.

Daniella arrived at Carl's house around 2 pm. She knew she couldn't stay there long as visiting hours at the prison were only from 5-7pm today and she wanted to see Leo to tell him what she'd been up to. As she parked, she noticed the laundry hanging out on the line and the fields of tomatoes and other vegetables. It seemed that Carl had a variety of things he was growing, but the plants looked a bit skimpy.

His horse stables did look great, though. She caught a glimpse of a beautiful stallion grazing outside the barn. He was jet black and obviously well cared for, as his coat looked shiny, which could only mean he was well nourished. She walked up to the house and nervously rang the bell. She heard a little kid scream from inside, "The doorbell is ringing!"

A woman walked quickly toward the door and said as she opened it, "I got it! I got it!"

She looked Daniella up and down in a very critical way and said, "Well Hello. How can I help you?"

Daniella took off her sunglasses and said, "I'm sorry to disturb you this afternoon Ma'am, but I'm here to see Carl Walters. I'm Daniella Pierce Sulieman. We went to high school together and he was a friend of my cousin Leo."

The country woman looked blank for a moment and then raised an eyebrow as she realized who Daniella was. Her name was Susanne, and she was a country girl to the core, complete with an apron, and flour on her face from all the baking she'd been doing. Her hair was a mess and her teeth were in need of a whitening treatment, but she tried to put on her best Southern manners.

Susanne quaintly said, "Oh my Lord! Yes, Carl's mentioned you before. Weren't you Leo's adopted sister that went crazy and married a sand, nigger? He said you don't even believe in Jesus Christ anymore."

She ended the question with such a big smile on her face that it left Daniella somewhat in awe. *Racism certainly is stewed to perfection around here*, she thought.

Daniella was so blown away she could hardly move, but

held her own, and replied, "Yep, that's me! The crazy adopted sister. Is he here?"

Susanne looked less than satisfied, hoping that she'd get more of a rise out of her, but instead confirmed, "Well you're gonna have to set a spell cuz he's out in the field. You can wait here in the kitchen if you want. You want some iced tea?"

"Why yes Ma'am. Tea would be nice."

Susanne brought the tea and said, "Well, if you'll excuse me, I still got a lot of work to do in here. It's not that I don't wanna be social or anything."

Daniella said, "No, it's fine. You go on about your business. I'll be fine in here."

As Susanne left, Daniella felt relieved not to have to talk to her anymore. She wasn't exactly the most charming creature in the world. She sipped on the tea, but not for long, as it was kind of funky tasting, obviously not made fresh, so she occupied herself by noticing all of the heads mounted on the walls. Carl had an unusually big collection of them, and one had to wonder why a man would need to display his kills so much. She was briefly reminded of a time that Carl was throwing rocks at squirrels outside their childhood home. He was trying to get Leo to join in, but Leo refused. Daniella remembered how proud she felt of Leo for refusing to take part in animal abuse.

Shortly after, Carl's kids, Carla and Bobby came bursting through the door. Carl followed them inside. He glared at the sight of Daniella sitting there but turned his attention towards the kids. Carla excitedly told her mother, "Mommy, Daddy showed us the baby horse today!"

Susanne replied, "He did? well, that's wonderful, Baby!"

Bobby kept on staring at Daniella, and it was in this

moment that she noticed little Bobby's piercing green eyes, as green as shamrocks.

Bobby said, "Daddy who's this?"

Susanne said, "Well that's a friend of your Daddy's baby. Now let's let them talk in private and go in the living room for a while."

Bobby felt offended and asked, "What's she got to say that she can't say in front of me?"

Carl snapped back, "Don't sass your mother boy! If you do, you know what you'll get!"

Bobby compiled, and as soon as they left the room, Carl sharply asked, "What brings you here Danny? Or do I even need to ask? It's about Leo, isn't it? Everybody knows what he did."

Daniella replied, "Oh that's Bullshit, Carl, and you know it! Leo may be a lot of things, but he's no murderer. You know this as well as I do. I know y'all have had your differences, but a murderer? Come on! Now help me figure out who may have done this to him."

Carl's fists and teeth clenched as he barked, "That son of a bitch is capable of anything! I'm surprised you're here for him Danny, after the way he treated you?"

He looks at her for a moment and continues, "If anyone had a reason to kill him, it's actually you. You had a reason to kill them both."

Daniella sadly laughed at this and replied, "Well, you're not wrong. Right before I came over here, I was telling my best friend in Dubai that if I had been here in the country when it happened, everyone would have suspected me, but alas, I wasn't here."

Carl looked at the floor and Daniella stood up. "Yep, you see that's the problem with accusing me. I wasn't here. I was halfway around the world." She pauses for his reaction and continues when she sees him look up with interest, "Where were you when Daddy was killed Carl?"

Carl's eyes filled with a violent hatred she'd never seen in him before. His eyes went black and his teeth clenched so hard that it looked as though he'd chip a tooth, and his fists were balled up. She found herself very frightened all of the sudden, and backed up for fear that he'd strike her. He looked at her with fury and said, "I thought I could be nice to you. I thought we could get along cuz of the fact we both share a hatred for that motherfucking bastard and his faggot father, but NO! You just had to accuse me! What about that other faggot? Mr. Hale! I bet you didn't even think of him. You came directly here to accuse me!"

Daniella could barely get words out of her mouth for fear of Carl. He moved towards her as though he wanted to hit her. She quickly replied, "Yes, as a matter of fact, I did go there, and he may be guilty, but somehow I don't think he's guilty of more than an ongoing man-crush on my father."

Carl glared in a threatening manner. His eyes were darkening, and she felt it was time to go. He came closer and looked menacingly at her, and then quietly said, "Get out."

She gulped, and felt frozen. She managed to get out only, "Carl, I..."

His eyes darkened further, and he screamed this time. "I said get the fuck out!!! I hate all you fucking Pierce trash fuckers! Out!"

She grabbed her purse and keys and ran out of his house. Her hands were shaking as she put the keys in the ignition. The second she was out, he screamed, "Fuck!"

He swiped a vase off the table and crashed it against the wall, and only calmed down when he saw his son creep out of the next room, terrified of what's made his father so angry. Carl took a deep breath and stretched out his hands, "Come here, son. Everything's ok. Don't be scared."

Bobby said, "I love you, Daddy."

A tear formed in Carl's eye, and he said, "Love you too son."

Daniella sped off, crying uncontrollably. *I gotta take off the rest of today. Tomorrow I've gotta be very strong, strong for Leo.* She thought. She knew she'd be no good to anyone today, not after that encounter, so she decided to call it a day and recover.

She saw a sign for a luxury lake resort, so she made the turn to go to it, and when she got there, she was overjoyed. The view was breathtaking—a beautiful lake cut through a plush green valley of trees, and the sky was the bluest she'd ever seen.

She took a room there for the night, called Katie to let her know what was going on, and relaxed for the rest of the day. The trial was going to take a lot of energy, and Carl had scared her to the core. She needed this, to unplug and refuel. Soon, her cares melted away, and that night she slept peacefully, but not nightmare free.

She dreamt of being behind a glass window, watching as needles injected the lethal poison into the arms of a young 10-year-old Leo. Tears were streaming down his cheeks as he called out "Danny!"

9

AND HERE WE GO...

The first day of the trial was tense. The entire courtroom was full, and it seemed like every type of person was there—country folk, business people, and the press. Aunt Rosie and Uncle Sheldon were there with Katie, and they all looked worried. The entire atmosphere in the room radiated anger mixed with satisfaction.

Mr. Hale was there, wiping the sweat from his forehead with the handkerchief he always carried. He made eye contact with Daniella and smirked as if to indicate that he was happy to be there to witness the downfall of the whole family. She understood that in his mind, Ross was the victim here, and his ungrateful children were to blame.

Carl was there alone, sitting in the back of the courtroom, looking smug and staring at Daniella with hatred in his eyes. Uncle Sheldon caught sight of this and whispered to Daniella, "That boy's got fire in his eyes! What's that all about?"

Daniella replied, "That's what I'd like to know."

Just when the proceedings were about to begin, Daniella saw someone that she didn't expect—Lizzie was there, and when she saw Daniella looking at her, she looked nervous. There wasn't time to deal with this now, as the bailiff announced the arrival of the judge. Daniella was behind Leo and his attorney, Mr. Hillard.

Leo turned around to see Daniella. *He looks so worried*, Daniella thought, and as she studied his eyes, she saw the little boy she used to know. Her mind wandered to a night in their childhood when it was just the three of them, Ross, Leo, and Daniella. On a school night, the two of them would normally go to bed by 8pm, but this night was to be like no other. Suddenly, Ross knocked on Leo's door, then Daniella's, to announce that they needed to get ready to go to town and see a movie.

Daniella replied, "But isn't it about time to go to bed? I'm really tired Daddy."

Ross scoffed and answered, "I swear girl, you are no child. You think like an old woman sometimes. Come on Grandma! Get ready." Leo cheered with happiness.

As they were in the car, driving to town, Daniella felt very resentful of the fact that she may not be alert at school the next day. She'd always taken her schoolwork seriously and didn't appreciate the interruption of her nightly schedule. Leo felt differently. He loved it. He looked admiringly at Ross as he drove and said, "Danny don't understand Daddy. I love going to a movie late at night! We ain't always gotta worry about school."

Daniella rolled her eyes and snapped back, "Danny doesn't understand! And there's no such word as 'ain't'. See, that's why you need school, Moron!"

Ross and Leo laughed at her, and she could see the strong bond between them getting more powerful. She rolled her eyes and muttered, "Peas in a pod."

Daniella snapped out of her memory to pay attention to

the Bailiff. He loudly commanded, "All rise!" Everyone stood up as the judge entered. The honorable Judge Bueford Belham was assigned to preside over the case. He was tough and had a reputation for being especially hard on those would commit "hate crimes."

"All rise as the honorable Judge Bueford Belham takes the stand!"

Everyone stood up. The judge sat down behind the desk and said, "Be seated."

After everyone sat down, the judge looked around the room with a stern grimace on his face and remarked, "I want it to be known that I expect order in my courtroom, and if any of the spectators or the press get out of line, I'll have them barred from these proceedings."

His brow furrowed as he looked around to be sure his message was received loud and clear, and then began. "Mr. Mitchell, please make your opening statement."

Mr. Mitchell, the attorney for the prosecution, stood up, looked pensive at Leo and said, "Ladies and gentlemen, you've been asked to review a shocking case. A case that involves not only murder but hate and intolerance for a minority. Ross Pierce was a pillar of the community, a peaceful man who brought nothing but prosperity to our great state and city. His only downfall was being a homosexual and letting Leo Pierce find out about it."

There was a loud roar of whispering from the onlookers, and this angered Judge Belham. He warned, "Now see, that's exactly the kind of nonsense I won't tolerate. Watch yourselves people." The silence was once again restored. Mr. Mitchell looked smugly toward Leo and his attorney and then continued.

"We will present you with many character witnesses that will prove beyond any shadow of a doubt, that Leo Pierce has a history of violent and abusive behavior and is the only suspect in this case that makes any logical sense. We will prove this young man willfully and maliciously planned and executed this horrible crime."

He moved closer to the jury, so he could look many of them in the eye, then finished his opening statement by saying, "As logical and reasonable members of this jury, you'll deliver the only possible verdict in this trial--Guilty as Charged."

Mr. Mitchell lingered for a moment, continuing to stare at the jury members for a few moments, then turned to go sit down. The judge turned towards the attorney for the defense, Mr. Hillard, and then said, "Mr. Hillard, your opening statement Sir."

Mr. Hillard stood up, thanked the judge and proceeded to go near the jury, not in a threatening way as Mr. Mitchell had, but more as a caring friend. Once he'd set the mood, he began to set the tone.

"Ladies and Gentlemen of the jury." He paused to gather his thoughts. "Yes, it's true; Leo Pierce is a bigot. He's also a philanderer and an all around Jerk. But, is he a murderer?"

He paused for a moment, tapped his fingers on his chin, looking pensive and reflective, then continued. "This is a capital trial, a trial for murder in the first degree, and for you to sentence this young man to death by lethal injection, you must be convinced beyond the shadow of a doubt this man has murdered his own uncle in cold blood."

He walked closer to the jury. "We will prove that the prosecution has no solid proof, and in fact, has only circumstantial evidence and has based most of their case on hearsay and speculation. You, as members of the Jury, must remember that being a jerk doesn't prove you are a murderer, and that's what's important here, proof."

He looked dramatically back at Leo. "The only verdict in this trial is Not Guilty because Leo Pierce didn't do it. He is *not* a murderer, and the character witnesses we'll provide will prove this to you. Thank you."

Mr. Hillard went to sit down beside Leo and the judge shuffled some papers on his desk, preparing to proceed. "Mr. Mitchell, you may call your first witness."

Mr. Mitchell called Henry Davidson to the stand. Henry was the police officer who was first called to the scene of the crime. He was African American, and had gone to school with Leo, and he also knew Ross Pierce very well. The bailiff ordered Henry to raise his right hand, and then asked, "Do you swear that the testimony you're about to give is the whole truth without omission?"

Henry replied, "I do swear."

Henry sat in the witness chair while Mr. Mitchell began to question him. He started simply by asking for his full name and exact position with the police force. Henry replied, "Lieutenant Henry Davidson, 2nd precinct, Atlanta City Police Department."

Mr. Mitchell carried on to ask if Henry had been on duty the night of August the 5th. Henry confirmed he was indeed on duty and things were going pretty smoothly until about 11 pm when he got a call because someone had been murdered at the Silver Linings Bar and Grill. Mr. Mitchell asked, "And what did you see? Please don't leave anything out officer."

Henry took a deep breath and explained the terrible scene he'd witnessed that night. He shuddered when he thought of it, and it became obvious to everyone watching him that he'd never seen anything quite so gruesome. He witnessed, "Well, I got there and heard lots of screaming going on, out in the parking lot. We cut through the crowds to see Ross Pierce lying on the ground dead. Somebody had beat his brains out with a baseball bat. Whoever it was must have run out of there in a hurry cuz they dropped the bat, or what was left of it. The victim was covered in his own blood and I remember thinking it was strange that no one seemed to have heard a thing. By that time, my backup officers arrived and they searched the premises and interviewed all the people who were still there, but confirmed no one saw anything at all that could help."

Once Henry finished explaining the scene, Mr. Mitchell pulled out some photos from the night of the murder to show them to Henry. Henry looked at them with a pungent mixture of disgust and pity. Mr. Mitchell asked, "Is that the body of the deceased, as you found him?" Henry replied, "Yes it is. That poor man."

Mr. Mitchell handed the pictures to the judge, and then began to ask Henry if he had known Ross Pierce personally, but Mr. Hillard bounced out of his chair with an "I object!" The judge knew full well what Mr. Mitchell was trying to do, but let him ask the question anyway.

The judge allowed Henry to state his opinion, because Henry had grown up alongside Leo in the same school, so it seemed reasonable to assume he may have some knowledge of any family "enemies" that were well known. Mr. Hillard's objection was duly noted by the judge, but turned down, so Henry was allowed to go ahead and tell the world what he *really* thought of Ross Pierce.

Henry maintained, "Well, even though no one ever talked about it, we all knew he was queer, but he seemed likable enough. I didn't appreciate how he called African Americans "niggers" though. Otherwise, he seemed pretty harmless."

Mr. Mitchell nodded his head in agreement, then asked

Henry if he had known Leo in school, to which he replied, "Yeah, I knew him."

Mr. Mitchell, detecting a bit of sarcasm in Henry's tone, followed up by asking, "Were you, friends?"

Henry looked shocked and sharply replied, "No way! Leo never liked any of the black students. He always said we were dumb niggers that should be shining his shoes, not sitting in his white school next to him."

The outrage in the court was obvious as the roar of the whispering voices became disruptive.

Mr. Hillard shouted, "Your Honor!"

The judge was compelled to ask Mr. Mitchell where he was going with this line of questioning, to which Mr. Mitchell said, "I'm simply trying to establish a pattern of behavior, Your Honor."

The judge, looking annoyed, replied, "Make your point and make it quick."

Mr. Mitchell asked, "Henry, you said before that you thought Ross Pierce was a bigot, but a harmless one. Would you consider Leo as harmless?"

Henry looked almost relieved to say it out loud, "No Sir, I don't think he's harmless at all. I have known him to be involved in many fist fights at school, and you don't even wanna know about the women he's hurt with his philanderin' ways!"

Mr. Hillard, obviously flabbergasted, said, "Your Honor, Objection! This is biased!"

The judge replied, "Your objection is duly noted. Mr. Mitchell, you have been warned." By this time, the buzzing in the courtroom had begun to severely annoy Judge Belham, so he gave the audience a stern warning as well. "One more outburst and I'll clear this courtroom! Now, carry on Mr. Mitchell."

Mr. Mitchell agreed to rephrase the question, so he stood and thought for a moment, all the while knowing what he wanted to ask, so he finally came out with it. "Henry, do you think Leo was capable of murdering his father after he found out about his sexual orientation?"

Henry thought for a moment and replied, "Well, I don't know really. He's a Godless man and I know he's capable of a lot of wrongdoing, but I don't know if he did this. I can tell you this, though. Whoever did this had to have really hated that man. No one beats a man to death like that unless there's some serious hate involved! So, it would have to be someone who knew him well, not a stranger."

Mr. Mitchell seemed a bit annoyed that he didn't get an absolute "Yes" from Henry, so he pushed a little more. "Given the right amount of anger, could Leo be capable of this?"

Henry looked at Leo, and Leo was peering back at him with ever darkening eyes, reflecting all the years he'd mistreated Henry and all of his friends. Even when his life was in jeopardy, Leo seemed unwilling to give him a longing or begging look, so Henry said, "Yes, maybe."

The buzzing in the court started but soon stopped as the judge gave them a stern grunt. Mr. Mitchell appeared to be pleased, then turned to Mr. Hillard and said, "Your witness."

Daniella's stomach churned due to what had just happened. Leo looked back at her desperately. Mr. Hillard stood up and approached Henry. "Ok, Henry I only have a couple questions for you."

He paused, then said, "Isn't it true that you and Leo got into a major fist fight in school, one so bad that everyone in school knew about it? And you lost?"

Henry wasn't happy to have this brought up again after all those years. "Yes, it's true. So what?"

"So..." Mr. Hillard pauses. "Don't you think that would make you a little bias against Leo after all these years? Perhaps you're enjoying the chance to get back at him?"

Henry snapped back, "No! I got in many fistfights over the years with many people! A lot of them folks are really good people now."

Mr. Hillard nodded in agreement and continued, "So, getting into a fight doesn't necessarily make someone a bad person? Look at you! You're a police officer now. No one is a better example of how people can change, how they can be better as an adult than they were as a kid."

Henry's mouth dropped open and he tried to retort. "Um, no wait. That's not what I meant. I meant..."

Mr. Hillard looked sympathetic and said, "It's ok Henry. We all make mistakes." He then turned to the judge and said, "No more questions, your Honor."

The judge smirked and said, "Mr. Mitchell, your next witness."

Mr. Mitchell smiled because he believed his next witness would be the ace in the hole, so he called Dana Johnson to the stand. Dana was a stylish woman, and she happened to be Leo's ex-wife. After the divorce, she had left Georgia, determined to never return, so rumor had it she was more than a little annoyed by the summons. She and Leo exchanged a dirty stare as she took the stand. The breakup had been an ugly one, as everyone in town already knew.

The Bailiff swore her in and Mr. Mitchell began his examination. "State your name fully for the court, please."

Dana said in the thickest Southern accent, "Dana Elizabeth Johnson."

Mr. Mitchell asked, "How do you know the defendant?"

Her eyes narrowed as she replied, "Well I was married to

him for a year. We divorced when I caught him cheating on me."

Mr. Mitchell said, "Ok, we'll get back to that, but first tell me how was his relationship with his Uncle?"

Dana said, "Well, it was good until he found out his uncle was a queer. They were so close before, especially since Danny left the country to go marry that Rag Head. Danny used to be his favorite until she turned her back on her religion and her country."

The roar of whispers in the court blew up again and this angered the judge. He said, "That is it! This is your last and final warning! I simply won't have this in my court."

Everyone settled down, except Daniella. She tapped Leo on the shoulder and asked, "What's up with this Bitch? Is she out for blood or something?"

Leo responded, "Na, she ain't got nothing but her bitching and moaning. It's about me, not you. But she's got no proof of anything."

Daniella sat back in her chair, hoping he was right. Uncle Sheldon was shaking his head slightly in disbelief, while mumbling, "You know what they say about a woman scorned."

Aunt Rosie snapped, "Shhh! Y'all be quiet! You'll have everyone staring at us."

Mr. Mitchell carried on, "Well I understand your sentiments, but let's stay on topic. My next question is... would you consider Leo, a bigot?"

Dana looked smug as if she'd finally get the chance to blow the whistle and say her piece. "Yes for sure he is! He's always hated Niggers, Jews, and Faggots. I can't hardly remember a day I didn't hear one of those words." She then gave him a damning glance and continued, "But he's a damn hypocrite. The woman I caught him cheating on me with was a nigger. God knows how many nigger girlfriends he's had!"

Upon saying this, her lips curled into a smile; she felt completely vindicated, as if she's been dying to embarrass him like this for years. Mr. Hillard jumped up abruptly and shouted, "Your Honor! She's obviously biased! I object!"

The judge nodded in complete agreement and said, "I'm about to put a stop to this. Objection sustained. Mr. Mitchell, you'd better get on to something relevant fast!"

Mr. Mitchell apologized for wasting the court's time with his antics and continued his examination. This time, in a more straightforward manner, he asked, "Ms. Johnson, where were you on the night of August 5th?"

Dana confirmed she was parked across the street from the Silver Linings nightclub. Mr. Mitchell, in an attempt to solidify this information to the members of the court, asked, "Isn't that a gay nightclub, Ms. Johnson?"

Dana agreed that it was indeed a gay nightclub, but she was parked across the street as she had just met a girlfriend of hers in the coffee shop next door. As she was getting back in her car, she saw Leo leaving the club. Mr. Mitchell pointed out what an oddity it was to see a man like Leo leave a club like that, given his feelings on the issue. Dana was very happy to explain the reason.

"Well, ever since he found out his Uncle was a fag, all he could ever do with his time was spy on him. He was obsessed with catching him in the act so he could 'beat his ass'. That's what he always told me! He said he was gonna find him with one of his 'froot loop' boyfriends and 'beat his ass to the ground.'"

Mr. Mitchell carried on to confirm Dana had never actually entered the club, as a classy and cultured woman such as herself wouldn't be caught dead in such a place. She was simply returning to her car as she had just left her friend at the coffee shop. Dana did confirm, however, "He left in a hurry. I do remember that. He looked like he couldn't wait to get out of there."

Mr. Mitchell asked what time she had seen him, and she confirmed it must have been around 11 pm. "I left for my hotel right after that, and I was only staying about an hour from there. I remember reaching my room around 12 midnight. I'm so sorry that's all I can remember. I wish I could tell you more."

Mr. Mitchell looked very pleased with himself and with her, then replied, "You've been very helpful Ma'am." He then turned towards Mr. Hillard and said, "Your witness."

Mr. Hillard got up, and it was a nervous moment throughout the courtroom, as people whispered and tapped on their smartphones, sending tweets about the case. Daniella was on the edge of her seat, thinking this looked quite horrible for Leo, and even Leo seemed nervous about what was going to come next, as his hands had started to shake a bit. *She certainly has made him appear guilty*, Daniella thought.

The courtroom was as quiet as could be, as everyone waited to hear what Mr. Hillard would come up with to come through this. Thankfully, he was way ahead of everyone and had been worth every penny of his exorbitant fees.

He approached, smiling at Dana's false sense of confidence. Like a tiger in the grass, he pounced with his first question, "Ms. Johnson, you testified under oath you left the Coffee Bean at 11 pm that night, on August 5th?"

Dana smugly replied, "Yes, that's right."

Mr. Hillard raised an eyebrow when he asked, "Well can

you tell me why the clerk doesn't remember you there that night?"

Dana said, "Well I don't know! Maybe she has a bad memory! How am I supposed to know? I know where I was!"

Cunningly, Mr. Hillard stared at her for a moment, and then softly asked, "Who was the friend you were there with?"

Dana snapped, "Ok I wasn't with a friend! I just didn't wanna look pathetic because I was watching him."

Mr. Hillard smiled slyly as he realized he had her exactly where he wanted her. He said, "Did you know that lying under oath is a felony?"

She looked up at him with large teary eyes, revealing by her look that she had no idea she'd just put herself at his mercy. Mr. Hillard went on, "Now Ms. Johnson, I want to ask you something else and I want you, to be honest this time. Isn't it true you regularly follow Leo?"

She closed her eyes and looked down at her hands. Even if it was ultimately true, she didn't want to be the talk of the town, and in a small town like this, that was almost a certainty. Nervously, she replied, "I don't follow him! If I happen to turn up in some of the same circles, that doesn't constitute following. Maybe he's seen me around a lot, and he's making up stories about me following him."

Mr. Hillard got close to her face, with every intention of intimidating her. Her big eyes and rapid breathing made it obvious that his plan was working. He asked, "Well isn't it true you'd like to see Leo put to death for this crime, whether he did it or not? You'd feel like he deserved it for what he did to you! Wouldn't you?"

Mr. Mitchell shot out of his chair like a bullet. "Your Honor! Objection! Speculation!"

The judge agreed and stated, "Mr. Hillard, that's strike

one for you. The members of the jury will disregard Mr. Hillard's comments and they shall be stricken from the record."

Mr. Hillard brushed it off with a nonchalant shrug of his shoulders saying, "That's ok your Honor; I'm done. No further questions."

The judge excused Dana from the stand, and she couldn't wait to get away from there. She hurriedly pulled herself together and walked past Leo with burning hatred in her eyes. Leo seemed pleased as he smiled and put his hands on his head to smooth down his hair, and as Daniella watched the smug look on his face, she couldn't help but wonder if Leo was learning anything from this terrible experience.

More and more she realized Leo was here in this predicament due to his womanizing ways. Of course, no one had any real proof of anything yet, but she felt it in her gut. Leo had somehow put himself into this, because he had pissed off the wrong person, someone who desperately wanted to blame him for the crime. She hoped the coming days would reveal everything, but hoped she was right about Leo's innocence.

The judge stated, "Court will reconvene tomorrow morning at 9 am." The gavel fell.

Daniella quickly moved near Leo, before he could be taken out of the courtroom, and said, "I'll be straight out there to see you. We need to talk before all this starts up again tomorrow, ok?"

"Ok, I agree. See you shortly" Leo said.

10

THE REVELATION

Daniella waited in the visiting room of the Georgia State Penitentiary and then saw a policeman leading Leo to the visiting cubicle. As they both sat down, they lifted the phones together and Daniella said, "Some day huh?"

Leo cleared his throat and replied, "Yeah, no kidding. So, what do you think my chances are?"

Daniella was more focused on the information he'd been hiding. Without wavering, she asked, "How come you didn't tell me about Dana? If you want me to help you, you have to tell me everything. Understand?"

Leo said, "Well you haven't exactly been here Danny. How the Hell are you supposed to know what's going on in anyone's life when you've been busy, shacked up with your fucking camel jockey?"

Daniella's eyes widened and her mouth dropped open, and she couldn't move. She'd come all this way, leaving the home she'd built, just to help this guy, and he had the nerve to say that? She shook her head and finally managed to utter the words, "I don't know how you can say that right now, and after all I'm doing for you. Don't you realize how much that hurts my feelings?"

He looked down at his hands, looked up at her with soft eyes, and then attempted to apologize in his own way. "I'm sorry Danny. I do appreciate you being here. I guess I've just got a big ole' redneck sense of humor. Guess I have been a real asshole to a lot of people. You know that's how he taught me to think. If I tried being myself, he'd raise his hand up like he was gonna slap me and call me a bleeding heart liberal faggot. He made me what I am."

Daniella appreciated the fact that he was reflecting on his behavior somewhat, as this may be useful for his future, and maybe he'd stay out of prison from now on. That is, *if* he gets out this time.

He tried to lighten the mood by smiling that same goofy smile that he did as a child and Danny couldn't stay mad. After all, she'd practically raised him. She smiled and said, "You are a big redneck alright!"

They share a moment of comfortable silence and Daniella thought to herself how nice this felt, to reconnect with her cousin again. She knew now exactly how much she'd missed him. They were so close as kids, and for the first time in a very long time, she realized that having this relationship with him was the missing piece in her life. *What a damn shame it is that it takes a tragedy like this to bring us together again.* She thought.

She felt tears wellingl in her eyes, but she knew that now wasn't the time to indulge in them. She looked straight up at the ceiling, to quiet them, and then said, "Ok now, we need to think. Do you know if they have any solid proof against you? That bat didn't have any identifiable fingerprints on it, as they only caught a few partial prints, not enough for identification, but the word 'Trust' was missing from the bat pieces. They believe that the bat was wiped hurriedly at the scene. So ... *what* could they have that proves a real case?"

Leo looked down at the floor, thinking of anything that he could remember, but frustration was all he could feel, especially when Danny nagged, trying to force him to remember anything. She said, "Come on Dammit! Think! I need to know if they have anything so we can figure out how to block them."

Leo looked frustrated as his eyes narrowed and said, "I'm trying! They arrested me the day after it happened, and no one's told me any details of the case, only what they *think* I did. As far as I know, all they have is the sighting of me at the scene."

Daniella replied, "Even your lawyer? He didn't ask the prosecution what witnesses they're producing? He's got a right to know that."

Leo said, "Well if he did, he didn't tell me."

"That's Bullshit!" Danny argued, "I'm gonna find out what he knows."

The guard pointed to his watch to indicate that their time was finished, and Danny started to get up. Leo said, "Thanks for coming Danny." He paused and continued, "Hey, I saw Carl in the courtroom today. I guess he's really gunning for me, huh?"

Daniella almost laughed, as that should be painfully obvious. "Well, you did screw his wife, my dear cousin. By the way, I can't believe you did that! What were you thinking?"

Leo shook his head, then thought for a moment and said, "Hey, speaking of people from the past, I saw Luwanda in the courtroom today too. Do you know her?"

Daniella had stood up before he mentioned Luwanda, but hearing her name mentioned made her plop down once again to her seat. A gutting feeling shot through her body, as many things were coming clear.

"I didn't see Luwanda there today Leo. How exactly do you know her?" Daniella already knew in her heart, but had to ask the question out loud.

Leo grinned a little in remembrance of Luwanda. "We were talking about people I fucked, remember? Well, Luwanda was my little brown sugar on the side for years."

Daniella huffed, "Oh my God Leo! You know she's got two kids! She claims that they were kids of a man who seduced her and left her high and dry."

She remembered how green Lizzie's eyes were, and how familiar they looked. Now, she knew that it was because they were Leo's eyes. Both Danny and Leo had striking green eyes, and Lizzie's were unmistakably the same.

Leo could tell that Danny was getting swept up in disbelief, and said, "You know I couldn't admit those kids were mine! They'd kill me here. You better than anyone ought to know that."

The guard interrupted and grabbed the phone, "That's it, Pierce!" He hung up the phone for him and took him back to his cell. As the guard did all but drag him, Leo looked back at Danny as she stood there in a state of disbelief. But just as he was about to turn the corner to go inside the cell block, Danny looked at him and saw that little boy's face of his again. She saw her little baby cousin being dragged off to a jail cell, and something inside her turned. He didn't belong there. He may be a womanizer, and a deadbeat Dad, but he was *not* a murderer. Danny felt it strongly in her gut.

That night she wanted to stay with Katie, so she made the two-hour drive to her place. She wanted to ask Katie if she'd known all along about Leo's children. As she sat there in the kitchen with Katie, they snacked on fresh roasted peanuts and drank iced tea. Katie shook her head in disbelief after hearing about all this and said, "Good God in Heaven! I've told that boy to stay away from those Negra girls. I knew he dilly dallied around a little, but I never imagined that he'd be dumb enough to father two bastards with one of them!"

Normally Daniella would let everything she said go because she knew that Katie was far too old to change, but calling the girls bastards seemed like one of those things that shouldn't go unnoticed. "Grandma, don't you think it's a little harsh to call them bastards? After all, you don't really know them, do you?"

Daniella went on to reflect, "They're actually sweet girls, just mixed up and resentful about the father that abandoned them. Do you think they know that Leo is their father? I wonder if Luwanda ever told them?"

Katie shrugged her shoulders, "I dunno Honey. I'm still thinking about how that cousin of yours is out of control. My God, he sure has messed up his life in all kinds of ways."

Daniella thought for a moment, as she took another sip of her tea. A burning sensation of curiosity bubbled up inside of her. She decided that she simply couldn't wait to find out, and decided to leave right away. Kissing Katie on the cheek, she said, "Oh Grandma, I'm so sorry. I thought I'd be staying with you tonight, but I have to find out what I can. I'll try to come back tomorrow. If I get tired, I'll just get a room in Atlanta tonight."

Katie hugged her and said, "Ok honey, be careful. You know Atlanta can be really dangerous at night. I sure wish you'd just go in the morning."

Daniella smiled a bit at hearing this. It was nice to have her concern, and it almost felt like she had her family back after all these years of being estranged from them. She kissed her again on the head and said, "I'll be fine. Don't you worry now. I promise I'll call you when I get there. I have to talk to Luwanda tonight. If I'm lucky, I'll catch her just as she's finishing her shift. I don't know exactly where she lives, so I think this would be best."

She got into her car and pulled away, but before she could get completely out of the driveway, she caught sight of the basement light flickering. The servant's stairs led up to a small window near the ground that was originally put there for ventilation purposes. The light flickered and then burst. She heard Katie shout from inside the house, "Stop doing that!"

Daniella was about to get out of the car to go back in and check on her, but Katie came out to wave goodbye. Daniella rolled down the window to her car and shouted, "You Ok, Grandma?"

Katie smiled and nodded, then started to shoo her away, so Daniella decided to forget it and head for the highway. As she was driving, she got a call from Mr. Hillard. Earlier, she'd called him because she was trying to find out what the prosecution had up their sleeve. Daniella always believed that the best defense was a good offense, so it seemed like the only logical thing to do.

Mr. Hillard said, "Well, I know you've been wanting to know what we can expect next and lemme tell you, it's not pretty. I tried hard to get it thrown out, but it's gonna come up tomorrow I think."

Daniella braced herself and asked, "Let's hear it. What've they got?"

Mr. Hillard continued, "Well, they've got a pair of bloody gloves, and unfortunately they were located in Leo's apartment. The blood on the gloves matches the blood of

Ross Peirce, so they were definitely the ones worn during the crime. They did some DNA testing on it too, to see if Leo's DNA was present, but the test was inconclusive, so that's good."

Daniella shuddered at the thought. Things were looking terrible for her cousin, and finding such a piece of evidence in his apartment wasn't helping him at all. She asked, "Could there have been a break in? Maybe someone planted those gloves?"

Mr. Hillard confirmed, " A glass window in his place was shattered, but the problem is that Leo himself has already admitted to shattering that himself in a fit of rage over his father."

Daniella rolled her eyes. Leo had always been a hot head, and this she knew all too well. Nevertheless, those gloves had to have been planted, she reckoned. There must be some other explanation. She asked, "Does Leo know about this? What's he said about it?"

Mr. Hillard replied, "Yeah he knows, and to his credit, he hasn't owned a pair of gloves for years, so the idea that someone planted them might fit. That's what I'm going to try to use, to cast some doubt about this to the jury."

Daniella said, "Well thanks, Mr. Hillard. I appreciate you getting back to me so soon, and I'll see if I can find out anything useful from Luwanda...Oh, did you know about those girls? Before I told you?"

"No, I can't say that I did." Mr. Hillard admitted, "Leo never told me I'm afraid, but it's really good that you know now. Try to find out if any of them had anything to do with it. I'll be standing by. Try to get some sleep later. I know you must be so tired."

Daniella agreed, "I'll see what I can do. As for sleep, I've basically stopped sleeping since I came here and this whole mess began, but I'll try my best." She hung up the phone as she drove on. More than an hour later, she was pulling up in front of the diner. Luckily, Luwanda hadn't finished her shift, so Daniella was very relieved to see her still there.

She walked in and sat at a booth, somewhere Luwanda was sure to see her before leaving. A waitress came over and asked to take her order. Not wishing to be rude, she simply said, "I'll just have a little coffee for now."

The waitress nodded and took the menu, writing down the order as she walked off. At the next booth, Daniella smiled as she remembered all the late nights spent with Faisal after they had first met. They were both young college students, and Daniella was very taken with his quick-wittedness and his strong stand on religion and politics. He was so different than most American boys, so serious and most of all, he stood for something. She looked at the booth and could almost see the younger versions of them over there, laughing and discussing everything under the sun.

One particular night came to mind, the night that Faisal finally admitted that he liked Daniella as more than "just a friend." When Daniella heard him say the words, "I would love to call you my girlfriend. I never thought I'd have these feelings for someone not from my country, but I can't control it. You're all I can think about. I can't stop."

"Then don't," Daniella said with a mooning look in her eyes.

Their hands reached across the table to touch for the first time, and the moment was electric. Daniella would later tell her children that this was the exact moment that she fell in love with their father, but it was only because she felt embarrassed to admit that she loved him from the first moment she saw him. *Kids today don't believe in love at first sight*, she thought.

The waitress brought her coffee and interrupted this happy memory. She asked if Daniella wanted anything else, to which she replied, "Well, I guess I'll have a slice of Pecan Pie."

The waitress smiled and said, "I made it myself. I'll bring a slice right over."

As the waitress left, Luwanda caught sight of Daniella sitting there. She was just finishing for the night, so she came right over. "Hey, girl! What are you doing here? You look so tired...you look like you've been up all night!"

Daniella smiled and replied, "Well yeah, I kinda have." The waitress brought the pie and Daniella thanked her. She was about to start the chat with Luwanda, but Luwanda's manager interrupted. "Wanda! Get back in here! We didn't get your schedule fixed for next week."

Luwanda excused herself and Danny smiled and nodded. "We'll talk when you're done."

Daniella was tired. She hadn't realized it until that moment. She couldn't keep her mind from wandering off, and this time her thoughts went further into her past. She remembered one of the famous Sunday mornings that Ross had with her and Leo. Sundays were usually spent going out to lunch and seeing a movie. Daniella and Leo looked forward to it, and for that one day a week, they felt like a real family.

Ross asked, "Hey Danny. What the Hell did you order?"

Young Daniella replied, "It's a Seafood Salad Daddy. My best friend Mary says it's good for us to order salads like that when we eat out so we won't get fat."

Ross grinned and looked at Young Leo. Leo said, "Well that's cuz she is hot for Mark Hobson in school! That's why she don't wanna be no fat heifer!"

"Shut up fart face!" Daniella said.

Leo laughed, "You shut up Butt Brain!"

Ross said, "Well you just go on and eat your healthy food girl! You can salivate while Daddy eats him a big ole steak!"

He took a big bloody bite, closed his eyes, licked his lips from side to side, then said with a groan, "Mmm! Damn that's good!"

Danny did feel a little jealous, but as a teenager, she was concerned with not gaining weight, so she tried to enjoy her choice.

"You kids ready to see that scary movie I done bought tickets for?" Ross asked as he cut into the char grilled Grade A steak.

By this time, the smell was making Danny's stomach rumble. She asked, "It's not too scary. Is it Daddy? I don't wanna have nightmares."

Leo said, "I love scary movies Daddy. I'm not scared like her." Ross looked on approvingly while they all carried on eating.

Luwanda broke the daydream by saying, "Hey Danny, don't you like your pie?"

Daniella looked down at the untouched pie and then up at the waitress who seemed to be waiting for her to taste it. Daniella said, "Please sit down with me a bit Wanda."

Luwanda joined her as Danny took a big bite of the pie. She smiled approvingly at the waitress, and that seemed to satisfy her need for a good review of her pie making skills.

Luwanda noticed that Danny was a little out of it as she asked, "Girl, what brings you out here at this time of night? I thought you'd be at your grandma's house."

"I was," Daniella replied as she sipped on her coffee, "I just had to see you, though, cuz I found out something interesting." Luwanda's body tensed and her breath hitched as Daniella asked, "Is my cousin the father of your kids?"

Luwanda's face dropped, and all the air rushed out of her lungs as if she had been holding her breath for years. She squared her shoulders, then took a gulp of air and replied, "Yep. He is Honey. I'm so sorry you had to find out like this. I should've told you before...Who told you anyway?"

Daniella said, "It doesn't matter who told me. The question I have is how come you didn't tell anyone?"

Luwanda said, "I wanted to, but I guess I was holding out some hope that your cousin could love me again, admit the way he feels about me, or at least love my girls. They both got his eyes you know. All the Pierce kids have shamrock green eyes."

"I saw that," Daniella commented, "and I guess it didn't really dawn on me that they were his until I was told, but to tell you the real truth, I think something deep in me stirred when I saw their eyes. On some level I think I knew... They're both so beautiful Wanda. Do they know who their Daddy is?"

Luwanda looked down at the table. "I recently gave in and told them. Lizzie was so mad! I never saw her so mad in all my life. She had such hate in her eyes."

Daniella felt something was sinister about this and probed further. "Who else knows? About their true parentage?"

Luwanda went on to say, "Just a few of my friends, and Carl."

Daniella nearly choked on her coffee, "Carl! When did you see him last?"

Luwanda thought for a moment, "Well it was just a few months back, after I told the kids. He came to see me and told me that I'd made a big mistake, but he's glad that I did. I still don't know what that meant, but I swear Girl, I've never seen more hate in his eyes. I don't know why he looked that way. Does he have a problem with Leo?"

Daniella huffed and blurted, "A problem with Leo?! Um, yeah! Leo screwed his wife and may have fathered one of his kids. So, yeah, I'd say that there's a problem, a big one!"

Luwanda reflected on that for a moment, "You mean he's got other kids?"

Daniella said, "Well I'm not sure Honey, but he's been around. That's for sure. I had no idea about all this until I came back. I don't know what made him like that....Well, I have *one* theory."

Luwanda gave her a questioning look. "Well? Let's hear it."

"I think that he's kinda proving that he's not like Daddy. If you know what I mean." Daniella watched her reaction carefully to see if she knew the truth about Ross's nature as well. After a moment, it became clear that she *was* aware of it. She nodded in total agreement and gave back a look of pity.

Daniella asked, "Hey, where are your kids now? I really need to meet them again, now that I know I'm their aunt. I'd like to get to know them better."

Luwanda looked touched, and Daniella noticed, "Hey Wanda, you look shocked. Did you think I wouldn't want to get to know them? Tell me about how my cousin and my father reacted when they knew about all this."

"Humph!" Luwanda blurted. "At first he was happy, but that happiness didn't last long when your Daddy threatened to cut him off without a dime. Leo may have loved me, but he loved the idea of hanging on to his money more. His Daddy was so angry at him when he found out what we'd done. You know how prejudiced he always was. He only thought of black folks as being good for cleaning his house, not for mothering his grandkids."

Daniella gave Luwanda's hand a squeeze when she heard this. She knew better than anyone how horrible Ross Pierce could be about anyone of color. She was still a little confused, though. "Ok, that explains the first one, but what about child number two? How is it that you got fooled twice?"

Luwanda went on to tell the sad tale of how she'd had to quit school due to the pregnancy and how her family had moved to Atlanta to escape prying eyes. Luwanda started working at the diner, and all was well for a few years until Leo found her. According to Luwanda, "That fool got down on one knee, engagement ring in hand. He told me that he was sorry for everything he ever put me through and swore that from now on, we'd be together."

Luwanda's eyes teared. "I let him have me that night. I was so happy and I thought we'd start our lives together and forget the world around us. I was so excited that Lizzie would have her father with her after all."

Daniella excitedly asked, "Well, what happened next?"

Luwanda tearfully admitted, "I woke up the next day and he was gone. He even took the ring with him. He was gone, just like all my hope. All he left behind was Sadie, his second baby with me. I don't know how I was so stupid Danny. I wanted to believe him."

Daniella dropped her fork on her plate and said, "I'm so sorry Wanda. If I'd known, things would have been so different. I wouldn't have let y'all live like this. Now that I do know, life is gonna change for you guys. You can be sure of that."

Luwanda smiled and felt for the first time that she was being treated compassionately. She remembered Lizzie. "My baby Lizzie used to see me so sad sometimes. She used to blame herself and say that if she wasn't born I could have been anything. I've told her over and over that it's not her fault."

"It's not her fault at all." Daniella interrupted. "I'll tell her that too when I see her. Speaking of which, where is she? I'd really love to talk to her."

Luwanda said, "Oh yeah, you asked me where they were before. The truth is, I don't actually know this place. Lizzie researched it and told me about it. It's a Summer Camp for underprivileged youth. I trust her cuz she's always been kind of a mother figure for Sadie, with me always being at work trying to pay the bills. Here's the card she gave me."

The card read, Firecrackers Summer Camp Program, 1590 Willow Creek Dr., Atlanta, GA 205-501-5555. Daniella took the card, trying to be careful not to upset Luwanda. The poor thing has been through enough without having to worry about what Daniella was suspecting. Her gut was telling her she's right, but her heart was wishing she was wrong.

She started preparing to leave. "Wanda, I need to get going now, but we'll talk again soon OK? You don't have to handle all this alone anymore. We've always been friends, and now you're family, so I'm here for you."

Luwanda seemed very pleased and asked, "Would you like a hot cup of that coffee for the road?"

Daniella looked relieved and said, "Oh yes! I'm mighty tired and have a lot of driving to do."

Luwanda brought the coffee and Daniella reached to get some money to pay, but Luwanda blocked her and said, "No Honey. This one's on me."

They hugged tight and Daniella left. She was going to drive to Atlanta tonight, determined to be on time for court the next day, but she was really very sleepy. As she drove, she was grateful for that cup of coffee, as its warmth and strong caffeine content was just enough to keep her alert. She never was a fan of playing loud music in the car, but she did love a great audio book now and then.

She put on her favorite book, the latest of the Game of Thrones series, sipped on her coffee and made her way back to her hotel. The court would be on time tomorrow, so she needed to get a decent night's sleep.

11

THE FIRST BATTLE

The courthouse was buzzing the next morning, and the local paper was selling more copies than ever, thanks to the gossip about the case and Daniella's presence. The fact that she was a Muslim and living in the Middle East seemed to be a very hot topic in the town paper, and the reporters couldn't understand why she had come back to town to help her cousin. The articles were speculating about Faisal, even suggesting he had taken her children and kicked her out of their Middle Eastern home. She chose to ignore all that rubbish for now and focus on freeing her cousin. She reckoned she'd enjoy suing them for libel when she had more time, but for now, there was work to be done. In true Scarlett O'Hara fashion, she told herself she'd think about that tomorrow.

As Daniella walked into the courtroom, Katie seemed to exhale a sigh of relief. Cameras were flashing as the reporters tried to get a clear picture of her entering. Leo looked like he'd been worried sick. He said, "What kept you? I was worried you weren't coming today, and you know I'm needing to know what you found out last night."

Daniella yawned, as it had been a long night, and then looked wearily at Leo. "Well, I had loose ends to tie up. Something you never told me until yesterday. Shall we call it *two* loose ends in fact?"

He looked down at the floor, obviously ashamed, as he knew exactly what she was talking about. He turned around to face the judge, knowing things were about to start.

Daniella asked Katie, "Hey where's Aunt Rosie and Uncle Sheldon today?"

Katie said, "Well they're not coming today because Sheldon's got that prostate problem that keeps on flaring up. I think he had to go to the doctor."

"Poor guy. Ok, here we go. I don't like what's gonna happen today."

Katie was confused and felt kept in the dark. She asked, "What do you mean?"

Daniella looked at her, but before she could answer, she spotted Carl in the back row. He was glaring at Daniella, and the look in his eyes gave her a cold chill. It was as if he knew something everyone else didn't, and to prove that, he smirked. Daniella's eyes narrowed. She wondered what he was up to.

The judge declared that the prosecution should call their first witness for the day. Mr. Mitchell called Peter Hamron, Director of the Department of Forensics, Atlanta County Police Department. Daniella again whispered, "Here it comes."

Katie was even more confused since no one had bothered to explain anything, but didn't say anything more. She watched helplessly as the Bailiff swore Mr. Hamron in. "Raise your right hand! Do you swear to tell the truth, the whole truth and nothing but the truth, without omission?"

Mr. Hamron replied, "I do."

He was instructed to sit down so Mr. Mitchell could begin his examination. Mr. Mitchell looked very confident today, walking with a swagger and keeping his head up high. He leaned in over Mr. Hamron and asked him to state clearly who he was and exactly what his position was. Mr. Hamron replied, "Peter Hamron, Forensic Expert, Department of Forensics, Atlanta County Police Department."

Mr. Mitchell's face hardened as he approached, whilst holding up a pair of blood stained gloves in a plastic evidence bag, "Ok now Sir, can you tell the court what that is exactly?"

Mr. Hamron answered, "They're gloves, found in the residence of the defendant on August 6th after a court warranted search of his apartment. They are splattered with blood that matches the victim. There's also fragments of bone found on the gloves believed to be fragments of the victim's cranium."

The people in the room roar with moans and sounds of disbelief. The judge became annoyed and barked, "Order! Order!"

People settled down a bit, but it didn't stop them from loud murmuring whispers. Leo was white from shock and whispered to his attorney. Mr. Hillard spoke up, "Your Honor, I object! How can anyone be sure that these gloves even belong to my client? They could have been planted in his apartment."

The judge shook his head and scolded, "Mr. Hillard, you know better than this. Your time for cross-examination will come soon. That's when you can ask these kinds of questions. Objection overruled."

Mr. Mitchell handed the gloves to the judge and requested that they be accepted as Prosecution Evidence

Exhibit C. The judge accepted, and Mr. Hillard's face became red and his jaw clenched.

Mr. Mitchell glanced over to the two of them and smiled sarcastically. Then, he turned his attention back towards Mr. Hamron, as he asked, "Just for the record Mr. Hamron, why wasn't the defendant aware of a search being done in his apartment?"

Mr. Hamron answered, "The defendant was arrested early morning on August 6th. He was already in custody when the search was conducted, and since he only rents this apartment, we are only legally obligated to inform the landlord, which we did. We did have a court order, after all."

Leo glared at Mr. Hillard, and Daniella worried that he was alienating the one attorney in this little Southern town who was gutsy enough to take on his case. In their little corner of Georgia, there weren't many people brave enough to take on Ross Pierce and his entourage. Leo barked in a loud whisper, "You suck! You should have thought to ask that! I didn't know anything about their investigation or what was coming up today. Why didn't you let me know?"

The judge was getting bothered and said, "I will have order in my courtroom, Mr. Pierce! You and your attorney can meet later to discuss what's happened today."

Leo got quiet and the judge asked Mr. Mitchell if he had any more questions for this witness. He said, "No Sir, no more questions." Judge Belham looked back towards Mr. Hillard and stated, "Now Mr. Hillard, you may begin your cross-examination."

Leo attempted to tell Mr. Hillard something before he stood up, but Mr. Hillard shushed him harshly. The last thing Mr. Hillard needed at this point was more insults from Leo or more unwanted distraction. He had to work hard to forget Leo at this point and focus *only* on finding any holes in Mr. Hamron's story. He made his way towards the witness box and asked Mr. Hamron the first thing that was on his and everyone's mind. "Mr. Hamron, how do you know these gloves belong to the defendant?"

Mr. Hamron asserted, "They are men's gloves, and the size that he would wear, and they look as though they've been used for a number of years. Also, they were found thrown on his bedroom floor. If they're not his, how did they get there?"

Mr. Hillard smiled and remarked, "Well that brings me to my next question. Is it possible the gloves were planted? Was there any sign of a break-in or unlawful entry?"

"There was broken glass around his door," Mr. Hamron continued, "but Mr. Pierce testified under oath that he broke the glass himself when he slammed the door too hard, out of anger over his father."

Mr. Hillard blurted back, "Yes, but would it have been possible for someone to slip a hand in using that broken glass as a way to jimmy the lock open?"

Mr. Hamron thought for a moment and had to concede, "Well, the glass on the door was quite high, far over the lock, but I suppose it could have been done with a reaching device of some kind."

Mr. Hillard asked, "Were there any fingerprints found in the apartment? Or DNA evidence found on the gloves to prove that Leo had worn them?"

Mr. Hamron confirmed the only fingerprints in the apartment that were found were that of Leo himself, and the gloves were, in fact, worn by more than one person over time, so the result of the DNA testing was inconclusive, but this doesn't prove they were not Leo's.

The courtroom buzzed with excitement at this, and then Mr. Hillard asked, "Mr. Hamron, is it possible that someone could have taken the gloves that may or may not have been worn by Leo, used them at the murder scene, and then planted them?"

"Yes, I suppose it's possible, but a bit unlikely." Mr. Hamron confirmed.

"What I asked you was, is it possible?" Reiterated Mr. Hillard.

Mr. Hamron nodded, "Yes...theoretically."

"No more questions, Your Honor."

That was about all the doubt Mr. Hillard could cast on this witness, but exhaled a sigh of relief to indicate moderate satisfaction with what he'd just pointed out. He went back to sit down next to Leo, and thankfully, Leo appeared calmer as his shoulders had loosened and his breathing became more steady.

The judge called for Mr. Mitchell's next witness. Mr. Mitchell announced, "Your Honor, the prosecution calls Carl Walters to the stand."

Daniella could feel her skin crawl and the hairs stand up on the back of her neck. After her last encounter with Carl, she felt creeped out by him, and his ranking as a suspect in this trial went up a few notches in her book. This suspicion only got worse when he smirked at Leo and Daniella as he passed them. *He knows something that we don't.* That's for sure. Daniella thought.

The bailiff asked Carl to raise his right hand, "Do you swear to tell the truth, the whole truth, and nothing but the truth, without omission?"

Carl vigorously agreed, "I do!"

He sat in the witness box, feeling very happy to be there. Daniella wondered if the other members of the court could see how eager this man was to hurt Leo in any way he could.

She was very glad that she'd filled Mr. Hillard in on the whole story the night before.

Mr. Mitchell began his examination by simply asking Carl to state his name and profession. Carl cooperated, stating he was a local farmer. That was the end of the easy questions. The drama truly started when he asked, "And how do you know the defendant?"

Carl honestly confirmed, "We used to be best friends for a few years when we were kids, even up to high school."

Mr. Mitchell paused, "*Used* to be friends? Can I take that to mean you aren't friends anymore?"

Carl calmly stated, "That's right. We haven't been friends for a while now, since before I got married."

Mr. Mitchell stood still, looking at him for a moment, and then he turned around to face the jury.

"Tell us about your friendship. Why did it break up?"

Mr. Hillard jumped to his feet immediately shouting, "Your Honor! Objection! Irrelevant!"

The judge didn't seem to appreciate that much and barked, "I'll allow it! Mr. Hillard do not raise your voice to me! Overruled!"

Mr. Hillard backed down and said, "Sorry, Your Honor."

Carl explained the reasons he had for ending the friendship. "I'm not friends with him anymore because little by little I could see what a bastard he was. He was just no good at all."

Mr. Mitchell replied, "Can you be more specific?"

Carl nodded and went on, "Well, he's really bad to women for one thing. God knows how many he's used and thrown away. Also, there's the way he treats his family. He hates his sister Daniella and he really hated his father. He's a no good bum! He only lives off his Daddy's money and doesn't do anything important like work or go to school."

Mr. Mitchell ran his fingers through his beard as if he was processing the answer. *What a crock*! Daniella thought as she watched him. She reckoned they had obviously rehearsed this scenario before and practiced it to ensure the most dramatic effect.

Mr. Mitchell probed, "Did he always hate his father? Or did something happen to break them up?"

Carl was excited to answer this question, although he pretended to be calm for the jury and the courtroom onlookers. Daniella and Leo could see the excitement in his eyes as he prepared to tell the baseball bat story.

"Well no. They used to be good buddies. Leo used to do everything with his father. In fact, they used to be pretty good buddies until Leo found out the secret Ross had been hiding his whole life."

Mr. Mitchell responded, "And what secret was that?"

Carl venomously replied, "That Ross Pierce was a faggot."

The murmurs in court began again and the jury became distracted by them, which upset the judge a great deal. Judge Belham said, "Order! Order! That's warning number two people! I will clear this court if I have to!"

Once they settled down, Carl went on. "I gotta admit, it threw me for a loop too! He always seemed like such a *normal* man. I never in a million years would have thought. But yeah, Leo went crazy when he found out."

Carl's thick country accent almost made his words funny, but Daniella was holding her breath, hoping today's testimony would be the worst of it all. She figured if she could get through this, everything would be downhill from here.

Mr. Mitchell asked, "What do you mean by 'went crazy'? What did he do?"

Carl cleared his throat, probably to be sure these words came out crystal clear to everyone, especially the jury. "He went crazy cuz he chased his Daddy up to his Grand Daddy's house with a baseball bat, threatening to knock his fool head off."

Some of the jury members turned to look judgmentally at Leo. Daniella whispered to him, "Don't react at all. Keep calm right now."

"What happened after that?" Mr. Mitchell asked.

"After that, he didn't want anything to do with Ross. They spoke less and less. Once Leo graduated from high school, he went off to the Army and then to college. Of course he didn't finish it, though." Carl confirmed, rolling his eyes.

By this time, even Judge Belham was propping his head up with his hand under his chin, listening intensely. The Pierce family was usually so secretive and private, and a story like this made everyone sit up and take notice in a Southern community. This was the flavor of the month, and all the gossip mongers were feasting on it.

Mr. Mitchell probed further, "But did they break up as father and son? Or did they seem to reconcile after some time?"

Carl said, "Well Leo seemed to go through a nervous breakdown. He'd do just about anything to piss his Daddy off."

Mr. Mitchell asked, "Can you be more specific?"

Carl explained, "Well he wrecked a few of Ross's cars, started getting drunk all the

time and he really pissed him off by dating nigger girls."

Carl smirked as he said that, feeling very satisfied. Mr. Hillard jumped up and shouted, "Your Honor! Objection! This is slander and hearsay!"

The judge agreed but didn't appreciate being yelled at again. "Mr. Hillard, I agree, but I warn you again to watch your tone. And as for you Mr. Mitchell, this is your second warning. Watch out for your questions."

Mr. Mitchell replied, "Yes your Honor. I apologize."

He turned back to Carl, who was still smirking and smiling ever so slightly at Leo. Leo was about to explode, and Daniella worried he'd cause a scene. She leaned into to whisper,

"Don't let this get the better of you. Settle down now. If you make a scene here, everyone will think of you as a violent man."

Leo calmed down and took a deep cleansing breath. He said, "You're right. I'm gonna hold it together, don't worry. I'll say my piece later, not now."

Daniella patted him on the arm, to reassure him, and Mr. Mitchell went on with his inquisition. "How did their relationship progress after the big news was revealed?"

Carl said, "Leo had that breakdown in high school, then went to the Army. I

heard that once Leo got back, Ross threatened to disown him, just like what happened to Daniella, if he didn't straighten up and lead a decent life from then on. And I know Leo's mind. He must not have liked hearing that at all, since Ross himself was living a double life."

Mr. Mitchell knew there was only one more question to ask, and by now everyone knew what Carl would say. Confidently, Mr. Mitchell posed the question, "Carl, there's one more thing to ask. Do you think Leo Pierce is capable of murdering his adopted father?"

Carl looked at Leo directly in the eyes and said, "Yes I do."

Mr. Mitchell said, "No more questions, your Honor."

The judge turned to Mr. Hillard and said, "Your witness Mr. Hillard."

Mr. Hillard patted Leo on the back and whispered, "Lemme at this fucker."

Leo smiled and did feel much better to see Mr. Hillard feeling strong and confident. As he approached Carl, he looked him up and down for a few moments, to create a sense of intimidation. Carl felt the stare, but straightened up and prepared to face whatever would be dealt to him.

Mr. Hillard asked, "Carl, would it be fair to assume that you and Leo have had a rocky relationship at best?"

Carl replied, "What do you mean?"

"I mean you actually *hate* Leo Pierce for stealing your girl from you! Isn't that right?" Mr. Hillard folded his arms, waiting for an answer.

The room started buzzing, although everyone was very careful not to get too loud, as the judge had already warned them more than once. They had to contain their laughter when they heard what Carl had to say in reply.

Carl said, "That ain't true! Well, the hate part is right but the stealing part ain't!"

Mr. Hillard was being purposefully condescending at this point, as he asked, "Well now you're gonna have to tell us what that means! The stealing part? You mean he didn't steal your girl?"

Carl blurted, "He had an affair with her, but I got her back!"

Mr. Hillard whimsically replied, "Oh, so he just borrowed your girl?"

The courtroom burst with laughter at this, even the police, and the jury members. Carl was mortified and to make matters worse, his face started to turn blood red. Even the judge was having a hard time keeping a straight face.

Mr. Mitchell feebly stated, "Your Honor, he's badgering my witness."

The judge replied, "Sustained. Watch it Mr. Hillard."

"I'm sorry your Honor." Mr. Hillard said, regaining his composure.

He turned back to Carl and asked, "Carl, I just have one more question to ask. Isn't it true you'd do practically anything to see Leo put to death?"

Carl was furious at this point. Venomously, he replied, "Are you trying to make me out to be a liar? It doesn't matter if I hate him or not! All that matters is he's a Psycho!"

Mr. Hillard said, "No more questions, your Honor."

The judge let Carl step down from the witness box, and he had a fire in his eyes as he passed Leo and Daniella. Both of them felt his cold stare. Neither one could believe this was the boy that they'd both known as children. He was obsessed.

Exasperated, Mr. Mitchell held his own face in his hands, but he quickly sat up straight and ran them through his hair. "Your Honor, the prosecution rests."

The judge said, "This court will reconvene Monday morning at 9 am. We will begin hearing the defense's testimony."

The Bailiff announced, "All rise!"

The judge's gavel fell. He and most everyone cleared the courtroom, and the attending officer snapped the handcuffs back on Leo. Before he had to go, he turned to Daniella and asked, "Well, how do you think it's going?"

Daniella sighed and said, "Well at this point, I'd say your chances are 50/50, but I'm working on a theory. I've got a lead. I don't want you to get your hopes up too high, but I feel positive about it."

She gave him a reassuring squeeze on the shoulder and

he nodded approvingly. He turned and left with the officer. Daniella was relieved today's proceedings were done. *It could have gone a lot worse,* she thought. She gathered up her things and looked around for Katie. She pulled out her phone to call her, but noticed Katie had texted her saying she had to leave in a hurry because she was over-scheduled and had to get home fast.

Just as Daniella turned around, with all her things in hand, she spotted Carl in the back of the courtroom, looking at her with menacing eyes. Daniella caught her breath, as he looked really threatening. She said, "Dear God! What are you doing just sitting there? Were you waiting on me?"

Carl said, "Yeah. I was. Look, I guess I was a little rough on you before. But you must know that your bastard cousin is not getting away with this. No way. And for the life of me, I can't figure out why you're helping him? After what he did to you? Why do you care?"

"Because he's my cousin! More than my cousin! He and I grew up as brother and sister." Daniella snapped. "I'll always love him even if I hate him! He's family."

Carl scoffed, then got up, preparing to leave. "Why don't you go back to your life Danny? Being here isn't *good* for you."

He continued to stare for a few moments, and one corner of his mouth started to curl into a smirk. At this point, Daniella was afraid, and a dark, ominous feeling washed over her. At first she thought Carl had shown some integrity because he apologized in his own way for being insulting before, but now, he was literally warning her to stay away, or could it be that he was warning her to stay *out* of his way?

She asked, "What does that mean?"

He shrugged his shoulders and smiled with that all-knowing look he'd had before. He turned on his heels to leave, and Daniella watched his every step as he walked out the door. After he had left, Daniella sat for a moment, trying to remember his face. She thought, *he knows something, and how is it that he was near Luwanda's children before all this went down?* She absolutely knew where she had to go next, to see Leo's kids.

12

THE KIDS

That night, a very tired Daniella pulled up to the entrance to the Firecrackers Summer Camp where Luwanda's kids were in attendance. It was getting late and had been a very long drive, but she couldn't waste any time. She needed to talk to them immediately, as court was scheduled on Monday morning. If these two kids knew anything or had anything to do with it, she needed to find out tonight.

Daniella walked in and, with the coordinator's blessing, she walked straight through to the campsite. Thankfully, she'd called ahead and arranged this meeting, otherwise seeing the girls may have taken far longer. The campsite was lovely. It was truly a rustic scene, filled with flowers, trees, and a brook. It was a perfect dusk, as the sun was going down. The environment was sleepy and relaxed. The smells of campfires and barbecue filled the air, and Daniella was nearly ashamed she had to end such a perfect scene.

Spotting the girls didn't take long. Lizzie was sitting by Sadie laughing and playing cards. The other girls were about to start some music, as she saw some instruments being brought out to a platform. Daniella saw the family resemblance right away this time. The curves of their faces were Leo's, and she'd seen him make a similar facial expression when he was a boy.

Lizzie caught sight of Daniella, and the smile left her face right away. She leaned down to whisper something in Sadie's ear, prompting Sadie to bounce away and start talking to another group of little girls her age. Lizzy marched toward Daniella with great determination, and barked, "What are you doing here? How did you even find us?!"

Daniella said, "Your Mama told me where you are, and I hope you're not mad because I need your help with something. I don't know what to do."

Lizzie rolled her eyes and sarcastically blurted, "What does the rich white girl need from me?"

She put her hand on her hip and stood leaning to one side, smirking like a true badass. Daniella wasn't deterred. In fact, she expected this.

She said, "I need some help understanding what to do with my nieces, considering that I only knew about them yesterday. I didn't know I had any on my side of the family." This time Daniella posed with hands on her hips, looking straight at Lizzie.

Lizzie fought to hold back the tears. She looked up at the sky. "You really didn't know?"

Daniella said, "No. I didn't. If I had, your life would have been remarkably different."

Lizzie nodded and processed, "I wasn't sure about you. My Mama always said that you didn't realise, but I wasn't entirely sure until now. Guess I always thought you knew and you didn't wanna know us, just like him."

Lizzie had obviously thought about this many times. Daniella wasn't sure what she'd been told about the Pierce family, but it didn't seem anyone had anything nice to say about any of them, including Daniella. Lizzy's misconception about how she would be received was quickly remedied when Daniella confirmed, "Now that I am sure we're blood, there's no way I'm gonna let you go, not you or your sister. You don't have to feel rejected anymore. I swear *if* I'd known, you never would have suffered for a single day."

Daniella stretched out her arms to her, but Lizzie hesitated. Daniella said, "I just want a chance to make things right. If you give me a chance, I promise it'll be worth it."

Daniella dropped her arms. Obviously, she'd have to work a little for this acceptance and trust. Lizzie replied, "How do I know you're a person who keeps you word? Look at what my own father did to my mother? And to my sister and me! What kind of people are you?"

Daniella thought for a moment and came up with a proposal. "Let's sit down and speak frankly with each other tonight. I'll get permission to take you and Sadie out for a nice dinner... I'm pretty sure I saw a Cracker Barrel on the way over here...We'll sit and talk about every concern you have over a nice meal, and relax a little. God knows I need it."

Lizzie looked at her with a discerning look on her face, thought for a moment, and said, "Well, I guess Cracker Barrel sounds a lot better than Hot Dogs."

Daniella smiled and said, "Ok, go and get your sister. I'll work on busting you out of here for a few hours."

The restaurant was warm and welcoming, and Daniella's stomach rumbled as she smelled the wonderful Southern food. The three of them sat down, ready to talk it out. The evening went along smoothly, apart from the occasional reluctance of Lizzie to believe that Daniella had sincere intentions toward her, her sister, and her mother. Daniella was able to learn about all the times their little family had gone without enough money, and how close Luwanda had come to disaster as a result of her abuses with alcohol. The depression over what Leo had done to her was at times, overwhelming, and both girls now suffered from severe trust issues. Sadie had been pretty quiet all evening, but finally spoke up. "So, why has Mama kept this away from me all this time? I would've liked having an Aunt. We've been by ourselves. Mama never talks about Daddy, and just shuts me up when I try to ask."

Daniella frowned as she heard this and said, "No anymore Baby. I'm so glad to find the two of you, and we're gonna be a family from now on. You guys have some great cousins you need to meet. My kids!"

"How do I know you won't just go back to Dubai and never think of us again? Why should I trust you?" Lizzie asked.

Daniella sighed. "I don't know Sweetie. I wish I knew how to get you to trust me. If we'd only had a chance to know each other before this, you'd understand I'm nothing like Leo. In fact, I'm kinda the black sheep of my family. As far as they're concerned, I've never been normal, like them."

Lizzie scoffed. "Normal? That's a laugh! At least you're trying, and if they're normal, I never wanna be normal!"

Lizzie's brow furrowed and her forehead crinkled. She looked worried. She took a gulp and asked, "So, I don't really know much about you or why exactly you're here. I heard that your father was murdered."

"Yeah, my father...So if you heard that, you know your father is being accused of murdering him."

Lizzie frowned. "Yeah."

"Let's get the check. You and Sadie had enough? Did you guys want dessert?" Daniella asked, changing the subject.

Sadie said, "We usually eat dessert every day, but my stomach hurts cuz this dinner was just too much food!"

Lizzie smiled at her and squeezed her arm. "I guess we're good. We had enough."

At this, Daniella paid the bill and they made their way to the car. Once inside, with seatbelts fastened, Feeling pleased, Daniella looked at Lizzie, as it seemed that she was making some headway with this girl, but something was amiss. "Honey, is there something you wanna ask me, or say to me? Whatever it is, nothing will change the fact that we're family. Do you understand? No matter what, even if you're ever in trouble. I'll help you."

Lizzie's tears couldn't hold back anymore. She cried and squeezed Daniella's hand, relieved the pretense was finally over. Lizzie sobbed and asked, "I hope you mean that. I hope you're for real."

Daniella earnestly replied, " No matter what, I'm your Aunt and I always will be. Your Daddy wasn't only my cousin. We grew up as brother and sister."

She pulled back her hand from Lizzie for a moment. As much as she experienced joy in her heart for this tender time, she had to ask the hard question. "Now Sweetheart...I must ask you something very important. Do you know a man named Carl Walters? He was a friend of your Daddy's."

Lizzie looked down, obviously very ashamed. Tearfully, she admitted, "Yeah, I know him."

They arrived at the camp, and Daniella put the car into Park so she could speak to the girls privately for a few more moments.

Daniella lifted Lizzie's chin up and looked at her

questioningly. "Have the two of you met recently? Before the murder? Is there something you wanna tell me about him?"

Lizzie panicked. She stammered, "I dunno. He came to me and said he hated what my father did to me and wished there was something he could do. Something he could do to set things right."

Daniella asked, "What did he mean?...wait, hold that thought. Since we're here, let's talk in the lobby."

The trio got out of the car and walked inside to continue their conversation. They sat down on the lobby sofas and Daniella said, "Ok Honey. Tell me what happened now. Please don't be scared." Sophie nodded and said, "Yeah, I wanna hear this too."

Lizzie looked as if she would burst. The tears welled up, and all of the emotion that was pushed down for so long found its way out. She grabbed Daniella's waist, hugged tight and began to weep. The tears fell like small waterfalls, and her chest heaved. Daniella sensed that something big was about to pour from her lips but patiently stroked her hair to give her a sense of safety and comfort. Finally, Lizzie spilled the story. Sobbing, she said,

"He said if Ross was dead and Leo was blamed, we could get rid of two bastards with one blow."

She started crying again, but this time Daniella coaxed her on. "Lizzie, Honey, now you've just got to tell me the rest. Did he put you up to something?"

Lizzie swallowed and said the rest while still holding on, unwilling to look Daniella in the eyes.

"He said society would be better off without such human trash and I could avenge what happened to my mother." Sophie teared up as she heard this. She never knew how much Lizzie had taken on, on her own.

"Does your mother know about any of this?" Daniella asked.

"No! She's the sweetest person in the world and would never have anything to do with killing anyone! I swear she had nothing to do with it, and knew nothing about it."

Daniella agreed with that. Luwanda was as gentle as a kitten, and no one who knew her would ever believe her to be involved in something so ugly. Carl had to be the one to instigate this. Daniella could see that this girl was emotionally unstable because of all she'd been through, and why not? It couldn't have been easy growing up biracial in Georgia, and if that wasn't bad enough, to know who her father was and to come to grips with the fact that he never acknowledged her. On top of all this pressure, the poor kid had to watch her mother struggle as a waitress all these years, just to make ends meet.

Daniella said, "Well I can easily believe that. Your mother is a good woman. I'm so sorry for what happened to her and to you girls. But Honey, I'm gonna need to hear the details. I need to know how it was done. Did Carl coax you into this? Or did he do it with your help? I've gotta hear the whole story, scene by scene. I swear by God I'll help you. I know you probably had your head filled with all kinds of ideas about us, even me."

Daniella insisted that they have something cool to drink, to take a small rest after revealing so much. She saw a water fountain and some Dixie cups nearby and filled a cup for both girls. Lizzie took a sip of water. Daniella asked, "Better?" She clutched her hand reassuringly and gave it a little squeeze. Daniella believed it would be best to send Sadie away for the moment, so she could get Lizzie to open up more. She said, "Sweetie, why don't you go back to your friends outside, and let me talk to your sister."

Sadie agreed, but she was worried about her sister. "Lizzie, I'll be inside, okay?"

Lizzie nodded, smiling at her in a reassuring manner. Once she was out of earshot, they continued.

Lizzie said, "Yeah, but I don't see how you could help me. God knows I regretted it every minute of every day that's passed after this and begged God to forgive me. I can't get it out of my mind and the guilt is killing me."

Daniella replied, "I swear I'll help you by getting you the best defense money can buy and make *sure* you get the lightest sentence. As for Carl, I can't promise the same. But for you

and Sadie my dear, I'll do whatever I have to, for you and your Mama too. You'll see. I'm not like the others Honey."

When Daniella smiled at her, Lizzie felt like she could open up. She only hoped that what she had to tell her wouldn't destroy the closeness they were sharing at the moment. Lizzie enjoyed the nurturing way Daniella was treating her, and it was nice to feel that she had an Aunt. Luwanda was an only child, so she'd never had an Aunt or an Uncle before. Still, Daniella had to be told, and Lizzie knew this was it. "Ready?" She asked.

Daniella said, "Tell me."

Lizzie took in a deep gulp of air and said, "I was at a coffee shop with my friends. We were having some lattes and talking and stuff. I saw him come in there, order a coffee, and I noticed that he couldn't stop staring at me. It was creeping me out, so I confronted him and asked him what the Hell his problem was. He just looked all cocky and said he was a friend of my father."

She paused to wipe a tear away. "Go on." Daniella urged.

"I told him that means he's no friend of mine and called him a Son of a Bitch. When I was about to leave, he grabbed my arm and said, 'I don't think you understand. I said I *was* a friend of his. Now, I hate him for what he did to you and your sister. If you let me, I think we can talk about how to get even.' So I listened to his plan. He wanted me to wear Leo's gloves and bash Ross on the head with that bat. I took the gloves but didn't even put them on. Truth is, I dropped them on the ground when I held the bat over his head. When Ross saw me, he was so smooth talking."

Daniella's breath hitched, then asked, "And then? What did he say?"

Lizzie carried on, "He said I shouldn't kill him because I had just caught him in such a vulnerable position, so that meant that I'd struck gold. I couldn't do it. Not because I wanted money from him. I just felt sorry for him. My hands started to shake, and he didn't look that bad, nothing like the monster Carl made him out to be. He was secretly something other than what he claimed to be, but other than that, he seemed kinda normal."

Daniella was extraordinarily relieved to find out Lizzie didn't do this herself. A huge weight was lifted from her shoulders when she heard Lizzie say it out loud. She knew now that defending her would be a far easier task. She asked, "Did Carl intervene then?"

Lizzie nodded her head in agreement, "Yeah, that's when he grabbed the bat from me and said, 'I should've known you didn't have the stomach for it, you little nigger bitch!' After that, he just started bashing. He seemed like he kinda liked it too! I couldn't believe what I was seeing. I thought my heart was gonna stop. I was so scared he'd kill me as well."

Daniella hadn't truly felt the impact of losing her father until that moment. Tears were welling up in her eyes now, as she couldn't understand why Carl would have wanted to kill him so brutally. Flashes of the kind moments with Ross appeared in her head, all in the blink of an eye, and suddenly she truly realized Ross didn't deserve any of this. Yes, he was a dark hearted person, and he was hiding a secret from everyone near him and had done some terrible things, but he did *not* deserve to be savagely murdered. Her anger started brewing for Carl, and she experienced a strong need for revenge, not just for what he'd done to her father, but what he'd done to her entire family.

Lizzie went on, "Ross looked horrified at Carl, but he didn't get a chance to scream before Carl started beating. He hit him with such rage that I was petrified with fear. When he finally finished, he exhaled loudly and looked satisfied that he'd finally had the revenge he'd dreamt of. He looked at me as I was shaking and sitting on the ground. He grabbed me by the arm and forced me up. I had splatters of blood on my face. I swear I couldn't even speak; I was so scared. He screamed, 'Now you listen and listen good Bitch! I want you to go somewhere private and clean up real good. Burn these clothes that have evidence on them and meet me in front of Leo's apartment at the address I told you.'"

Daniella asked, "What address did he mean?"

Lizzie said, "Leo's apartment. He wanted me to slip the gloves and the missing piece from the bat in the broken window and let them drop on the floor. Carl already knew that he'd smashed a window in his apartment. He said Leo was a miserable slob that not only wouldn't clean up the glass, but he'd most likely just walk right past the gloves without even noticing them on the floor. I guess that's kinda what he did. I'm so sorry. He said if I double-crossed him, he'd pin the whole thing on me, and claimed that no one would believe a half breed nigger over a respectable member of society like him."

Daniella could see Lizzie was getting exhausted. Reliving this was taking the wind out of the poor girl. That bastard Carl had played on her anger and sense of abandonment to get her to take part in his sick plan. *He needs to pay*, Daniella thought.

Lizzie noticed Daniella's eyes and how they were filled with hatred. She said, "When I finished doing as he said, I told him to leave me and my family alone, but he didn't take kindly to being threatened. He grabbed my arm and told me that he owned me now, just like a nigger owned by its master. He said he can crush my life at any time he wants. He's got a recording of me saying that I'd like to see him dead, and a video of me walking up to Leo's apartment the night I dropped the gloves in his door. I tried to grab his cell phone from his hand, but he flaunted it over me and screamed again at me to call him Sir and obey him any time he would call on me. Otherwise, he can have me locked up."

At this point, Daniella reached into her bag for a cigarette. She'd been trying hard to stop, but a revelation like this called for special help. Taking a big drag off the cigarette seemed to calm her nerves a little bit. It didn't seem to please the camp counselors, however, as it didn't even take a minute for her to be asked to put the cigarette out. Daniella grumbled but complied.

She was putting out the cigarette when Sadie came bursting through the doors. She was getting nervous that Lizzie was taking so long, and really wanted to urge her to come back to the group.

Sadie's excitement faded, however, as she saw Daniella. The whole idea of her being part of a white family was still very new to Sadie. Lizzie had known for far longer, so she'd had time to process the whole thing. Daniella said, "Come over here, Baby. Let me have a good look at you. I'm so sorry that we didn't get much time to talk at dinner."

When she came closer, Daniella gently reached out to stroke the hair out of Sadie's face and touched her cheek. She said, "What a lovely girl you are! Tell me what you've been doing out there."

Sadie let her boundaries drop and said, "Um, I was outside at the Barbeque. I told them I'm full, but Jerry told me that I have to try a hot dog, but he dropped one. I told him no one would eat that one, but he didn't listen. He picked it up and put it right back on that grill! He said the ten-second rule, whatever that means! Lizzie, what does it mean to say ten-second rule?"

Lizzie laughed and gave her a hug. Daniella said, "Everything will be ok. Don't you two worry. I'm gonna fix all this somehow. You two both need to come with me, so I need you to go get ready." Sadie looked disappointed, so Daniella confirmed, "Honey, I'll get you something healthier to eat than those nasty hot dogs." They all shared a smile.

Once the camp coordinators called Luwanda and confirmed that Daniella was indeed their Aunt, and once they understood how complicated this story was, they reluctantly allowed Daniella to take the girls with her, even though it was very late at night by that time. The two of them came through the doors with a load of luggage, and Sadie was already in her pajamas.

As the trio walked towards the car with their bags, Daniella spotted a few photographers near the entrance. One of them stepped out to snap a few photos of her with the two girls. This angered Daniella, and she shouted, "Don't you have anything better to do?"

The photographer shouted back, "Have you lived in

Hadleyville Georgia? There's not a whole lot happening there, lady!" Another man stepped forward and started taking pictures, then the others followed. As far as Daniella remembered, there was only one actual newspaper in Hadleyville, Georgia so she couldn't imagine where the others would be from. Regardless, she wasn't going to let herself think of that right now, because she had to get the girls back to Atlanta right away.

Once they were in the car, Lizzie called Luwanda on her cell phone as they drove off towards Atlanta. Luwanda was frantic with worry, but trusted Daniella must have good reason for picking them up. Lizzie didn't tell her mother everything, as Daniella believed firmly that the news of Lizzie's involvement in the murder would make her faint or worse. She figured if Luwanda was going to pass out, it might as well be around people who care about her, so the plan was to let her discover the truth alongside everyone else.

Lizzie said, "Mama...Yeah, we're ok. We're so happy, maybe for the first time in, gosh I don't even remember."

She finished telling her all about how the three of them were going to Katie's house to hang out and get to know each other better, then she asked, "Mama, can you meet us at the courthouse by 9 am tomorrow. Aunt Danny says it's extremely important you pick us up from there because something came up and she can't get us home afterwards. I think it's something with the trial...Ok, Mama, we'll see you there. I love you too."

Lizzie hung up and said, "Ok, it's done. She doesn't know anything about any of it, just that we all know about each other now."

Daniella said, "Good. The last thing we need is to have to rush Wanda to the Emergency room right now. There's no time. I've gotta get the two of you to Mr. Hillard and tell him the whole story. I hope to God this makes a difference. We can get your father out and get Carl arrested. Was there anything else suspicious on that tape?"

Lizzie shook her head, then looked back at Sadie, who was drifting off while listening to music with her headphones on. She shrugged and said, "I dunno really. I can't remember saying anything else, but there is something I need to share with you. I don't know if it would be in my favor, or used against me, but I have something from the crime scene, something that does prove I was there."

Daniella is intrigued. "What's that Honey?"

Lizzie pulled something out of her pocket. Daniella struggled to keep her eyes on the road and to see what Lizzie had with her. Lizzie cautiously took it out of her pocket and put it carefully in Daniella's hand. When she saw what it was, she almost had a wreck. She pulled over and stopped the car so she might examine it safely. It was the missing shard from the bat, the piece with the word, "Trust" carved in the wood.

Daniella couldn't believe it. It was the missing piece everyone had been looking for, but sadly, Lizzie was right about it being a toss up as to whether this would be a good thing or a bad thing for her. She said, "Does anyone else know that you have this?"

Lizzie shook her head and said, "No...Do you think it will help me in any way?"

Daniella said, "I don't know. I need to talk to Mr. Hillard, and don't worry, everything we say to him is confidential. He can't reveal it without our permission, so one way or another, this won't come out unless it will be good for you."

She pulled out on the road again, and as she drove, she went through a mix of emotions. There was joy for having time with her nieces, but a great deal of worry for them. She thought of Leo, and her emotions turned to embarrassment for the way he treated Luwanda. No doubt was in her mind that Leo initially just set out to prove he could enjoy a little "Brown Sugar" and get away with it like many guys from her hometown. Luwanda had been one of the prettiest girls in school, full of potential, but she had to work very hard waitressing to make ends meet, and to support two kids all on her own. Daniella appreciated what a great job Luwanda had done with her daughters. After all, it's a wonder these two girls turned out so well, considering what they've been through.

Her thoughts also started to turn to Faisal and how much she missed him and her own kids. Her three kids were enjoying the last days of their Summer break, and she was sure that Faisal was taking them to all kinds of exciting places. Dubai was a desert wonderland, and she enjoyed picturing them going to the water parks, malls, and the big ice skating rinks. *God how I miss them all! I wonder what they're going to do when they find out that our family is bigger than we thought. Somehow, I want them all to know each other.* She thought.

She made a mental note to call Faisal when she got to her hotel room. He must be so worried about her, and she'd been awful about not calling, but the trial and her investigation had taken a lot of energy out of her.

Finally, they arrived in Atlanta, and Daniella wondered why Lizzie and Sadie had been so quiet the whole time. She looked at them and realized they had both fallen asleep. *I guess camp is like any other sleepover. No actual sleep happens.* She thought. She gently nudged Lizzie and was a little unnerved by how Lizzie jumped, startled. "Sorry Danny. I guess I forgot where I am."

"No problem Honey. I'm gonna take y'all up to meet with Mr. Hillard now. That's his office up there. I'm sure we're gonna work all this out." Daniella smiled reassuringly.

After Mr. Hillard heard the whole story, he fell back in his chair, completely blown away. He asked, "So these are Leo's children?" He looked at Lizzie. "Well young lady, I believe your story, but we need to work on your testimony. Even if we convince the jury you're telling the truth, you may do a little time in a juvenile detention center."

Lizzie looked unnerved by the idea of it, but said, "I guess I deserve that. I had hoped that I wouldn't have to, though. I'd hate to put Mama through the drama."

Daniella put a reassuring hand on her shoulder. "If God's willing, you won't have to. We'll try our best."

Redirecting her attention to Mr. Hillard, Daniella asked, "Did you find out if the Silver Linings Club had any CCTV footage of the parking lot that night?"

Mr. Hillard replied, "Yes actually they did, but interestingly, the footage was damaged." He snapped his fingers in revelation and said, "Now that I understand Carl did all this, I'll go back and ask if anyone saw him in the club that night. We need a continuance so we have time to get our ducks in a row."

He thought for a moment and said, "I need to make a few calls, but I think I can get the next court session delayed at least a day. That'll give me the time I need to place Carl at the scene. I'd also like to find any of your friends to confirm that he had met you previously as well."

Daniella liked the way this was going. Everyone agreed another day of getting the story straight was a great idea. Mr. Hillard successfully managed to make it happen, so the team went to work, building a case against Mr. Carl Walters. Their next court session would be a game changer.

13

GETTING THE RIGHT GUY

Daniella woke up to a ton of messages on her phone. She knew they were messages because the beeps sounds from her phone woke her. This fine day was provided by Mr. Hillard, a day that would be crucial, and she was glad to have this continuance, however, the list of missed calls and messages was considerable, as she had forgotten to tell everyone. Time after time, Faisal had tried to call, as well as Katie, Aunt Rosie, and even Nay. The messages were all frantic, as everyone was wondering why the court session had been delayed for a day. Groggily, she read them as she looked at the girls, who were still sleeping in the hotel room's second bed.

Slowly, she got up and made her way to the room's complimentary coffee. She poured herself a cup and took a slow deep breath, enjoying the rich aroma of the French Roast. Suddenly, the phone rang. It was Mr. Hillard.

"Good Morning! I'm sure you already figured that I've put this all on hold for one more day so we can prepare our case. Can you and the girls come to my office right away this morning?"

Daniella pursed her lips, "Yes, we'll be there. I'll get them up for some breakfast now. As soon as we're done, I'll be there with them straight away."

She hung up with Mr. Hillard and got the girls up. They were very confused at first, not knowing where they were. Daniella handed Lizzie a cup of coffee, and she started to sip on it slowly. "What time is it?"

"Early," Daniella murmured. "I think we should hit up the so-called 'continental breakfast' around here, then high tail it to Mr. Hillard's office."

Lizzie nodded in agreement, and the three started to get ready. After a hearty breakfast and a few laughs, they found themselves on the way to Mr. Hillard. Daniella was the first to knock on the door and she was really surprised to see Mr. Hillard answer his own door. His secretary was typing something frantically on her computer. While ignoring his secretary completely, he said, "Come in Y'all! Come on in! I have some very exciting news for you young lady."

Daniella and the girls took their seats and listened intently to what Mr. Hillard had to say. He seemed so excited, as if something significant had happened. He hurriedly pulled up a chair so he could look them all in the eye. "Since you told me the story last night, I've been up all night doing some digging of my own. You see, I really didn't want this young lady brought up on charges herself. After all, she withheld evidence, and that alone is a crime, as you know, so to prove that she was scared, we had to put Carl at the scene."

Daniella remembered, "Yes, but you said earlier that there was no parking lot footage of the night of the murder."

Mr. Hillard smiled broadly and said, "Yes Ma'am, but it turns out that there was filmed footage of Carl *inside* the bar."

Daniella asked, "How? I thought the bar reported that their CCTV system was broken, so they had a whole lotta nothing from every angle."

Mr. Hillard replied, "Well yeah, that's true, but do you remember when the police put out a notice to all the people who were reportedly there on the night? When they wanted anyone with any knowledge of the crime to come forward?"

Mr. Hillard didn't wait for an answer. He went on, "Well, I remembered that one person there actually had a video they took on their phone, because as it turns out, one of their friends was celebrating his birthday that night. Well....I asked to see the video again, and sure enough, Carl was there. What makes it better is that the video kept rolling long enough to catch him following Ross out to the parking lot. Not directly after him of course, but it showed that he was stalling until there was some distance between them."

Daniella smiled. "Ok, that's great news right?"

Mr. Hillard replied with guarded enthusiasm. "Well, yes it's good news, but it's not a smoking gun that links Carl directly with Lizzie. Of course, at this point, our chances are better than his." He thinks for a minute and remembers to tell them, "I sent the missing shard of the bat to the forensics lab, to check if anything would come up, anything we can use. We'll have to wait a little for those results."

He sat for a moment with his lips pressed into a hard line, tapping his fingers on the desk, then commented, "Well I guess our best bet is to cut a deal with the District Attorney. She's a minor after all and a minority. Our D.A. is sympathetic to cases like hers. Maybe I can get hold of him tonight."

Daniella asked, "Who's the D.A. now?"

Coyly, Mr. Hillard replied, "Oh I think he's another high school acquaintance of yours."

Daniella looked surprised. She thought about how she wasn't the most popular kid in school and how she knew the D.A. could be a bad thing or a good thing. With guarded anticipation, she asked, "Well? Who is it?"

Mr. Hillard said, "Jerry Hobson...Hey, I heard he used to date you. Is that true?"

Daniella frowned. "Yeah, it's true, but he treated me like crap. He broke up with me for Gena Ramsey. My father wouldn't let me go to any school dances, so he thought I was boring because I wasn't ever allowed to do anything. He just never understood that my father was very strict... Well, anyway, I guess you can say he *owes* me for the maltreatment, but we're talking about one of the most self-absorbed people I've ever known. I'm sure he'd rather die than admit to wrongdoing."

"Well, that's who we need to go visit right now. Get the girls and let's go." Mr. Hillard demanded.

They all piled into Mr. Hillard's large black SUV. He was a lawyer, but a country guy at the same time. According to insiders, he said he wanted a black SUV because it was useful for intimidation. Mr. Hillard always said that every time the government was coming, they were always in a black SUV. Daniella really hoped that they looked intimidating enough today, but she thought the sympathy vote was more of what they should be going for.

The district attorney's house wasn't far from the office, a car ride of only 6 minutes, all the way to North Street, Hadleyville, Georgia. The road felt long to Daniella though, as she remembered high school days. Jerry was the only boy in school that seemed like he had a brain in his head.

She remembered how proud she was, walking down the halls with him, and how she enjoyed the fact that this was the only time she wasn't jealous of "the popular girls." Jerry was smart, and although he was one of the most handsome boys in school, he was also one of the most romantic. He gave her flowers and candy on her birthday and dedicated songs to her. He even made her a sweet mixtape once, with all the songs that reminded him of Danny.

The happiness didn't last, however, and what he did only served to solidify her growing distrust of men in general. He surprised her one weekend by taking her to her favorite seafood restaurant in Atlanta. In spite of Ross's reservations, she happily went with Jerry to Atlanta, for that really special night out.

As it turns out however, he only wanted to ease the blow. He and Gena had been secretly meeting at Lion's park to attend school dances and go parking. Gena was also one of the many girls who had no problem letting go of her virginity in her teen years, so Jerry happily accepted the challenge of being one of the lucky boys she'd share her *whole* self with. He had been through a whole year of dating Danny, who wasn't allowed to go to high school dances or even be out later than 9pm, and the thought of giving up her virginity was unthinkable. Danny firmly believed in waiting for marriage to have sex, but that made Jerry think of her as a prude.

Her trip down memory lane was broken unexpectedly as Mr. Hillard came to a sudden stop in front of the building. "Did he marry Gena?" Danny asked.

Mr. Hillard's lips formed a hard line, as though he was hesitant to answer, but said, "Yes he did, but she divorced him 5 years later. Poor bastard. She took their two kids and half of his money. I heard that he cheated on her regularly with a girl that bore a strong resemblance to you. Some say he never got over you, little gal!" His mouth turned up into a sneaky grin as he said this, and it made Daniella feel uncomfortable, but surprisingly vindicated, even though she had been half a world away.

They all made their way into Jerry's office, and he was surprised by the visit, as he had only expected Mr. Hillard. Daniella had expected to see a handsome and dapper older man, as Jerry had been one of the most desired boys in school, but she was very surprised to see a balding overweight man who bore a slight resemblance to the dashing young face she'd been so swept away in as a girl. She almost felt sorry for him. "Jerry? Oh my God. How long has it been?" She asked.

Jerry seemed pleased with her pleasant demeanor. He replied, "Hey Danny girl! You're still just as good looking as you were in high school Sweetie! How in the world do you do it?"

His smile was charming, and for a moment, Daniella remembered this boy from high school. She realized that he must have had a very tough time in life—the divorce, fighting for visitation with his kids, all while struggling through law school. She smiled warmly at Jerry, determined to avoid causing him any more pain. She said, "Oh well, I guess it's just clean living Hun. How've you been?"

He grinned broadly, and even though he was very professional, she could see that he still had a little "thing" for her, even after all these years. He motioned for everyone to sit down on his black leather sofas, and once they were all comfortable, Mr. Hillard began the negotiations.

"Jerry, let's face it, we're talking about a minor here, one that's been through one Hell of an ordeal. She was influenced by the *real* criminal here, and I think we ought to be able to make a deal for her, seeing as how she's willing to turn over on Carl. What do you say? Probation? Community Service? Juvenile Center?"

Jerry leaned back in his chair, taking in Mr. Hillard's words, and after what seemed like an eternity, he exhaled loudly and said, "I don't wanna put her in Juvie, particularly since she didn't go through with it all. I will need to put her on probation for at least 2 years though."

He saw that Daniella and Mr. Hillard were both becoming far too excited too fast, so he qualified his previous statement by saying, "Provided that she testifies against Carl of course."

Lizzie couldn't help but jump into the conversation when she heard that. "I'm very happy to testify against that scumbag. You can count on me. I promise."

"Well then! It looks like we got a deal!" Jerry exclaimed. He had a look of fondness as he looked at Daniella. She was gleaming, knowing that Lizzie would be OK. She caught herself glancing at Jerry, thankful for what he'd said.

"Jerry, this will solve everything. Thank you so much for helping my niece." Daniella looked at Lizzie and felt dismayed to see her staring down at her fingers. "What's wrong?" Daniella asked.

"I don't know how my Mama is gonna react when I tell her about all this." Lizzie murmured.

Daniella smiled reassuringly and then put an arm around her. "It's ok Baby, I'll tell your Mama so you won't have to. Probation isn't a picnic, but it beats the Hell out of prison. Two years will pass before you know it, you'll see."

"Yeah, I guess you're right." Lizzie paused. "You called me your niece."

"Sure I did!" Daniella said.

"Your Daddy was more of a brother to me than my natural brother, and even though we've had our differences, a good Southerner doesn't turn their back on family, and neither does a Muslim, which is what I am Honey. You understand that right?"

Lizzie looked thoughtfully at Daniella, blinked at her, and said, "I've never met a white Muslim before. I think it's amazing actually. I'd love to see where you live one day."

"Well, that can most definitely be arranged! Let's make a deal—Just as soon as you're free from your probation, you, your Daddy, and your Mama will all come over for a nice long visit. Deal?" Daniella gleamed at her, as this was the kind of thing that she'd been anxious to say for a very long time. She'd longed for her family to see where she lived.

Lizzie grinned and hugged her. "Deal. Thank you."

"Your more than welcome Honey." Daniella pulled back and asked the girls and Mr. Hillard to go wait for her in the car while she had a private moment with Jerry.

Once alone, Daniella murmured, "I can't tell you what this means to me. I've got a good family in Dubai, but I need my family here too. I actually believe it's possible now. I wanted to let you know that I only wish the very best for you, Jerry."

He looked as if he would swoon. Daniella considered that the poor guy probably hadn't enjoyed any positive attention for years. He exhaled and said, "You're most welcome Danny." Then, a smile washed across his face that made Daniella uneasy. He admitted, "I shouldn't have ever broken up with you. Seeing you here today made me realize that. That rotten *thing* I married only brought suffering to my life. You would have brought me nothing but happiness."

Daniella swallowed and politely replied, "Well I don't know about that Jerry. I've always believed things turn out the way they are meant to be. God knows, things in my life aren't perfect, but I try to focus on what I have instead of what I don't. It's not an exact science, but it seems to work for me."

Jerry looked down at his feet, a little embarrassed that he brought it up. After a moment, he replied, "Well, that guy you're with sure is a lucky guy! I want you to understand I have never once bought into the whole racist thing. I know if you love him, he's a great person, and it doesn't matter where he's from."

This really pleased Daniella as this was the first time anyone in town had really lent their support like this. She smiled and blurted, "Thank you for that Jerry. Hey, I just know it's gonna happen for you again. There are a lot of pretty ladies around here, and you're the D.A! With a prestigious position like that, it's only a matter of time. You just gotta put yourself out there."

He smiled sweetly, lapping up the joy of a compliment. Afterward, Daniella excused herself as it was time to go prepare Lizzie for her day in court. As she left, she couldn't help but to look back at him once more, that boy who broke her heart in high school, and a dark part of her enjoyed the longing look on his face as she turned away.

Once back to Mr. Hillard's office, the phone rang and Mr. Hillard answered immediately. "Hillard here. Got some news?"

He paused, and a smile came across his face. Daniella felt her heart pounding with excitement as she watched him nodding and smiling. She knew this had to be good news. Finally, he hung up, and she couldn't hold her breath anymore, and blurted, "Well????"

Proudly, he announced, "The forensics lab found a partial fingerprint on the shard, and I'm happy to report that we found a 10 point match to none other than the elusive Carl!"

Shouts of happiness rang through the office as Daniella, Lizzy and Sadie jumped up and down, reeling with excitement. Mr. Hillard looked at Lizzie and said, "It's a good thing that you knew better than to wipe it clean all this time. That was a smart move, young lady. With your testimony, plus Danny's, the video, and the fingerprint, I do believe that Carl has seen his finer days. Yes, Sir, he has."

14

DAY OF RECKONING

As the entire family sat in court, awaiting the judge, Leo turned around to face Daniella. She knew he was dying of curiosity, and she badly wanted to fill him in on everything. Mr. Hillard hadn't had time to fill him in because he was working so vigorously on building a case against Carl for the last two days. All she could do was give Leo a reassuring smile, one that promised everything would be all right.

He looked apologetically at Lizzie and Sadie, and his eyes pooled as he thought of how much he'd let those girls down. The girls seemed to be smiling at him kindly, and Leo didn't know what that was about, because, in his mind, he thought he deserved nothing but their hatred for what he had done to them and their mother.

He didn't have much time to dwell on the past, because the judge, the honorable Beauford Belham, was taking his seat, as the Bailiff shouted, "All rise!"

Once the judge was firmly in his place, everyone sat down, preparing themselves for a dramatic day, full of promises of final justice being served. Daniella discreetly turned to see Carl in the back row, who was unaware of the new developments, still believing his revenge will be complete today. Daniella smiled and relished the thought of this bastard finally getting what he deserved.

Mr. Hillard blurted, "The defense calls Mr. Carl Walters to the stand."

Carl looked really shocked to hear his name being called. Reluctantly, he got up feeling puzzled and angered by the smirks on the faces of Danny, Lizzie, and Sadie. He gave Lizzie a damning look as he passed by. Lizzie didn't let herself feel intimidated and stayed strong as he took the stand, raised his right hand, and was sworn in.

"Do you swear to tell the truth, the whole truth, without omission?" The Bailiff asked.

Carl sounded unsure as he weakly replied, "Yea, I do."

Mr. Mitchell looked worried as he saw Mr. Hillard walk to the witness box with such confidence in his stride. Mr. Hillard opened his questioning with, "Mr. Walters, where were you on the night that Ross Pierce was murdered?"

Carl looked offended as he snapped, "I've already made a statement to the police that I was at home with my wife, and she's testified the same."

Mr. Hillard gave him an all-knowing smile and asked, "Are you sure about that? Is there any chance that you forgot you were at the Silver Linings Bar and Grill that night?"

Carl snorted, "No! I'm not a faggot. I wouldn't go in places like that."

Mr. Hillard's mouth turned into a crooked smile. "You do know that lying under oath is perjury, don't you Carl? I suggest that you change your statement now. Otherwise, you'll have another charge brought against you."

"Another charge? What the Hell am I being charged with? I told you I wasn't in that Faggot bar!" Carl snapped.

Mr. Hillard shook his head slowly, showing his obvious

frustration, then solemnly said, "Ok, I guess we'll have to do this the hard way. Your Honor, the defense would like to enter this video as Defense exhibit number one. We ask that it be reviewed and shown to the jury."

Carl slumped down in the witness box, realizing he'd been seen and caught on video. Mr. Hillard caught sight of his defeated face and asked, "Would you like to say anything Carl?"

Mr. Mitchell jumped out of his seat like a flash and snapped, "Objection! Your Honor, I think we need to review this video first to be sure that this evidence is admissible. I knew nothing about this."

The Judge thought for a moment and concurred, "Objection sustained. We will recess for one hour to review the video. Go and get a coffee everyone."

He pounded the gavel, and at that, he got up as the Bailiff said, "All rise!"

During the break, Daniella had gone to get a coffee with the girls, and as she was coming back, she brought one for Leo. He looked at his police guard and got the nod of approval to accept the coffee. Taking it carefully, he inhaled the comforting scent while closing his eyes. After a moment, he took a sip and eagerly commented, "Wow! Who knew courthouse coffee could taste this good."

"Yep, not too shabby," Daniella muttered.

Leo's mood suddenly became serious, and he asked, "How are my daughters? Do they hate me?"

Daniella replied, "No, trust me, they don't. They resented you for a long time, and once you hear the whole story, you'll know why. It's Carl that's behind it all."

Leo looked down at his hands and shook his head in disgust. "Who would have ever thought that regular o'le boy we once knew would lose his shit like that? I never would have thought in a million years that he'd be capable of a violent murder."

He paused and Daniella could see Leo was feeling real grief for the first time. He looked as though he would sob as he said, "No matter what he was doing, he didn't deserve that, and it's all because that Shit Son of a Bitch wanted to get revenge on me! Why? Why didn't he just try to kill me?"

Daniella put her hand on his back and looked at him sympathetically. "Well, I think that he may hate you so much he wanted to punish you, and death simply wasn't enough. I'm telling you, Leo, you didn't see him the day I went over there. He was seriously psycho. Somehow, we missed the fact that this guy was quiet, but deadly."

"Daddy wasn't all bad you know. I know you didn't see much of his good side, but I did." Leo reflected.

"I know," Daniella muttered softly.

The Judge and jurors' return to the courtroom interrupted their conversation. Everyone rapidly went back to his or her seats, and Daniella and Leo were equally delighted to see Aunt Rosie, Uncle Sheldon, and Katie come to join them. Daniella had called them early and urged them to be there for the day that would change their lives forever.

The Bailiff bellowed, "All rise!"

The Judge entered and took his seat behind his desk, then sat down as everyone in the court sat simultaneously. He looked perplexed with what he'd seen, so Daniella felt relieved, but didn't want to get too confident yet.

Judge Belham said, "Mr. Walters, you can come right back up here. I already have good cause to charge you with perjury and I might do that unless you decide to do the right thing here."

Shocked and terrified, Carl slowly made his way back

to the witness box. As he passed Leo, they both stared angrily at each other. Daniella thought they looked like two junkyard dogs, about to fight for territory. Carl reached the witness box and was reminded that he's still under oath.

The judge gave Mr. Hillard the go-ahead to continue his questioning, so Mr. Hillard confidently walked up to Carl, giving him a stern look. Carl decided it was time to admit his presence in the bar, as he was absolutely positive they had nothing else on him.

"Ok, I admit that I was there, and I was watching him, but I didn't do this."

Mr. Hillard, looking satisfied with this progress, replied, "You've wisely chosen to tell the truth, Carl, at least about this."

"Objection!" Mr. Mitchell blurted.

"Sustained. Mr. Hillard, watch your mouth." The judge reminded.

"Yes, Sir. I apologize." Said Mr. Hillard, then, turning his attention back to Carl, he asked "Have you met Leo's daughter, Elizabeth? She's right over there."

Mr. Hillard pointed at Lizzie. There was a wavering look in Carl's eyes, and he started tapping his foot on the floor. Mr. Hillard could tell he was nervous and desperate, so he took full advantage.

"You do know her, don't you Carl?" Said Mr. Hillard.

Carl nodded and solemnly admitted he did, but then tried to dismiss the significance of this. "I've met her before, but I don't know what you think is so strange about that. Her mother and I were classmates at one point."

Mr. Hillard replied, "Well Carl, I'll tell you what's so significant about that. Elizabeth is prepared to testify that you recruited her to murder Ross Pierce, and when she couldn't do it, you did it yourself and threatened to frame her if she didn't keep your secret."

Carl was fuming but wasn't stupid enough to lose it, as Mr. Hillard hoped he would. He remained calm, and thoughtfully said, "You have no proof of this."

Mr. Hillard smiled broadly, produced the shard, and retorted, "Well now Carl, that's where you're dead wrong."

He turned to the judge. "In fact, your Honor, I'd like to submit this as defense exhibit B."

The judge looked at the shard, and Mr. Mitchell blurted, "Objection! Your Honor, we know nothing of this piece of evidence and haven't reviewed any forensics performed on such evidence."

Mr. Hillard replied, "Your Honor, we had to finish all this in a hurry, and there simply wasn't time. I have the forensics report right here."

The judge took a moment to examine the report and agreed that it was legitimate. "I'll allow this. Proceed Mr. Hillard."

Mr. Hillard went on to explain, "This shard is the elusive 'missing piece' of the murder weapon, the part that ironically says, 'Trust', and fortunately for all of us, Elizabeth had it all along, wrapped carefully, so as not to disturb the fingerprint that it bears—Your fingerprint Carl."

Carl stood up and exploded, "That's a lie!"

"Is it? Is it Carl?" Mr. Hillard stood forcefully over Carl as he cowered and sat back down in the witness box.

"Isn't it true that you met Elizabeth many times prior to the murder to coax her into doing it as a means of getting revenge against her father and her grandfather, for abandoning her and her sister? You coaxed a vulnerable young girl into killing her own grandfather!?"

Mr. Mitchell shouted, "Objection! Conjecture!"

The judge said, "I'll allow it. Answer the question Mr. Walters."

Mr. Hillard dug into him harder. "You just hated Leo didn't you Carl? You hated him so much that you tried to talk his own daughter into killing her grandfather so Leo would be blamed for the crime! You knew about him chasing his father with that bat. You knew about it all along and knew that would make him look guilty."

Mr. Mitchell blurted, "Objection! Badgering the witness! Your Honor?"

The judge said, "Objection sustained. Stop this path your walking down Mr. Hillard, or you'll be in contempt. You've been warned."

Mr. Hillard said, "Yes, your Honor. I only have one final question."

He looked squarely at Carl and said, "Carl, I will remind you that you are under oath and the evidence against you is overwhelming, and we've got plenty more where that came from so I would advise you not to add perjury to your crimes. Now, did you kill Ross Pierce?"

Carl started to cry and his hands started to shake.

So solemnly, he said, "I killed him."

The entire courtroom gasped and started whispering loudly. The judge banged his gavel. "Order! Order! I will have order!"

Everyone tried to keep quieter after that, as they knew the judge hadn't closed the case just yet, and there'd be more to see. This case was making front-page coverage every day, and people from all over the area were waiting to hear the news. All at once, there was a flurry of journalists picking up their smartphones and tweeting to their readers.

Leo and Carl were looking at each other, Leo with hate in his eyes and Carl with deep regret. Mr. Hillard said, "Your

Honor, in light of this new evidence, I move for an immediate dismissal and ask that the defendant be released."

The judge said, "Officers, take Mr. Walters into custody and arrest him."

The officers did as they were instructed. The judge waited until Carl had been taken out of the room in handcuffs before he said, "Mr. Hillard, I'd still like to hear the testimony of Elizabeth before I decide to dismiss. After all, young lady, if what he says is true, you've had a big part in this, and we all need to hear it."

"Yes, of course, your Honor." Said, Mr. Hillard.

Lizzie cautiously approached the stand and was sworn in. Leo looked at her with a swelling heart, and by the time her testimony was done, he was crying for her. The guilt of all those years of neglect weighed on his mind and pulled his heartstrings hard. The judge was nodding, processing all that she'd said. Finally, he said, "Elizabeth is an unfortunate victim of circumstances here, and I have spoken with the District Attorney and am fully aware of how her cooperation has been pivotal in getting to the truth."

He paused for a long while and came to a decision. "I'm going to let her go with 2 years of probation and 100 hours of community service. That's the best I can do for her, and at least she'll avoid any jail time. Y'all should be glad she's a minor."

Leo was overjoyed that his daughter wasn't going to prison. He whispered to Mr. Hillard, at which point Mr. Hillard asked, "Your Honor, in light of the new evidence that's been revealed today, I move that my client be dismissed of all charges."

Judge Belham asked Mr. Mitchell, "Mr. Mitchell, what do you say?"

Mr. Mitchell reluctantly replied, "Your Honor, the prosecution drops all charges against Mr. Pierce."

The shouts of relief were loud and joyful. Everyone was there, hugging Leo and congratulating him. Aunt Rosie, Uncle Sheldon, Katie and a few of Leo's friends were there. They rejoiced with tears in their eyes, but none more than Leo. His eyes were full of tears as he hugged Katie very tightly. His eyes found Daniella, and his heart swelled. She was standing in the middle of the room and crying for joy. He ran to her and grabbed her for a huge hug. Daniella started to cry loudly, finally able to breathe relief after all the drama this case had drummed up. For a few moments, it seemed as if they were the only people in the room, and they were right back to being those children that had escaped the horrors of what their parents had put them through.

"Thank you, Danny. I know this wouldn't be possible without you." Leo admitted, with deep sincerity in his voice.

Daniella knew the road to recovery had begun for them, and this experience, as bad as it was, made it possible for them to resume the adoptive brother and sister bond that they'd had before. Daniella replied, "It was a wonderful and terrible experience, Leo. I was so worried about you. I know you're good, deep down. I've always known that. I hope we can start again now, and let bygones be bygones."

Leo nodded solemnly and added, "And I *really* need to get to know my kids. They seem like sweet girls."

"They are," added Daniella.

"I promise that from now on, we're gonna be a family. Hey, and you know what?" Leo asked.

"What?" Said Daniella tearfully.

Leo smiled and said, "We are gonna all get our act together and come visit you over there in your Arabian home. I'm so sorry I'm just thinking about doing that. I should have done that earlier. I should've helped you when you needed it, supported you, and I should've still been your cousin, no matter what."

Daniella had waited years to hear something like this. She didn't realize how badly she'd missed having a family, a family of origin, all those years in the Middle East. Not having any of them around made her feel like an orphan. There was only one thing about what Leo had said made her a bit upset.

"Leo, do me a favor and never call yourself my cousin again. You're my brother. We were raised together, and now we're together again. You're closer to me than my real brother, just like you've always been.

Lizzie approached with Sadie. Lizzie looked at Leo cautiously, feeling very afraid of what he may say and how he may react. To her delight, his mood was warm and welcoming, and quite relaxed, especially now.

He smiled warmly and said, "Hello my beautiful babies. I'm thanking the Lord for seeing your sweet faces right now."

He reached out and grabbed Lizzie in a joyful hug, then freed a hand to stretch out to Sadie. "Come to Daddy baby." Daniella looked on with pride and happiness for Leo and the girls then decided to break the silence. "Hey, you guys, what do you say to getting out of here and getting something to eat? Maybe some ice cream?"

Everyone thought that was a great idea, and they happily left the terrible ominous courtroom, together, as a family.

15

FAMILY REUNION

The family gathered at Katie's house, and all the right players were there. Katie, Uncle Sheldon and Aunt Rosie, Leo, Lizzie, Sadie and Daniella were enjoying a beautiful evening sitting around the same large dinner table that they'd gathered around since their family began. They were feasting on a banquet Katie had made, consisting of Beef Casserole, Mashed potatoes, green beans, carrots, and a lovely split pea soup with a tossed salad. She had promised one of her famous lemon meringue pies if everyone cleaned their plates. It wasn't long before Luwanda rang the doorbell which startled Lizzie and Sadie. Lizzie said, "That's Mama. Oh God...I hope she's not gonna freak out."

Leo got up from the table and came around to where they were sitting. He crouched down beside them to look at them on eye level. "Don't worry. You know I'm dying to see her. I've never told anyone this, but your mother has always been the love of my life. I'm so sorry I was too chicken shit to admit it before today."

The girls both smiled shyly and he gave them both a gentle kiss on the head. Daniella said, "Well, is anyone gonna get the door and let the poor gal in? Gosh! Y'all have lost all manners, I swear!"

She got up and opened the door for Luwanda to find her with a wild look on her face. Luwanda blurted, "Danny what the Hell is going on!? Where are my girls!?"

Without waiting for an answer, she pushed inside and rushed up to Lizzie. Concerned, she asked, "Baby, is it true? Did that bastard talk you into what they said? Oh God, now I know why you were acting so badly. You haven't been yourself for a long time."

Lizzie replied, "Yes Mama. I'm so sorry, but I hope you also heard that I *couldn't* do it. When it all came down, I just couldn't hurt him. That's when Carl jumped in and did it himself, and now he's the one in jail instead of my father."

Luwanda looked at Leo, still crouched beside the girls. He stood up, and when their eyes met, it was obvious to everyone in the room that there were still feelings between them. However, regardless of what her heart told her, Luwanda's mind knew that Leo abandoned her and the children, and the damage from that action had a horrible impact on their lives. Without much emotion, she said, "Hello Leo, long time."

Leo moved closer to Luwanda, extremely close, so he could look her into her eyes. "Wanda, I can't tell you how grateful I am to our beautiful girl right now. Lizzie's got your courage, that's for sure. God help me if she'd been anything like the rat I've been all these years."

He paused briefly to get a reaction, but Luwanda stood strong. Her eyes pierced him like daggers, and his pain was evident as his eyes drooped. After a long and painful pause, Luwanda said, "She's more like me, but maybe that's a bad thing since it made her go after revenge in the first place."

Luwanda held her head down in a surprising show of

shame, which was unlike her. She said feebly, "I shouldn't have talked to her about it, about how hurt I was. I guess that's what made her listen to Carl. I'm sorry."

Upon hearing this, Danny and Leo rushed to her side, eager to comfort her. Daniella said, "Oh, Wanda! Don't you dare think any of this is your fault! You had every right to confide in your own family about your pain."

Leo couldn't agree more. He added, "My sister's right. You were in a bad way, all because of me. If I hadn't listened to Daddy and had paid attention to my feelings for you, and been a good father, none of this would have happened. I brought it on myself."

Katie chimed in, "Well I guess it's Ross's fault. Y'all are not mentioning the obvious here!"

Daniella replied, "In the Middle East, they have a story, a story about a snake that was drowning and spotted a woman passing by. He begged and pleaded with her to rescue him and promised not to hurt her. She rescued him, and as soon as he was safe, he bit her. In shock, as she started to die, she asked, 'Why did you do that? You promised not to hurt me.' To which he replied, 'I'm a snake after all.' We can't blame Daddy for what he was. He was naturally bad, and so was Carl. Looking back on it, I don't think that boy was ever good. Even when we were kids, he was only nice to you because he was jealous of you Leo."

"I guess I always felt it, but you know when we're kids we don't realize." Leo reflected.

Luwanda nodding, added, "Yeah, I always felt his jealousy for you, Leo. You were the star in high school, and he was your sidekick. That's how all of us saw it."

Leo smiled at Luwanda and said, "I've missed you. I really have."

The look on his face was one Luwanda had fallen for

many times. His smile was sparkling, his perfectly straight teeth, his dimples, his gorgeous green eyes—Luwanda was taken in by it yet again. She smiled back shyly but quickly looked concerned as her eyes closed and her breath hitched.

Leo held her hand with both of his and looked deeply into her eyes. "I know I've put you through a lot. Even if I work all my life to make it up to you, it wouldn't be enough. God knows, I know that. But, I wanna try. Please let me try. I still love you, Wanda."

Luwanda looked at him and a small smile curled on her lips. She squeezed his hand back and looked back at him with large longing eyes, then said, "I want to believe you... Please don't hurt me. Please no more."

Leo hugged her tightly and declared his devotion."I promise Baby. I know you don't have any reasons to trust me, but I swear it's all changed now. This is a new day. Nothing's gonna be the same, so anything's possible."

Daniella looked on in wonder and thought of how much easier all of their lives would have been if these two had been free to express their feelings for each other openly. They would have been a happy family right now, and Leo could have been in Daniella's life all along, but then again, God always knows best and has a plan for everything and everyone. "Allah Kareem" she said, which means, God provides.

The evening went on with everyone getting along and catching up on old times, and it seemed that all was finally well in the Pierce family. Then, the doorbell rang again, startling everyone. If there was one thing to be sure of, it was that no one was ready for any more drama.

Katie said, "I'll get it. Y'all just relax. I sure hope everything's ok."

She made her way to the door and opened it cautiously.

The look of surprise on her face was classic, and everyone was eager to see what she was so happy about. As the door crept open everyone gasped to see Brian, Daniella's half brother, standing there. Katie invited him in, and he said, "Thank you, Grandma. It's certainly great to see you. I've really missed you."

He hugged her tight and Katie was beside herself with excitement. She thought about Ross Sr. and how happy he would have been to see the family all together like this. It was such a shame it took a tragedy to make it happen. She smiled at everyone and felt the warmth of gratitude in her heart.

Daniella ran to Brian and grabbed him for a huge hug, and blurted "Oh my God!! I'm so happy to see you! Where the Hell have you been? My brother is home at last!"

Brian was so excited to hug his sister for the first time in years. He smiled widely and even though he was an attractive man, as well as big and burly, he looked emotional, and even though no one there could remember a time that they witnessed Brian crying, one could swear his eyes watered *just a bit*. Everyone looked on with approval except Leo. Brian, after all, was Danny's brother by blood, not her cousin, and he'd always had a privileged life. He had been born with the proverbial silver spoon in his mouth. However, in spite of his feelings, Leo remained courteous.

"Hey there Brian! We're all shocked to see you."

He felt all the eyes in the room studying him, tracking him for signs of disapproval, so he decided to try and recover from what he'd just said. He stepped forward to shake hands with Brian. "Hey, we are shocked but happy! Really happy! Gosh boy, I haven't seen you in a Coon's age! How the Hell are ya?"

Brian smiled, and when he did, all the women in the

room were reminded of how dazzling he really was. He had Carol's deep dimples in his cheeks, so he was simply magnetic to everyone, especially females. He looked at Leo and said, "Well Bro, I've been studying, still at Oxford actually. I've got about a year left on my Master's Degree in International Studies."

He paused thoughtfully and said, "Truth is, I heard about your situation, and at first I didn't answer when Grandma called me, but she kept up with trying to get through to me. And...well...finally she did, and I have to tell you all I feel really bad about not getting here sooner. I'm glad you're OK now Bro. Guess we all have to be thankful for having such a strong sister."

Daniella blushed a bit, as she wasn't really used to getting compliments from her family, and said, "Oh come on now! That's all water under the bridge, so get on in here and join us for some food. You know Katie's got a feast in here. She just can't help herself."

Katie replied smiling broadly, "It's true. I can't. I'm so glad to have someone to cook for right now. I felt like my skills were getting rusty."

They all really enjoyed the rest of the evening, forgetting about any past arguments, the color of anyone's skin, or anyone's permanent address. The food was delicious, as the table was spread with Casseroles, green beans, corn on the cob, tossed salad and ambrosia, with 3 different kinds of pies. Daniella looked around the room and felt a glow in her heart. This truly was the missing piece she'd been looking for all these years. All her years in the United Arab Emirates were great, but she'd always felt like an orphan, like she appeared there from thin air.

She wondered if this happy family reunion would last for long, and how everyone would feel when it was time for her to go back to the home in the Middle East that she'd made for herself. Eventually, she'd have to tell them it was time for her to truly go home. Would anyone visit her there? All her American friends who were married to Emirati men had enjoyed visitors like their moms, their sisters, brothers, etc., but Daniella had never had one single appearance by a family member, which left her feeling very alone from time to time.

She decided that now wasn't the time to deal with all those fears; now was the time to enjoy the moment and be grateful for having the family all together, getting along. The laughter, the stories, the food, the iced tea, and heartfelt and loving moments swept through the air like a dove's wings flap through the night sky, and all was well *for the moment.*

16

INTERNATIONAL TIES

Daniella woke the next morning in her childhood bed to the sound of birds chirping in the apple orchard outside. She slipped on her robe and slippers and made her way to the kitchen. Katie had already put out some coffee and toast for everyone, but she wasn't anywhere to be seen. Daniella helped herself to some coffee, enjoying the lovely French Roast smell. She thought about how she'd probably learned such an appreciation for coffee from Katie, who didn't believe in preparing instant coffee, and not even store-bought filter coffee, only gourmet.

Taking a sip from her stone mug, she opened the screen door to the porch and stepped outside. She smiled warmly at the sight of Katie picking apples in the orchard, undoubtedly to make her famous apple tarts for breakfast. The thought of this made Daniella's stomach growl. She blurted, "Hey Grandma! Do you need some help?"

Katie turned back and shouted, "No Sweetie Pie, I got this. You go on back inside."

Daniella smirked and said, "Yeah, I'm not buying it." She went back inside, took another deep swallow of her coffee, and changed her clothes. She went outside and Katie couldn't hide the look of joy at seeing her. "Well OK, if you insist. Grab that basket and go over there and pick a few. There's bound to be some ripe ones there cuz I didn't get to those yet."

Daniella started to turn and walk toward the trees when Katie remembered, "Oh, and please watch out Honey, cuz there's a snake or two in here sometimes. When your Grandpa was alive, he kept them away pretty good, but now that I'm alone, I just have to pick around them."

Daniella couldn't believe what she was hearing, and thought about it. *This tiny old lady picks apples around the snakes in her orchard? How could it be that no one knew this, least of all, Leo?* She said, "Ok Grandma, please stop and come back to the house with me for a minute."

Katie looked up in bewilderment, "Why Darlin'?"

Daniella replied, "Please just trust me, Ok? I promise it's only for a little bit. We'll get those apples."

Katie looked bothered and bewildered as to why Daniella was determined to stop her from finishing her apple picking, but didn't complain as she gathered up her basket and went inside, muttering, "I don't know what's gotten into you child. You never had a problem with me picking them before."

Daniella heard her and muttered back, "There were no snakes in the picture before."

She then called Brian and Leo to the kitchen. Once they were standing there at attention, she started to speak when she saw Luwanda coming out of Leo's room, fumbling to close her bathrobe, looking like a woman who'd been making love all night. She caught sight of Daniella and smiled a guilty smile. Daniella looked at Leo and put her hands on her hips. Leo shrugged his shoulders and said, "Well, I still want the girl, OK?"

Daniella didn't budge from her accusatory stance, so he became a little nervous. "We've got kids together, so I thought you'd think of it as a good thing. I can see myself with this girl for the rest of my life."

Daniella cracked a small smile, and Leo could tell she was only messing with him. Irately, he said, "You're just fucking with me, right?"

That moment stimulated a full-fledged laugh from them both. Daniella caught her breath long enough to say, "Na Leo, I think it's great. I hope it works out this time. But, I swear to God, if you hurt her anymore, I'll be there this time to kick your ass."

Just as he was about to reply to her, Daniella's cell phone rang. The ringtone was loud and intrusive, so it shocked her a bit. She grabbed it from the kitchen countertop and answered, surprised to hear the concerned voice of her husband. Faisal had a certain tone in his voice, the tone that always let Daniella know he was pushed to the edge of his limits. He was always a worrier. He said, "I'm really wondering what's going on, Habibti. You haven't called me, and I'm worried all the time about you! We only Skyped once, and then you just disappeared! You're not even answering your phone!"

Daniella felt guilty. Weakly, she said, "I'm sorry Baby. I've been under a lot of stress here. You know that."

At this point, there was only awkward silence on the phone, as Daniella didn't have any words to follow up with. He went on, "I just need a call now and then so I know you're ok. That's all. Is that too much to ask?"

"No," Daniella replied. "I'm sorry I worried you. I'll try to be more considerate."

The silence on the phone that followed was deafening. She carried on waiting and finally heard an exhale that might have sounded like a small concession. Reluctantly, he said, "Well get back safe. The boys and I miss you. That's all I wanted to say." After that, he hung up without another word, and Daniella's heart sunk.

She sat down on her grandpa's old chair, feeling defeated. There was no winning when it came to talking to Faisal. He knew how to psychologically dominate in every conversation. Even when he seemed to concede an argument, he ended up making her feel like she was too aggressive. In all their years together, she'd always ended up feeling a little worse for the wear each time they'd gotten into it. As she sat sulking, Leo put a reassuring hand on her shoulder and said, "Relationships are never easy are they?"

Daniella looked up at him and said, "Nope."

They were silent for a good long and awkward moment, and she finally said, "I guess I'm gonna have to call him back at some point. He's a great man, he really is, but I guess they all get insecure sometimes, and I have been away for a while." She thoughtfully paused a moment and continued, "Well, I think I'll just text my apology first. There's something quite safe about typing words, right?"

He smiled back at her, and gave her an agreeing nod, and said, "Well I'll give you a minute to do that while I get dressed. Hey, what did you want me and Brian to do?"

Distracted, and already beginning to type her apologetic text, said, "Yeah, I want you two to somehow snake proof the orchard so our sweet Grandma doesn't get bit by a rattlesnake to bring us fresh apple tarts."

Leo scoffed and said, "Ok Sis, I'm on it."

Before she could finish the text, they all heard a loud scream come from the orchard. Daniella dropped her phone and ran out the door with her brothers to find Luwanda running with Katie away from the orchard up onto the porch. No one had even seen her go out there, so she had no idea of the snake danger. She wanted to get closer to Katie, who had ignored Daniella's directions and gone back out there again. When Luwanda offered to help her pick apples, they encountered a snake.

Luwanda got Katie up on the porch to safety, and they ran so fast they were both panting. Leo started to stroke Luwanda's back, hoping to sooth her breathing so she could speak. After a few moments of actively trying to catch her breath, she finally said, "We saw a snake. Oh, sweet Lord! This poor woman was inches away from getting bitten by a bona fide Diamond Back Rattler! I spotted it and thank God I caught her eye long enough to motion for her to take a step back so he couldn't reach her when he struck."

Every kid growing up in Georgia, Alabama, or Mississippi knew a rattler could only strike the distance of its own body, and thankfully, the diamondback was small, small but deadly. If Katie had gotten bit, she surely would have died. This brought home the danger in all their minds. Daniella said, "I had a bad feeling. I knew it! Grandma why didn't you listen? I didn't think you'd be going off in there again! Good heavens!"

Katie said, "I'm sorry Darlin'. I swear I didn't think there'd be any out there today." Daniella rolled her eyes.

Brian said, "I've got a buddy that takes care of things like this. I'm gonna call him right now and get him over here. I've lost a mother and a father, so I'm not ready to lose my sweet Grandma now." He reached over and touched Katie's chin. She smiled warmly.

Katie said, "Ok Y'all stop fussing over me! Let's get in the kitchen and have whatever breakfast I can scramble up, now that I don't have any dang apples."

That pulled at their heartstrings, so they went inside and had a lovely family breakfast. Of course, it was a little awkward to everyone when Daniella refused to eat Bacon. Leo said, "Well, I'm not gonna say anything. I've learned my lesson, and thanks to you, I'm here and free. So eat whatever tickles your fancy Hun!"

Brian wasn't as accommodating. "Well, I think it's little nuts, but I have met some good Muslims in Europe."

He looked at her thoughtfully for a moment and continued, "I don't know Danny. It's just so weird, though, you being one of them. When you're over there, do you wear that black *thing* on your head? And that black cape thing?"

Daniella looked at him as one who'd just had her toes stepped on and blurted, "Well Yeah, as a matter of fact, I do! And, I'll have you know Sir, that those 'Black Things' are quite stylish, at least in our area. Some of them are extraordinarily well made and quite comfortable. The *cape thing*, as you call it, hides the extra pounds and the hair wrap hides a bad hair day very well, so that's always a good thing."

Everyone smiled politely at this, but it was becoming obvious to her they were trying hard to be polite so as not to ruin the new found harmony they'd been enjoying since Leo's freedom. Daniella decided to let it be for the moment and finish her breakfast in peace. She knew that soon she'd have to start texting Faisal all sorts of apologetic messages, because after all, she'd have to go home at some point soon, and the last thing she needed after all this madness was an irate husband to go home to, and a family here in Georgia that she'd have to say goodbye to again.

Luwanda and the kids came to the table and joined

them, and everyone enjoyed a nice leisurely morning, and as the hour went on, it became apparent to everyone that Leo and Luwanda were going to be an item from now on. They were getting chummy with each other, holding hands and looking flirtatious towards one another. Daniella was very happy to see them like that, and had to feel somewhat good about herself for having been a catalyst; however, all good things must come to an end, and Daniella didn't have to wait long to know when the right moment would come to tell them she'd be leaving soon. Katie brought up the subject for her.

"How long are we gonna have you with us Honey? Faisal and the boys must be missing you." Katie asked, with a tilted head and a scrunched brow.

Daniella felt them all staring at her for an answer. "Umm, well I was gonna bring that up. I've already been off work for more than a couple weeks now, and this is a busy season for us, so I'm afraid I can't be here too much longer, maybe a couple more days?"

Leo looked the saddest, which surprised her a great deal, but she considered how much he'd been through lately. Katie was the first one to speak. "It's not fair. You just got here, and we're all sitting together like a real family again. Isn't there any way you can stay a little bit more?"

Brian chimed in, "Yeah Sis, I'm sorry I said that thing about the black cover you wear. I feel like I want a little more time with you too. We haven't been under the same roof for years. It's kinda nice."

Daniella smiled at the attention and said, "Well I guess I can try and make it three more days. I'll talk to Faisal tonight about my ticket, but you know what? You guys should think about making a trip over there to visit with me for a while! I've got plenty of room at my house to put you all up during your stay. You wouldn't have to pay for any hotel, and of course, we'd be mostly eating at my place too. That only leaves the ticket."

Katie laughed out loud, "Hahaha! Oh, Honey, you can't expect me to go all the way to Arabia! I've never even been on a plane before. I've always said I'll only go on a plane if I can keep one foot on the ground."

Leo blurted, "I'll come! I'll come very soon, but I wanna bring Wanda and the girls, just as soon as Lizzie's probation is over. I promise I'll come."

His warm smile made Daniella beam. This was indeed some of the closure she needed, and she realized that for the first time in many years, her heart was mending. But her heart wasn't all that had to mend. Ross needed a proper funeral, and the morgue released his body for burial to Brian. He started making the arrangements from the moment his plane landed and had tried to avoid bringing it up, but he had to let everyone know they had a funeral to attend tomorrow. When the news sunk in, Daniella thought about how she'd feel when she went up to the casket to pay her final respects.

Ross was a man who had rejected his daughter wholeheartedly after finding out she was living a lifestyle that wasn't to his liking. All his life he'd had issues with women, first his mother, his wife, and then his daughter, but now he's dead, and everyone will need to say goodbye. Daniella had mixed emotions about how she was going to feel, but for now, she was enjoying the feeling of acceptance from her family that she'd longed for.

Brian broke her chain of thought with even more news, "Danny, we also have to deal with Mr. Hale and Daddy's Will. Mr. Hale probably told you that you didn't inherit a thing, but that's not entirely so. None of Y'all knew it, but Daddy had regrets about how he treated Danny."

"What do you mean?" Said Danny.

Brian looked around to see many surprised faces and spoke up as Katie planted her hands firmly on her hips, in full reprimand mode. Almost chuckling at Katie, he continued, "He contacted me about 6 months ago and said he'd changed his Will. It's true he had cut you out years before, and I'm sure Mr. Hale was happy about that. They always had wanted it all to go to me, and if I was the asshole a lot of Y'all think I am, I could be keeping all this to myself now, and just keep all the family fortune. But that wouldn't be right."

Daniella looked aghast and murmured, "You mean I'm not cut out? I inherited a portion of the company? What about Leo?"

Brian looked sadly at Leo and said, "I'm sorry Buddy. He was pretty firm on you not getting anything. I'm really sorry."

Leo shrugged it off and said, "Hey Bro it's all good. I knew he hated me. No matter what I ever tried to do to make him happy, that old Bastard just hated me."

Katie pinched Leo's arm, and he yelled, "Oww! What'd you do that for Grandma?"

Katie said, "It's ill-mannered to disrespect the dead. I know he was a handful, but he was your Uncle and your adopted father, and now he's dead. He can't hurt anyone anymore."

Daniella hugged him and whispered in his ear, "If I did get some of this, I'll share. Don't you worry now."

Brian went on to explain the situation. "He really did start to regret how he treated you, Danny. He sent me a new copy of the Will, and he left it all to you and me, equally, so it looks like you and I have some property to split."

The smile on his face was one of pride, pride in doing the right thing. Daniella was touched because she never imagined that her father still cared anything about her. She was stunned and stood there absolutely paralyzed. Never in a million years did she imagine that her father would still care for her at all. He'd made it so abundantly clear he didn't care if she lived or died. The same sentiment went for her kids, as he'd never even asked to see a picture of them.

Brian couldn't stand seeing her stunned like that, so he finally said something. "Danny, are you ok? This is a good thing. You do understand this, right?"

Daniella snapped out of her look of shock to say, "Yeah, I'm Ok. I only wish he'd told me. If he had only picked up the phone one time...just one time."

She perked up when she remembered Mr. Hale, and said, "Oh my God! Does this mean we can go stick it to Mr. Hale? Please say Yes." She had a huge smile on her face as she remembered how rotten Mr. Hale had treated her, and how much she was going to enjoy putting him in his place. Leo loved it. He looked on with great approval, nodding as if he could read her mind.

17

THE FUNERAL

The day before had been a wonderful bonding experience for the Pierce family, and for the first time in many years, they felt connected. Each one felt it, and as they all went to Aunt Rosie's, the visit was so much better. Everyone spent the day relaxing on Uncle Sheldon's deck, sipping iced tea, rocking in the swing, and catching up on all the news.

But today was not to be the same, not even close, as today was the day everyone had to pay their final respects to Ross Octavian Pierce II and lay him to rest. It wasn't a surprise to anyone that his funeral had to be a closed casket ceremony. There wasn't any funeral parlor in Georgia that knew how to make heads or tails of how smashed in his head was.

Everyone in the county was there, old classmates, all of the prominent families of the community, and all of Katie's close friends from Church. Everyone seemed unnerved to see Leo there, but he held himself strong and confident, since he had been proven innocent of the murder. Reverend Bobby Fisher, the same Baptist reverend that had been there since Daniella and Leo were children, delivered the eulogy.

Reverend Bobby's eulogy was warm and wonderful, as he referred to Ross as a *pillar of the community*. Daniella knew he was just being kind, as Ross had never done a charitable thing in his life, and most of the charitable acts Reverend Bobby referred to were the acts that Ross Sr. had performed.

Ross Sr. had started a charity to help the newly released prisoners get back on their feet by paying for the expenses of a halfway house. Only the immediate family knew that Ross Jr. had wanted to cancel this program to save money, and it was Mr. Hale who convinced him to keep it or lose face in the public eye.

After the eulogy, Reverend Bobby asked Daniella and Brian to come forward to say something about their father. Brian decided that it would be easier for Daniella if he went first, so he bravely stepped forward and took his place behind the podium. True to form, Brian talked about what a good stepfather Ross had been, how he had spared no expense for the boarding school education that enabled him to pursue a wonderful career as a successful stock broker. Brian expressed his regret that Ross didn't live to see his beautiful wife and children. Then, to everyone's surprise, he ended by saying, "But I wasn't ever his real child. Daniella and I shared a mother, and Ross adopted me, but my sister Daniella is his only true born child. Only she had the privilege of being his natural child, and it would be an honor if she'd come forward and say her piece now."

Daniella hadn't prepared for this, so she was very nervous, and not quite sure of the path to take. *Should I tell the truth?* She wondered. *Everyone would know what kind of man Ross Jr. really was. Or should I do what Southern aristocracy would agree is the "honorable" thing to do?* She decided on taking Katie's most commonly offered advice —"if you can't say something nice, say nothing at all."

With a gulp and a silent Islamic prayer for strength, she began. "I'm glad to be standing here in front of all of you today. Standing here to say goodbye to my father."

She fought the tears hard, and it was a very difficult battle, but she found the strength to carry on. "As many of you already know, my father and I had many disagreements, although early in my life, I was the apple of his eye, his perfect child...Well, I stopped being his perfect child when I moved to the Middle East, and everyone by now knows why, but I don't want to talk about that today. Today we're here to honor my father, and the good points he embodied."

As she paused, she looked around the room, and Katie, Uncle Sheldon, Aunt Rosie, and many others were nodding in somber approval, understanding what she was trying to do. She gulped and found the power to carry on.

"I remember once when Leo, Brian and I were little, he tried to make one perfect Christmas for us. Yes, it was only one Christmas he went to all this effort, but I'll never forget it. We woke up and found the most beautiful train set I'd ever seen all set up and running around the Christmas tree. There were presents everywhere. He really went all out."

By this time, it was hard for Daniella to hold back tears as she remembered the sweet look on Ross's face as he presented the perfect Christmas to his kids. He was like a sweet little boy himself, and it was her favorite memory of him. Seeing his face in her mind's eye was heartbreaking, as she had wished for many years to see this look of love and acceptance on his face again. The memory was heart wrenching. Sobbing, she went on.

"I'll never forget his face that fine day. He was my Daddy that day, and he loved my brothers and me. We ate pancakes and we laughed as we enjoyed the enormous bounty of gifts he had for us. Today my heart aches knowing I'll never see that sweetness in his face again, sweetness I always knew he was capable of. That one single day taught me that in his heart, he had a wonderful and loving side. I hope he's at peace where he is now, and he knows I never stopped loving him, no matter what happened between us."

The tears were streaming down now, and it was obvious to everyone she couldn't continue. She ended her speech with, "Bye Bye Daddy. I love you."

Reverend Bobby walked her back to her pew and helped her sit down by Katie. Then, he looked towards Leo and asked if he'd like to say anything. Leo agreed and stepped forward to the podium.

He cleared his throat and began, "I'm also glad to be here today, to say Goodbye to the man that raised me, the only father I've ever really known...I know a lot of Y'all thought the worst of me, and I'm sorry my past behavior has brought that on."

Leo looked at Daniella supportively, smiling warmly. Then, he went on. "I remember that day Danny. It hadn't been long since I lost my parents, and that day was the best day of my entire childhood. Ross was *my* Daddy that day too, the Daddy I always wished for, and I'm grateful for it... I'm also grateful to be a part of this family. Ross did the best he knew how I suppose, and I've learned from my sister to see the positive in things now, so praise the Lord. May he rest in peace."

After that, Leo sat down by the family and Reverend Bobby finished the service with a prayer. It was then time to transport Ross to the cemetery to lay him to rest. His pallbearers were Leo, Brian, Mr. Hale, and two store employees Mr. Hale brought along to make it a total of 6 as it should be.

As Ross was lowered into the open grave, Daniella and the rest of the family looked on and one by one, they laid a rose on his coffin just before the dirt was piled on. It was almost surreal. The great Ross Octavian Pierce II was dead and buried. Katie suggested that everyone make their way to her house where there was going to be a gathering for the after funeral occasion.

The reporters were standing at a respectable distance, as they were not allowed into the church for the ceremony. Within minutes, the story was all over the internet.

18

AFTERMATH AND WHO GETS WHAT

The next day started quietly, but no one had seen Brian all morning. No one seemed particularly bothered by this for the time being. Everyone sat in the kitchen quietly sipping tea and reflecting. Daniella had her return ticket booked for the next morning in Atlanta, so she knew her day would need to be spent packing for the trip and maybe shopping for a few personal items for Faisal and the kids. She had been up almost all night the night before on Skype with Faisal at the neighborhood Internet Café. Katie didn't have Internet access in her house. When asked about the lack of internet in her home, she said, "I don't like computers Baby. You know I've never been partial to such new-fangled things."

Suddenly everyone heard Brian's car drive into the driveway and Leo said, "Well I wonder where that fella's been all morning? It ain't like him to just run off like that... Or maybe it is. None of us has seen hide nor hair of him in so long before all this mess."

Daniella snickered and turned full attention to Brian as he burst into the house, smiling from ear to ear. He blurted,

"Oh Sister dear, I've got some good news for you! I've been with Mr. Hillard this morning reviewing the Will that Daddy left behind, the updated one, and you'll be very pleased to know that you have indeed inherited half of the whole kit and kaboodle!"

Daniella's jaw dropped, and for a time, she was beyond stunned. Leo was also in a state of total shock, and it took a moment for him to recover enough to look towards Daniella, and see the smile that was beginning to form on her face. She looked truly touched as she whispered softly, "He really was sorry. This was his way to apologize."

Katie blurted, "Oh my God! Well, Baby, it looks like your Daddy wasn't a hopeless case after all. Come to think of it, around those last days he did look nervous like something was on his mind. He was going out a lot, and he did mention you once or twice."

Daniella asked, "Well, why didn't you tell me earlier?"

Katie replied, "I guess it just slipped my mind. I'm sorry Honey. But he looked busier than a one-legged man in a butt-kicking contest. Hmm, now let me see...Oh yes! I remember him saying something about making things right, and he did wonder what those boys of yours looked like, and he hoped they looked more like you."

Daniella sensed she was holding something back there, and asked, "And? What aren't you telling me? I know that face."

Katie put her hands on her hips, as she always did when she was nervous, and revealed, "Well, I just hate to speak ill of the dead, but he did say that he hoped the boys looked like you instead of like a couple of camel jockeys....I'm sorry Honey. I just don't think he could help it."

Daniella snickered, "Yea, you're probably right."

Leo, wanting to change the subject, said, "Ok, well I

think we've got some nose rubbing to do girl! What do you say? Let's go and harass that old bastard, Mr. Hale!"

The sneaky look on his face was appealing and reminded Daniella of when they were kids, so she couldn't help but agree. She rushed to get ready, and off they went to reclaim what was rightfully theirs. True to her word, in time, she split her share with Leo, and appointed him as her spokesperson in the company, as she knew it would be too hard to maintain regular contact from out of the country. Leo was overjoyed to take the job and was determined to be a wonderful success. Brian was far more able to make regular visits to Georgia, so he kept a more vigorous role in the company's affairs, but also trusted Leo to be CEO. They kept Mr. Hale on board as a Vice-President, much to his chagrin. He still muttered on and on from time to time about what spoiled little shits Ross's kids were, and how he could have run the company so much better. Leo enjoyed hearing his rambling from time to time and considered it great payback for all the chiding he'd suffered from as a child.

Daniella and her brothers were finally in a good place again, and the trio vowed to stay in contact regularly when Daniella returned to Dubai. This made them all feel a lot better about each other, but Katie was a point of concern. She was getting up there in age, and with no one living in the house with her, there was concern that one day she'd be unwell and no one would know until it's too late. Katie needed a sense of purpose. She had enjoyed having everyone there so much, and it was definitely because it made her feel needed again, so Daniella had an idea. She invited her brothers out for coffee to discuss it. She had wanted to take them to lunch, but Katie wouldn't hear of them skipping a meal as long as she was there to cook for them.

They met at the only coffee shop in town, a little joint named, "Cup of Joe". Daniella began by saying, "You know guys, I must say, I admire this place for being possibly one of the only towns in the world with no Starbucks."

"You ain't kidding girl," Leo replied.

They sat down and ordered some drinks, and each one was surprised at what a great rich flavor they were tasting, and the comfort of that was pleasant. Leo asked, "Ok, so why are we here Danny? What's in your head now?"

Daniella said, "Well, I know Y'all are just as concerned about Katie as I am. She's getting on up there, and she's having a hard time dealing with the fact that there's no one around for her to take care of. I mean, let's face it, if we leave her like this, God only knows what may happen. Leo, you live in town, but you're gonna be super busy with the company. Brian, you live in another state, and I live in another country. So, Katie needs something to do, and someone who's there all the time….I have an idea."

Brian and Leo leaned in closer to pay attention; both intrigued by what she'd say. Daniella carried on, "I've been staying there with her while I've been here, and I don't think Y'all know just how beautiful the house really is. It's got Southern Charm and grace, and it's got a built-in mother figure for weary travelers. I think it should be made into a Bed and Breakfast Inn, and I think Katie should run it."

Brian shook his head, indicating he may not be ok with that. "I dunno Danny. She's an old woman, and you wanna put her in her house alone with strangers? What if an axe murderer came to stay there?"

"Yea!" Leo blurted.

Daniella scoffed and said, "Oh come on! Would I do

that? No, I thought that we should also hire a bouncer security type fella to stay here also. He could be here to assess and manage any security threats."

She looked at the both of them staring back and was quite happy to see them start to nod and smile in agreement. She continued to drive the point on, "The house will look beautiful, fixed up in traditional antebellum Southern style, very antique, and Katie would be over the moon to supervise a Southern menu for the guests! Oh my God! It would be so totally cute. She'd love it and she's bound to make a lot of money. She could even dress up in traditional Southern clothes, as well as all the employees."

Brian started nodding, getting totally sold on the idea. Leo chimed in, "I wonder if Wanda would like to help. You know my woman is the best soul food chef in the world, right?"

"Damn right she is!" Daniella agreed, smiling broadly. "I think Wanda would be awesome here! Between Grandma and Wanda, we'd have the best Southern menu in the state. This place would be a legend in no time!"

Brian asked, "Well Sister Dear, are you gonna stay here in town to set all this up? You own half of this house too now, so don't you wanna supervise this yourself?"

Daniella thought for a moment and replied, "Gosh you're right. I couldn't leave this to anyone else. I really need to do this myself, that is if you trust me to handle it. You own half of this house too."

"I trust you. But please make sure you give Katie and Wanda key positions and you hire a strong and very dependable security guard. We can't take chances on something bad happening. There's a lot of sickos out there, even in a small town like this." Brian said.

Daniella confirmed that after she got back home to

Dubai, she'd arrange another trip there soon to begin the renovation and refurbishment the property. Brian and Leo were happy because they'd see her again soon, and from now on, she'd have a more active role in their lives.

Later that day when they told Katie, they were delighted to see how positively she reacted. "I'm gonna be a working woman again. You know I was a lunch lady once. Long before I met your Grandpa. That was back when my first husband was alive. I was really good at my job."

Daniella said, "Well I'm sure you're gonna be awesome here! Hey, I'm not gonna call it Katie's Southern Bed and Breakfast for nothing!"

Katie beamed with delight, as it had been a very long time since she felt needed. This was exactly what she needed, and just to be sure everything got up and running properly, Daniella decided to extend her stay a bit longer, rather than book a whole new trip, long enough to see the doors open for the first time. It was a day that would make history in their little corner of Georgia.

19

BACK IN DUBAI

The flight back to Dubai was long and tedious, but at least Daniella flew back with a sense of closure that she hadn't had in years. There was only one thing she hadn't resolved. She hadn't let herself truly mourn her father. Since she'd been in Georgia, she had had little time alone, so it was just sinking in that her father was gone. He hadn't been so bad all the time. When she was little, he was actually pretty fun as a Dad. He took her and Leo to the movies every Sunday as he wasn't a big fan of the church. She only had one memory of him ever setting foot inside a church, and he seemed very regretful he'd gone afterwards, but that was most likely due to all the people staring at him the entire time. *Poor guy*, she thought, when she remembered how the whole town was talking about his one appearance in church, especially when it wasn't his "established" church, the one that was mostly for the rich and white.

Hadleyville was a place where everyone knew everyone, and Ross was often a victim of that. When he wanted to have fun, he went to Atlanta to find more like-minded people. Daniella remembered fondly all the fun times they had enjoyed in Atlanta, like going to Six Flags over Georgia. Ross was a great vacation Dad. It was almost like he became a different person when they were on a trip together. He went on rides, bought them treats and gifts, and made sure they had all the fun that they wanted. Tears fell down her cheeks as she remembered a beautiful Teddy Bear that Ross bought her one time. He got it because she had just tried to win the same bear in a Carnival game, but lost. When she started crying because she wanted the bear, he presented it to her with a big smile on his face. *A real Hallmark moment*, she thought.

As the needed tears of mourning fell freely, she looked over at little Sadie, who was sitting beside her, and smiled fondly. Luwanda wasn't happy about the fact that it would be so long she'd have to wait to see her little girl again, but she was delighted to let Sadie have such a great opportunity, to see another country, all expenses paid. Sadie was beaming with excitement when she found out she'd get to go. Lizzie was very jealous, but happy for her sister. Daniella cushioned the blow by assuring her that her turn would come immediately after she'd finished her probation.

After the plane landed, Daniella and Sadie excitedly walked through the gate and went through the immigration line straight to their luggage. They were flying through these procedures because they couldn't wait to see Faisal and the boys. Daniella's heart was beating as she saw the automatic doors swing open.

There he was, the love of her life, and her beautiful sons, Ahmed, and Abdullah. Ahmed was 16, Leila was 13, and Abdullah was only 12, just on the cusp of his teen years, so he was probably more in a position to understand Sadie. They were all beaming to welcome "Mom" back home, all except Leila. Even Nay came to greet her, and she was gleaming when Daniella walked up to them. She squealed with delight. Faisal stretched out his arms and hugged her tight.

"Welcome, home Baby. We missed you so much."

He turned to Sadie and flashed a warm, welcoming smile, then said, "Well, you must be Sadie. Welcome to UAE Habibti. I hope you'll enjoy your time with us."

Shyly, she replied, "Thank you, Uncle Faisal. It's my first time to visit a foreign country."

Ahmed chimed in, "Oh you'll love it here. Just wait till we get home. Hey, do you like any video games? Abdullah and I have all the good ones."

"I like games," Sadie said. "Do you have Super Mario Kart? That's what Lizzie and I play a lot."

Abdullah replied, "Oh yeah! I like her. That's a good one."

After a huge hug from Nay, Daniella was pleased to see the kids getting along already, and said, "Let's get home guys. I'm so tired I could just pass out." She turned to Nay, blew her a kiss, and said, "I'll call you in a couple days girl! Love you!"

"Back at ya Babe!" Nay called as she was turning to go, leaving Daniella to spend time with her family.

They all piled into Faisal's Land Cruiser and headed for home. When Sadie got her first look at Daniella's house, her jaw dropped open. "Aunt Danny, is this your house?"

Daniella replied, "Yes Sweetie. Do you like it?"

Sadie said, "Oh my God! It's so big! I love it."

She paused a moment to stare longer as they drove into the driveway and muttered, "Aunt Danny, are you rich?"

Faisal chuckled a bit at this and Daniella smiled at her warmly, then replied, "Not really Baby. We're comfortable, but not rich. We didn't always feel comfort, though. There was a time when I first moved here that we lived in a dump. We even had rats running around outside."

"Rats!? Ewww!!" Sadie blurted.

Everyone got a little chuckle when she got grossed out hearing about the rats. Faisal replied, "You're never gonna let me forget that, are you?"

Daniella grinned, "Nope. I put up with a lot, and you know it. I wasn't gonna put up with disgusting rats."

Faisal nodded mockingly, and said, "Yeah Yeah, we know, we know. You were the princess and I was the street rat."

She leaned in for a little kiss, just a peck on the lips, and said, "Well not anymore."

"Damn right." He agreed as he gave her a little wink.

They went to the door and Fahani, their housemaid, was there to greet them. She hugged Daniella tight and exclaimed, "Mama! I'm so glad you're home! The house is not nice when you're not here. Mama Sophia came over every day and told me I wasn't cleaning right."

Daniella smiled, but Faisal gave her a glaring look. Fahani recoiled and knew that she mustn't speak badly about Baba Faisal's mother. She grabbed one of the suitcases, and was gleaming when Daniella excitedly said, "Hey Fahani, I got you some lovely things from America! I just know you're gonna love 'em!"

After settling in, the kids began to get along beautifully. They were playing their favorite video games in no time, and Daniella was handing out all the gifts. For Faisal, she got a new phone, as phones were considerably cheaper in the USA, and Faisal loved getting the newest gadgets out there. She also got him a metal detector, just like he'd always wanted. She had looked high and low for one in the UAE but had no luck at all.

He was beaming, and said, "You got it! Hey, look at that! You know I've always wanted to go to the beach and see if I can find anything cool."

"I know Sweetheart. That's why I got it for you. Well, that and the fact that I'd pay good money to see you get to the beach with us." She murmured.

"Ha-ha, Smartass, very funny." He blurted.

For Ahmed, she brought a number of new books on the paranormal and an EVP recorder, as he had just joined an online group called the Society of Paranormal Organization and Observation of Kindred Spirits, or SPOOKS, for short. He had become a member of an online society of teens who believe they have a unique connection with the supernatural.

"Thanks, Mama! These are great! Once I get a break in my study time, I'll start reading these right away."

Abdullah didn't seem happy with his clothes, even though they were very stylish ones. He wanted a cool gift like his father and his brother. Daniella brought clothes for everyone, including Fahani, and they were all happy with their gifts, but Abdullah always felt a bit swept by the wayside by Ahmed, as he was always the one in the spotlight, thanks to his self-proclaimed gift to communicate with the world of the unseen. Daniella said,

"Sweetie, you don't seem happy. Are you ok?"

"No Mama, I'm OK. I just thought...nothing...I like my clothes. Thanks, Mama." He sulked.

Daniella smiled at him knowingly and said, "You didn't think that was *all* did you?"

His head bounced up and he gleamed with excitement. She reached in her carry on bag to reveal a robotic toy that could be used with his IPhone. This little gadget was a hovering camera, and could fly above anything or anyone and take pictures for Abdullah. He loved his IPhone and thought a robotic hover camera was just the thing. Daniella was relieved to see the look of contentment on his face.

"Wow! Thanks, Mama! This is great! Can I go to my room and try it?"

"Sure Baby, go right ahead. Have fun." She said.

As for Leila, Daniella's 13-year-old teenage daughter, Daniella knew she could expect maximum drama, as this is what she'd learned to be good at lately. First of all, it was obvious that she blamed her mother for spending so much time away from home. The all too familiar look of resentment showed on her face. It was the same look of complete bitterness that made Daniella long for the days when she was a cute and sweet little girl.

In an effort to make things go smoothly between them, Daniella offered Leila her present. Leila reluctantly came forward to accept it. The gift was wrapped in bright red wrapping paper with a big cream-colored bow on it. It was ostentatious, just what Leila liked, and Daniella was pleased to see that the extravagant wrapping was doing the trick. Leila tore into the gift and was pleasantly surprised to see the Apple MacBook Pro she had always wanted. All her friends had one, and now so did she. Leila looked surprised and very happy, and then, in a rare show of affection, Leila came to hug her mother sweetly. *Thank God for the power of the bribe*. Daniella thought.

"Thank you." Leila said quietly, then she went upstairs to her room without another word.

"Your welcome Honey. I love you." Daniella said softly.

Daniella saw Sadie sitting by Faisal and was amused to see him trying to explain to her how his metal detector worked. *What a charming sight they are*, she thought. Sadie had never seen anything beyond the continental US, so now

Daniella felt it was her mission to show this young lady a really good time, as she promised her mother she would. She made a mental note to take all the kids to the Dubai Mall Ice Skating rink this week, as well as the Aquarium. Sadie would be sure to love that. Sadie had grown up in a very underprivileged environment, and was sure to be very appreciative, she thought, unlike her children, who've grown up with a silver spoon in their mouths.

However, before she could let Sadie enjoy any of the fun UAE had to offer, she'd need to perform the obligatory visit to Faisal's family tomorrow, as it was Friday. They didn't go there for lunch every Friday, but tomorrow they were expected, especially since Daniella had just come back. She wasn't very fond of the idea, in spite of the fact she had learned how to handle his family at last.

In the beginning, when she first came there, she bent over backward to please them, to be the perfect wife, to the point that she almost disappeared altogether. She remembered thinking that if she could be like one of them, maybe they wouldn't pick on Faisal for marrying an American, but much to her dismay, she found that the more she changed, the more they wanted her to change, and the more they voiced their disapproval of her. She was made to feel very insecure because she wasn't an "Emirati", and those feelings of insecurity and the lack of belonging used to keep her up at night, but not anymore.

Now, she had learned that she may never be able to win their approval, but she could win their respect, simply by being herself. Step by step, she started to assert her own personality by going out with her friends more, by working, and by making a name for herself in the country as a publisher. She found that the more she expressed herself, the happier she was. She wasn't mean to Faisal's family, or disrespectful, she simply put herself as a priority as well.

In fact, this was another similarity between Southern families and Arab families when she finally let herself think of it. As much as the men in her husband's culture spoke of demure women, it seemed that they actually valued the strong-willed woman far more.

20

A BIG FAT ARABIC FAMILY GATHERING

Sadie was dressed up beautifully for the family visit. She was feeling nervous about meeting a lot of Arabs for the first time, and it didn't help that when she walked in, everyone seemed to stop dead in their tracks to stare at this little girl. Daniella often felt irritated no one over there seemed to share the American belief that staring isn't polite. Over the years, she'd gotten used to it, but this was Sadie's first time.

In spite of the staring however, they all welcomed Sadie inside and bid her to have a seat. Immediately, Sophia had the maids start bringing in sliced fruit for everyone to snack on until lunch. Sophia was a domineering lady, and could barely keep a maid working for her, but once she actually found one, for reasons that were beyond anyone's understanding, they renewed one contract after another.

Faisal's brothers were there. Malak was the oldest, and everyone considered him to be the "boss" of Sophia's children. He was about 5ft. 10in. tall and 160 lbs—a proud and cocky man with a booming voice. His favorite thing to do was "pick" on other family members by quipping insulting things. For example, he often teased Daniella by saying she was *old* now and Faisal needed to start looking for his second wife. Unfortunately for him, Daniella had learned to deflect such quips by shooting them directly back at him. Once, following the comment that she was now "old," Daniella came back with "Ok Grandpa, whatever you say." Malak was, in fact, a grandfather several times over, so it was a perfect reply. The trick to dealing with Malak was to never let him see he had caused a reaction.

Faisal's other brother Abdullah, the middle brother, was the proud father of 6 children, and was far easier to get along with. He was about 5ft. 5in. tall and weighed about 170lbs. Even though he was a bit of a *chubster*, he was polite and courteous, and by far the most religious of the brothers. He made everyone feel a little bad about themselves like they weren't trying harder to be a good Muslim and was the one who took the best care of his parents. Daniella often wondered how three brothers could be so different. Faisal was the happy medium between the two, modest and mild-mannered, but not completely straight-laced. He always seemed more "real", which is one of the things she found so appealing about him in the first place.

Saleema, Faisal's sister, weighed about 200 lbs, and was only 5 foot. tall. As the proud mother of 5 children, she was the eldest of the group and was a very domineering woman, just like her mother, although she'd never admit that, not in a million years. She was actually the eldest child of the family, and because of that, she often clashed with Malak over the role of the "boss", not overtly of course, but in each and every family discussion, Saleema and Malak would inevitably take opposing sides to every argument and argue it out until they were both blue in the face. Faisal and

Abdullah would usually stay out of it and drift on to other subjects.

Finally, there was the proud patriarch of the family, Faisal's father. Hameed was a tiny man, one of the tiniest men Daniella had ever seen, standing at only 4ft 11in. tall, and weighing in at only 120 lbs. He wore a thick white mustache and a thick beard. He and Sophia didn't speak a word of English and preferred it that way. They both thought Daniella should always make the effort to only speak to them in Arabic. In the beginning, that was hard, but in time she didn't really mind, as it was a great way to learn Arabic in a hurry. She often thought Hameed was kind of picked on by Sophia, as it was clear she ran that house and made absolutely all the decisions, even though tradition demanded that she treat him as the head of the household.

Daniella often chuckled under her breath at how *little* he was, and wondered how a man that tiny could have ever been considered intimidating to the likes of Malak and his abrasive personality or Saleema and her domineering insistence that she was always right no matter what. Thinking of that now and then reminded her of her grandfather, Big Ross Sr. and what a gigantic man he was. Of course, that would also lead to the ironic realization that Big Ross was also dominated by Katie, and everyone knew Katie was the real power in the house, as she had Big Ross wrapped around her finger. *Did those women know something I don't? Maybe it's because they always let the men "think" they were in charge?* Thinking about this gave her a deep feeling of respect for both of these women, Sophia, and Katie. *What a shame that they never had a chance to meet*, she thought.

After all the introductions were made, Sadie politely sat down on the floor with the whole family as they sat around a giant Arabic feast. Her eyes popped open at the sheer amount of food available. Daniella helped her take a reasonable portion of Biryani, an Arabic meat and rice dish, and some Tabouli, a Middle Eastern salad. Sadie looked at it cautiously and took a tiny bite. The little smile that followed let Daniella know she actually liked the dish and would be just fine.

The afternoon seemed to be going great, and even though it was tough, little Sadie endured all the probing questions from the kids about her parents and how she was related to Daniella. Daniella often answered for her, rescuing her from their investigation at every opportunity. After lunch, everyone settled into their cup of Chai, or Arabic tea served in a tiny glass with a tiny saucer. Sadie took a picture of it with her phone to post to Instagram. Even though she was pretty young, she had a very active Instagram account and didn't let her followers wonder where she was for long. When she snapped the picture of something as mundane to them as a tea glass, some of the children snickered. Daniella flashed them a "No No" glance, but it didn't seem to help. Thankfully, Sadie was so wrapped up in her own little world she didn't notice they were poking fun.

Finally, it was time to go and Sadie dutifully bid them all goodbye, one by one. Daniella had given her a crash course on Arabic manners, and she was glad she did. Even Sophia looked impressed and they managed to leave with no dramatic outbursts, so that was a great accomplishment. When it came to drama, Arabic families were only rivaled by Southern families. This being another ironic point Daniella often thought of since she was in a unique position to see both sides for the way they actually were. In fact, she often thought about how wild the similarities are. Arab families sit around sipping their Chai, and Southern families sit around sipping on their iced tea. Arabic families almost always have a strong Matriarch and so do Southern families, one strong woman that the family would fall apart without. They also both share that one old crazy, batty woman everyone just agrees with out of courtesy. Arabic men are proud and strong-willed; fiercely protective of their country and their mothers, wives, and sisters, and exactly the same can be said of Southerners. They both like big food, big cars, and big homes with big gardens and luxury surroundings with lots of hired help to prevent overexertion from any dreaded manual labor. Well, of course, cooking was the sole exception to this rule, as both Southern women and Arabic women took enormous pride in their dishes and would never trust the outcome to a maid.

There was one more similarity—hospitality. Both Arab families and Southern families are the best hosts and hostesses one could ever want.

Faisal knew this ball was in his court now, so while the afternoon was still young, once they were all inside the car, Faisal proposed that the family go out for a trip to one of UAE's most amazing attractions, Dubai Mall, the biggest mall in the world.

"What a coincidence!" Daniella said. "I was thinking the same thing. Sadie will be blown away by how big it is."

She turned to Sadie in the back seat and asked, "Honey have you ever been ice skating before?"

"Um No, not ice skating, but I've been roller skating." Answered Sadie.

"Are you good at roller skating?" Asked Daniella.

Sadie reluctantly answered, "Well, kind of. I fell on my butt a few times the last time we went with our church group."

Abdulla was great at Ice Skating, better than Ahmed, so he felt like he should rescue the poor girl. So, being the Hero, he confirmed, "Don't worry Mama. I'll take care of her. I won't let her fall."

Daniella was proud of her little man. He was stepping up to take care of a damsel in distress, another fine Southern quality.

"My little knight. Of course, you won't. That settles it. Sadie, you just follow what Abdulla does. He's really good at Ice Skating. I'm sure you'll get the hang of it in no time. After Ice Skating, we may take you guys to the Aquarium."

The day was going well until Daniella spotted one of the journalists that had initially printed a story about her and her family. She had printed some pretty unflattering things about Ross so this would be a chance for Daniella to redeem her father's image, especially since he had redeemed himself shortly before his death. The reporter's name was Shaneen, and she worked for an international online news syndicate.

"Hey! Shaneen right?" Daniella blurted.

Shaneen looked very surprised and curiously relieved to see Daniella. She murmured, "Oh Ms. Sulieman, I'm glad to see you today. I've been trying to call you, but your answering service wouldn't let me through."

Intrigued and surprised, Daniella replied, "Oh? I hope it wasn't to write another bad story!"

Shaneen shook her head, "No Ms. Sulieman. And, by the way, I'm really sorry for that article, especially since the details of the case have been revealed in the press. I'd like to write something about people reconnecting with their past, as a way of making it up to you if you'd let me."

Daniella was surprised and moved by this gesture. She was always one for giving people second chances, so she simply extended her personal business card with her private line, and said, "Give me a call in a couple days. I'm taking a little time off to show my niece around, so I'll need a little time with her."

Shaneen looked relieved, took the card, and said, "Oh thank you, Ma'am. Again, I'm really sorry."

Daniella gave her a courteous smile and said, "No worries. That's what it's all about. Making things right."

Daniella went back to her seat, and Faisal, who had observed the whole thing, said, "See? Most people are pretty good at the end of the day."

She smiled and nodded, and they both turned their attention to the kids, who were having a lovely time playing on the ice. Sadie had a lovely look of joy on her face, and this pleased Daniella a great deal. She found herself wishing her own daughter would be able to appreciate life as much as this sweet little girl. *Emirati children are very pampered. God, I love my kids, but they don't realize for a second how good they've had it compared to others.* She thought.

The day went well, and the Aquarium was a huge hit with the kids. Of course, Daniella's kids had been there before, but not with Sadie. Her enthusiasm was infectious. There were a few new exhibits to add to their already impressive collection of aquatic life. The idea of seeing such an impressive aquarium in a mall was unreal to Sadie. Dubai was an impressive place; there was no doubt about that.

On their way home, Daniella's phone rang. Enthusiastically, she answered, "Hello?"

But the enthusiasm quickly washed out of her face, and a pale, sick look replaced it. She listened to what the caller had to say, and with a quivering voice, said, "I can't believe it. I just got to know her again. She was so happy."

Faisal was worried, and the kids listened on, frozen with fear over what she might be discussing. Then, the real tears began, and they were all frantic with worry. Faisal was only waiting for her to finish her phone call.

"I understand. I'll book a flight for tomorrow if I can. I'll call you." Daniella said.

She hung up and started crying profusely. Everyone in the car was holding their breath and trying not to make a sound. Finally, Daniella mustered up enough courage to tell them.

"My grandmother just died," She said with a whimper.

Faisal's eyes filled with water, but he held strong. He asked, "Who was that on the phone? Who told you?"

Daniella weakly replied, "Brian."

Sadie started to cry. It was easy to understand, as she had just gotten to know her as well. Daniella looked back at her and said, "Don't worry Baby. We're going tomorrow if I can get the tickets."

Faisal said, "We're *all* going."

He looked back at the kids and found them nodding in agreement, then looked at Daniella and squeezed her hand reassuringly. "We're going. There's been a death in our family, so we're going to act like a family."

Daniella was deeply touched. It had been so long since they felt like a united family, but what a cost! Two lives were lost, and that's the price these two families seemed destined to pay to become one united force. Faisal made a quick call to his travel agent and was delighted to find that Emirates Airlines could accommodate them all the very next evening. Of course, this meant Faisal would need to work fast to get an emergency entrance Visa. He didn't seem overly worried, as his connections were quite good. Daniella certainly didn't plan to go back to the USA so soon, but these dire circumstances demanded it.

Within hours, they were on their way, in business class this time, since it was all booked at the last minute. No one seemed to mind, however. Daniella, Faisal, and their three kids were all going to pay respects to a great woman, and to unite the two families into one.

21

ENDINGS AND NEW BEGINNINGS

The Sulieman family arrived at the Atlanta International Airport, and Daniella immediately spotted Leo there waiting for her. She rushed up and jumped into his arms for a tight hug. They stood there embracing each other, providing the needed comfort for such a moment. Leo was fighting back the tears, trying to stay strong for Daniella, especially when he caught sight of her family with her, including little Sadie.

Sadie rushed up to her Dad, so he released Daniella to grab her up for a big hug. She started to cry, which upset Leo. He said, "No Baby, don't cry as soon as you see Daddy. Everything's gonna be alright."

"Grandma Katie...Is it true Daddy?" She had such pain in her voice.

Leo hugged her gently and reassured her, "She went to Heaven, Baby. One of the last things she said was how much she enjoyed meeting you and your sister, so don't cry Darlin'. You made one of her dreams come true."

With Sadie calmed, Leo moved on to greet Faisal. They shook hands as men do, firm and confident. Another thing

Arabs and Southern gentlemen shared was the belief that a man's handshake can speak volumes about his character.

"It's great to meet you Brother, but I'm very sorry it's under these circumstances."

Leo appreciated Faisal's words and replied, "I'm really happy to meet you too Bro. I'm so sorry that I've been such a jackass all these years. Danny's a happy woman, and I should have known better. I wasted a lot of time."

Faisal put his hand on his shoulder in a reassuring way and said, "To borrow an expression from my beautiful wife, 'It's all water under the bridge now.' We're family, and it's never too late for a family to come together."

Brian listened to this, and chimed in with his response, "Well said Faisal."

He grabbed Faisal's hand with another strong Southern handshake, and confirmed, "We're all brothers now. I know you've got brothers in the UAE, but I do want you to know you can add two more to that roster."

Faisal leaned in to hug both of them, and they were huddled together like a three-man football team, and then, as the brawny men they were, they broke formation and shared a couple of small nods of approval. Daniella's heart soared to see them getting along so well. All the years of fitting into his family were not in vain as now she was witnessing Faisal's attempt to fit into hers.

Once they were all back at the family home, the group all took seats around the same dining room table where they'd shared many meals together, but this time it was without Katie's bouncy personality lighting up the room. She had been a wonderful grandmother, but she had also acted as their mother, taking care of all three of these siblings for many years. The house seemed empty and cold without her, even as residents of the newly formed Bed and

Breakfast bustled about. The place was missing its key ingredient, the sweet Southern grandma that was at the very heart of it.

"How did she go?" Daniella said quietly.

Brian said, "She died in her sleep, Honey. The doctor said it was probably an aneurysm, and she probably passed on quickly, and relatively painlessly."

Leo's eyes formed a few tears, and one by one they trickled down his cheeks. Faisal was also getting misty hearing about this. He said, "God, how I wish I could have met this amazing woman. She was the glue that held this family together. Danny has said the most wonderful things about her."

Daniella sighed and asked the question that had been haunting her, "Did this have anything to do with the hotel? Did she work too hard? I swear I set up a top notch staff here, folks she could really count on."

Leo grabbed her hand and blurted, "No Danny, don't do that to yourself. Your hotel idea is what made her die a happy woman. She was bouncing off the walls, excited about how well things were going every time I saw her over the last few days. I swear she was a new woman! She couldn't stop talking about it, and the customers just loved her! They chatted on and on about how they wished for a mom like her."

Daniella couldn't help but smile at the thought. Images of her sweet smiling face came to mind, and her bringing in a new dish she'd just cooked with pride. "They don't make 'em like her anymore." Danny murmured.

"Amen to that." Leo agreed.

"So what happens now, guys? What are we gonna do?" Daniella asked.

Leo thought a moment and said, "Well, I think we gotta

take care of funeral arrangements, and we need to make this special. She was a great mom to us, and her funeral needs to be a hero's funeral. After all, that's what she was. I think there's not one of us that would've turned out halfway decent without her. Hell, she was the reason you came back to us, Danny! And God knows, I would have been dead without her, so I'm ready to make this a real way of honoring her and all she represented."

"Damn right Man," Brian said. "I'm in! Call the Brown Funeral Home. I've heard they're the best."

Leo got out of his seat and said, "I'm on it. Calling them right now."

Daniella asked, "I love the way you guys think. Ok, what should I do? How can I help?"

Brian looked at her knowingly and said, "I don't think anyone can write a better eulogy than you. You're an eloquent person Danny. I think you should speak for her and let everyone in attendance know what an extraordinary person she was."

Daniella smiled, pleased with such a wonderful compliment. "I'm honored by that, and I'm pleased to accept. I promise it'll be good. No, It'll be great!"

Faisal said, "Well if you guys don't mind, I'd like to chip in for the cost. I'll leave the beautiful words and arrangements to you three, and I'll pick up the cost."

Leo heard that and said, "You and me brother, WE will pick up the cost. I'm in as well."

Brian agreed, "Well I've got a third of that. We're brothers, so we'll share it."

Faisal felt warmly welcomed into this family and was touched by the gesture. The expression on his face couldn't hide how deeply affected he was. "I want to say something. I'm sorry we haven't come together before. I'm just so happy to be here and to have more family now. If I had only known, I would have come out here with Daniella long ago."

Brian and Leo came to Faisal and both of them grabbed him for a strong manly hug. Leo said, "Hell Boy! It was *our* fault. We missed out on you all this time. I want you to know I'm a changed man now."

Daniella blurted, "Hey guys! You're all killing me. I can't believe what I've seen today. God sure does work in mysterious ways. Let's all get to work now. I can't start my crying now when I know I've got a lot of tears to shed when I write this speech."

"Ok Honey, you get on to it then," Brian said, then tapped Faisal on the shoulder and said, "Come on man, let's go into town and visit the funeral home to see what we gotta do."

The three of them got into the car and took off into town as the children played in the yard, oblivious to all the plans. Children always seemed to have such a wonderful way of brushing off the gravity of a moment to make time and energy for play, and today was no exception, in spite of the dark circumstances. Even Leila seemed to be warming up to the situation, but she seemed bothered all the same. She had a strong urge to see her mom.

As she crept into the house, she looked around past the staff and the guests of the hotel to finally find her mom sitting at the dining room table staring blankly at a white piece of paper. She said, "Mama, are you OK?"

Daniella looked up at her daughter, and Leila was suddenly struck with the sight of her mother with tears in her eyes. Daniella said, "I'm fine Baby. I'm just trying to find the words to describe a great lady, the only real mother I've ever known. I hope I won't let her down."

Surprisingly, Leila had great insight on the subject. "You

won't Mama. She was your hero, like you're mine. You'll do her proud because everything that comes out of your heart is good. Just write from your heart and you can't go wrong."

Daniella's mouth fell open. She was in awe of how this little girl had delivered the words of wisdom she needed to hear. She said, "You're such a sweet girl. I love you, Baby." She gave her hand a little squeeze, and added, "Now go play. I'll come out there soon to get Y'all when we go out for Dinner."

When Leila went back out, she sat down and wrote the words of her life, from her heart, just as her daughter had encouraged her to do. When she finished the speech, she gleamed with pride and looked up at the sky. "I hope you like it, Grandma. I love you."

The men had, in only 24 hours, pulled off the funeral of the century in the small town of Hadleyville, Georgia. The church was decorated with the most beautiful flowers anyone there had ever seen. The coffin was the most expensive and comfortable looking anyone had ever been buried in, and Katie looked so beautiful that guests commented they couldn't tell she was dead when they passed by to pay their final respects. Daniella, Faisal, and her brothers were deeply honored to hear all the complimentary things people in town had to say about their beloved grandmother.

Everything proceeded well, and the Minister delivered a perfect funeral service. Then, the moment of truth finally came. It was time for Daniella's eulogy. She had delivered speeches to royalty and heads of industry in the UAE, and never felt the slightest bit nervous, but this made her shake with fear. She felt her throat tighten as she looked through the audience, finding every face she'd ever attended high school with, every bully that ever tortured her with the words "nigger lover," every popular kid that had ever ignored her, and she felt for a moment she couldn't breathe.

She looked to her family for support and found Faisal's face. He was sweet and very supportive, but she couldn't keep looking at him. As much as she loved this man, he wasn't the best at dealing with embarrassment. In fact, she became even more worried and frightened that she would embarrass him somehow and have to see his judgmental eyes after.

The one face that helped her snap out of her "deer in the headlights" moment was Uncle Sheldon. He was sitting there smiling so calmly, exuding the confidence Daniella needed at such a critical moment. His eyes were almost dancing, they were so full of joy and pride. Seeing him there made her smile back, and suddenly, she was just fine. She cleared her throat and began.

"I'm very sorry that I'm having a hard time. It's hard to begin a goodbye to someone as special as my grandmother... She wasn't my grandmother by blood. How many of your knew that? None of my family had any blood relationship to this grand woman we're laying to rest today. Biologically, she was a stranger to us."

She waited for a moment to listen to the uncomfortable shifts people were making in their chairs and the inevitable whispering. Their potential for gossip and rumor telling was astounding, and Daniella found their growing discomfort amusing. After another couple moments, she put them out of their misery by continuing.

"It just goes to show us that blood is not thicker than water, not necessarily. Although she didn't share any biological connection to me, I couldn't have asked for a more perfect grandmother."

The sighs of relief in the audience were more than audible.

"Even as I say 'grandmother,' it doesn't begin to cover all that Katie was to me. My brothers and I have come to agree that this woman was, in fact, a hero. Without her, our family would have surely broken apart, and my grandfather, Ross Pierce I (the first), wouldn't have been alive for at least the last 10 years of his life.

I remember the story of how they met. He was a lonely widower and she was a widow. They both went to the senior's dance club, The Good Ole Days, in her hometown. God knows I don't know what she saw in my grandfather since he was at least 400 pounds back then."

She paused for a moment as she let them have the notion that Katie was in it for the money. It didn't take long. She saw one of her former classmates rub their thumb and index fingers together as if they were counting money.

"I know some of you think the only thing she found attractive about my grandfather was his big bank account, because there's no way she could have loved his big overweight body, but I'm here to remind you that we are more than our bodies or our bank accounts. We are our souls and our deeds. Those of you who think they were together for convenience never really knew my grandparents. You never saw how kind and considerate they were to each other.

Katie could have asked for the Moon and Sun to be put into her hands, but she never asked for one single material thing from my grandfather. Everything he gave her, he gave to her with open hands, and every single time he gave her a gift, he saw her roll her eyes and remind him that she has never asked for such extravagance... I know a lot of you may have seen him buy her Lincoln Continentals and big diamond rings and think you were right all along, but what you didn't see was how lovingly she looked after his health and well-being, how she made him laugh and how she made sure every day of his life after that was never lonely; but full of life, family, good food, and good times.

I wish it had been me who gave the eulogy for my grandfather, because I would have had the opportunity to tell you about his generous heart. I bet none of Y'all knew about his housing projects he let families live in for twenty dollars a month, or loads of free peaches from his farms that he donated to charity, or his generous donations to Goodwill Industries. Ross Sr. was a big man, but his heart was bigger, and none of Y'all saw how he almost ate himself to death after my blood born grandmother died. And you certainly didn't see my darling Katie come along to save his life.

You saw a gold digger accepting lavish gifts. We saw a kind-hearted angel who loved our grandfather and saved his life many times over. Big Ross showed his love and care by buying things for people, and that shows just how big his love for Katie was because her gifts were the biggest he had ever given, bigger than him.

Her care for Big Ross wasn't all she did. My brothers and I can attest to that. When she came to live with our family in the beginning, that poor lady couldn't have ever known what she was getting into. She came to us at a volatile time. My father got shot by my late mother, which landed her in an insane asylum. If it weren't for the generosity of Big Ross and Katie, my mother would have surely died in prison. Instead, she died knowing her children still loved her, and with a man that truly loved her.

Katie took care of my father for 70 days in the hospital, as his intestines had to be completely reconstructed, and to boot, she got to accept responsibility for three scared and psychologically damaged children that she cared for like a mother. She cooked for us, cleaned up after us, nursed us when we were sick, and made sure we all did our homework every night. For me, being the only girl, she became my female role model and taught me how to hold my own family together and care for my own children. For that, I'm eternally grateful, and would never be able to pay her back for all she did for me.

My brother Brian learned how to be a great businessman and entrepreneur from Big Ross, and married a lovely woman from a close family, possibly because he wanted to have the kind of family Katie would have been proud of. She was always proud of him, and I'm proud of him, proud he accomplished that.

My brother Leo knows well what he owes Katie, as many of you do. He wouldn't be sitting here today without her intervention, as I wouldn't be standing here, delivering a hero's eulogy for her. She called me back, and by doing so, she healed me and helped me far more than I helped her or Leo.

Quite simply, our grandmother was a living angel, the very glue that held us together, and now that she's gone, the world will be a little darker, as a light has burned out. But she wouldn't want any of us to get mired up in our feelings like this, and I can just hear her now telling me 'Oh Honey, that's all just water under the bridge now! You all have to pick yourselves up and move on. Y'all need to be sweet to each other because you're family, whether you like it or not.'

Ironic isn't it? Is blood thicker than water? Or do we make our family, no matter where we are? I think Katie would have agreed that God deals us all a hand of cards and we just gotta do the best with it that we can. So that's what

I'm gonna do now. I'm gonna keep on playing my hand, the best way I know how...And to my darling Katie, I love you, and I'll see you again, so this is not Goodbye. This is Thank you; Keep watching over me, and I'll see you soon. The old South will try to keep your memory alive, the best we know how, because to us, you are the South, and everything beautiful about it."

She finished by blowing a kiss upward to Heaven, and there wasn't a dry eye in the house. Even the harshest, most rugged guys in the room were emotionally touched by her tender description of Katie and Big Ross. Daniella felt like she'd done her grandma proud, and turned to sit back down with her family. Just then, there was a creaking sound as the big church doors opened. To everyone's surprise, Brian's wife Kelly and their daughters Betty Kay and Betsy walked through the door. They looked charming, dressed in their matching black dresses and hats. Kelly was English, and unbelievably, this was her first trip to the USA. She had been scheduled to come in much earlier. Brian had a chauffeured limousine waiting for her at the airport so he would be at the funeral on time, and now that they had finally arrived, he could stop looking at his watch.

Kelly and the girls came to sit with the family, and Brian embraced them warmly. Kelly whispered, "I'm so sorry Darling. The flight was delayed due to bad weather outside of London." She stroked his face with the back of her hand, and her blue eyes looked misty, emotional and sympathetic for her husband, now that she was next to him again.

"I've missed you and my girls, but let's get through this first." Brian looked at her longingly, and the emotional ride he'd been through lately seemed to bubble to the surface, now that he'd seen her lovely face. He fought back his emotions, telling himself there would be plenty of time for all that later.

Reverend Bobby wrapped up the ceremony with a prayer, and then it was time to lay Katie to rest. Leo, Brian, and Daniella arrived at the graveyard, each holding a sunflower, Katie's favorite flower, in their hands. They walked up to the open grave and watched as Katie's coffin was lowered into it. Daniella's tears couldn't be restrained any longer, and it was as if the floodgates opened. Her children stood next to her, stroking her back as she started to wail.

"Grandma," She said, sobbing.

Ahmed kept staring at a nearby gravestone. Betty Kay noticed him and thought it odd the way he kept on staring, and finally said, "What are you looking at?"

Ahmed looked beside him for a moment to be sure the grownups wouldn't pay any attention to what he was saying, then commented, "Grandma Katie is standing over there. Of course it's not her, not really; it's her companion. She's looking at me and waving."

Betty Kay became scared and turned white. She hugged her father's waist and seemed to want to get away from Ahmed, now that she thought him to be a very weird little boy.

Daniella gently tossed the sunflower onto the coffin, as did her brothers, and then they watched as the dirt was shoveled onto her, bit by bit. The reality of her passing truly hit the three of them, and before it was over, they were all weeping for their loss.

When all was said and done, the three made their way to Katie's Bed and Breakfast for an after-funeral gathering. The staff had made finger foods and prepared a few flavors of iced tea for all the guests. People from all over town came to pay their respects. Faisal stood next to Daniella, her brothers, and their wives, hearing everyone rave about the funeral and how perfect it was and how Katie truly was a good woman who left the world far too early.

Security had been posted outside of the church to keep reporters out, and the hotel security had been instructed to do the same at the gathering, but one managed to get through anyway.

The tiny man with the mustache that had asked Daniella all the terrible questions about Leo when she first arrived was there. Since he was an acquaintance of the family, he managed to get in without any questioning, especially since he didn't have a press badge on or any visual recording equipment. Daniella spotted him, and he spotted her. It was hard to tell if he was grinning, as the mustache on his face was rather big, and effectively covered up his facial expressions, but she could have sworn she saw a slight grin underneath that thick hair.

She approached the little reporter and said, "Look, I hope you're here only as a guest paying their respects. None of us are in the mood for an interview."

The little reporter, whose name was Earl, said, "No Ma'am. Don't you worry your pretty little head Darlin'? I'm only here cuz I wanna honor a wonderful woman. You're Grandma was as sweet as she could be, and I just thought the world of her."

Daniella's fears were quelled for the moment. She nodded an acknowledgment of his respectful words and proceeded to sit down. It had been a really long day, and she was curious as to what her kids were up to. She saw Abdullah and Leila helping to greet people, but couldn't find Ahmed. She looked around a bit, then decided to look upstairs, but the tenant's quarters produced no results.

Finally, she decided to look in the basement. Going down there immediately struck fear into her heart, considering the fact that some strange activity had been witnessed down there. Her face went completely white when she descended far enough down the stairs to see that the light had blown out again. She walked past the broken glass, all the way down to the basement.

The basement was ominous, or at least that's what she had always thought as a child growing up there. There was something that always made the tiny hairs on the back of her neck stand up when she went down those backstairs, the only way to reach the basement. In the old pre-Civil War South, this area of the house was the servant's quarters, and those stairs were how the servants were allowed to go up and down floors, as they were not allowed to use the main staircase. At the bottom of the stairs were a few tiny rooms, where the maids used to sleep, and to her surprise, that's where she found Ahmed with Sadie and Lizzie. Ahmed stared at the air, between Lizzie and Sadie. She called out, "Honey what are you doing?"

He remained frozen, and so did the girls. Daniella felt the fear creep up into her heart and it felt for a few moments that she couldn't breathe. The air felt heavy, and she started to feel her energy draining. She tapped Ahmed on the shoulder, and he turned around to face her, but for a split second, she felt it wasn't Ahmed. His eyes opened big and a strange smile crept across his face as he said in a deep Southern accent, "Who are you? How did you find me?"

Daniella said, "Bismellah Araman Arahiem! Stop this now! Ahmed! Ahmed!"

She shook him and he fell down. Terrified, she grabbed him by the shoulders and said, "Oh my Baby, are you ok?"

She felt the hairs on her neck stand up again, then

turned around to see Lizzy and Sadie staring blankly at the two of them, with white eyes, frozen in the same spot they were before, seemingly unaffected by the fact that Ahmed just fell. Then the same creepy smile started to wash over their faces at once. Daniella felt her heart pounding, and again cried out, "Bismellah Araman Arahiem! Get out of these girls! Leave them! In the name of Allah, leave them!!"

Lizzie, or rather the spirit occupying Lizzie said, with someone else's voice, "We will always be here Madame. This is our house. YOU get out."

Then, the two of them fell, just like Ahmed, their energy drained. They all felt weak, but thankfully, they were all Ok. Daniella kept nudging Ahmed and the girls to wake them back into full consciousness, and finally Ahmed started to come around. Wearily he said, "Mama, where are we? What happened?"

Daniella's heart dropped into her chest at the realization that her son had just had a supernatural encounter. She'd indulged all his adolescent fantasies about being a ghost hunter for a while now, and supposedly; he had recently joined an online group called "SPOOKS." Supposedly, they were all teenage kids like him who had all encountered supernatural experiences. As far as she knew, Ahmed had never encountered a real being of any kind. How could she even talk to anyone here about it? No one in the South had ever heard of "Jinn." They believed they were experiencing ghosts.

She cradled Ahmed's head in her hands and tried to comfort him.

"What happened down here Sweetheart? Was someone here with you and the girls?"

Ahmed came to full alertness and looked thoughtfully into her eyes and said, "Yes, there was someone. At first they only spoke to us. Here, listen to my EVP recorder. I got some voices."

Daniella grabbed the recorder rather forcefully, more forcefully than she had intended. Ahmed didn't seem alarmed by it, as he was just recovering from his attack. Daniella played the recording, and at first it seemed like white noise. After a few moments, she heard, "Get out."

The voice was a male voice, and she struggled with whether or not she'd heard a Southern twang in his voice. As she listened further, she got her answer. She heard Ahmed ask, "Who are you?"

The voice said, "The Captain."

There was something "old" South about the way he said "Captain."

Ahmed went on to ask, "Captain? What do you want? Do you need help?"

"I need you to leave. They are mine. You won't take them from me." He responded.

Ahmed's voice asked, "Who is yours?"

Then, there was the recording of Lizzie's voice as she said, "Oh my God! What the Fuck is that?!"

Followed by the sound of a thud, the recording became silent, and even the white noise sounded quieter. Daniella was as white as a sheet after hearing this, but she held it together as the two girls were picking themselves off the floor. Sadie rubbed her eyes sleepily and looked around, unable to focus, but Lizzie got up with a start and said, "What the Hell? Ahmed, what did you do?"

It was obvious none of the kids remembered fully what had happened, so Daniella thought that in the interest of keeping any peace of mind, she'd better get them focused on something else. She said, "Ok guys, let's get up. There's no one here. See? Just look around...no one. You kids let your imaginations run away with you. I knew I shouldn't have gotten you that stuff. Let's get upstairs. We've got a lot to do today."

The kids listened and went upstairs. They all seemed ok, but quiet. Daniella was very thankful none of them witnessed her brow furrowing. After all, she had only set up the hotel a short time ago. *I wonder if anyone's had encounters.* She thought.

When she told Leo about it, she was surprised to hear his reaction. "Hell girl! That's good news! You haven't been out of the South so long you forgot how valuable a haunted hotel can be, did you?" Her lips formed a hard line, as she replied, "Um, Oh my. I guess I forgot about how many ghost stories there are here."

She thought for a moment and asked, "Well, don't you think we should do a little research to find out who this 'Captain' was? And what about the two women? Sadie told me she felt like an old black woman. I think if we find the story on them, we can get some help with this. I mean, Yeah, it's good for the hotel and all, the publicity, but I don't want anyone to get hurt."

Leo wondered, "Hey, I wonder if this is somehow connected to the bullet hole that Big Ross always kept in the front window! Remember how he said it was good to keep a bullet hole that was left by Yankees, to remind us of how close we all came to disaster?"

Daniella hissed as she exhaled remembering the bullet hole. "Oh my God! You might be right! I'd forgotten all about that bullet hole! Ok, can you do a little digging for information when you get to work tomorrow?"

"Yep, I sure can." Leo agreed.

He was away for a while, because the next day, as the family sat down to lunch in the hotel, they were complaining of Leo being late. Daniella hoped he was late because he was wrapped up in the research he needed to do. She made photocopies of a protective verse of the scriptures and laminated them so all the kids were able to keep a copy on them at all times. Reluctantly, they agreed, even if they did think Daniella was just being an old fuddy-duddy. She didn't mind that they thought this and felt really good that none of them remembered the "encounter."

Leo finally came through the doors, and walked straight past the enquiring faces of Luwanda and the kids to ask Daniella if they may speak privately for a moment. Daniella said, "Y'all excuse us, please. We need a few private words, but you all go ahead and eat. We'll be along directly."

Leo led her to the front Hall where the bullet hole was, as he really thought that would be the perfect place to tell her. Unable to contain himself any longer, he said, "This place is definitely haunted. I'm really surprised we never felt anything when we were kids, or maybe they weren't here then? I dunno, but they're here now."

"Who? Who's here now?" Daniella asked, feeling exasperated.

"Captain Rowan Adams! He was a slave ship captain or more like a pirate, and his main goal was to catch runaway slaves, mostly women, but rumor has it that he had a soft spot for one, in particular, a lovely young lady he had a child with. I think the two females that y'all experienced were his lady friend and his illegitimate daughter. He tried to pass them off as house slaves, but his shipmates knew the truth."

He pulled out a copy of an old picture of the Captain that Leo had printed from the Internet.

"There he is! Our Captain."

Daniella was floored. It was easy now to see why this

entity felt kindred spirits here. Shaking her head in disbelief, she said, "Should we tell everyone?"

"No!" Leo snapped. "The paranormal group I talked to said that for now, we need to do a proper investigation to see if he's friendly, someone we can negotiate peace with."

"Did you find out if this bullet hole has anything to do with him?" Daniella asked.

Leo said, "Oh yeah, that's the other part of the story! Evidently, some of his shipmates tracked him down here, and they were really pissed because he'd just left them there and abandoned the boat and all the crew. Some were Hell bent on killing him because they saw it as Mutiny, and it took them a really long time to find this house because he kept it a secret from everyone he knew and it was far from the shore. They eventually tracked him down and shot him through this very window."

Daniella's fingers outlined the bullet hole, almost hoping she'd be able to feel some of the story there. "I wish I was Psychic. I envy those who can sense the story when they touch something, don't you?"

"I never really thought about it," Leo replied.

Daniella thought about the Captain and what he'd been through. *No wonder he's so angry.*

"That's a really sad story in a way, don't you think? The guy realized the error of his ways, and he got killed. I guess they killed the ladies too?"

Leo confirmed, "Yeah, they did. It seems like this house attracts people who've come around about the whole black and white thing. I'll get some teams over here tonight to investigate and try to make contact again. We may have a harmless entity with us. If he's not, we'll find a way to put him and his women to rest so we can run our hotel in peace."

Daniella nodded in agreement. "Ok, maybe it's best to keep it to ourselves for now then until you've done everything. God knows Ahmed is far too into all this stuff. I don't wanna draw his attention to more or encourage him again."

She snapped her fingers in alarm, as though she had just remembered something vital.

"By the way, how did you find out about all this?"

Leo said, "I asked around at the Public Library, and as it turns out, one of our ancestors wrote a book of memoirs."

"No way! Who?" Daniella blurted as she cocked her head to one side.

"William Pierce, our great-great-grandfather. Yep, it seems he was quite a writer! Maybe you'd like to take a look?"

Leo handed her the book. She looked at it with wonder. All this time that she'd been a publisher, she never imagined there had been an author in the family. She glanced over a few pages, amazed at how eloquent the writing was. He described the history of the Pierce family and the adventures they had been on since their immigration from Greece, centuries ago.

"We were Greek? All this time I thought our origins were Irish! It says here that the original family name was 'Persis.' The name means, 'from Persia.' Wow, that's amazing! Don't you think?"

She read on to find out their ancestors were originally Greeks who immigrated to Scotland. Later, they moved on to Ireland, and that's where they became known as the Pierce family. Then, due to lack of work and poor conditions, they moved on to America. They bought this house at an auction after the Captain was shot. That's why the bullet hole was never repaired.

"Kinda adds even more charm to the place. Wouldn't you agree?" Leo beamed.

Daniella really couldn't argue, but she couldn't have Captain Adams trying to possess anyone, so she decided she'd hang pictures of the Ayat Al Kursi, a powerful protective verse, in every room, and ask the staff to burn Frankincense and Sage throughout once in the morning and once at night. She knew this would have to be kept secret, just between her and the staff, as the family would not likely understand.

For now, Daniella and Leo agreed to keep the haunting quiet but thought later on about adding this information to a special tour the guests could take throughout the house. *That actually may be helpful in attracting a bigger crowd to the hotel.* She thought. After all, everyone loves a good ghost story, she figured.

The two of them joined the rest of the family, and dismissed what they'd been doing as just "business". Brain didn't buy it, but they all let it go because everyone was hungry. The staff had prepared a big Southern meal, at Daniella's request. The table was set and their eyes feasted on many Southern delights. Katie would have been proud of the crispy fried chicken on the table, with buttermilk biscuits, corn on the cob, mashed potatoes, apple pie, and plenty of sweet tea. Ahmed unknowingly said, "Wow! It looks like a KFC exploded in here."

Every head whipped around to glare at him, and suddenly, he felt very embarrassed and nervous. He said, "I'm sorry?"

Leo blurted, "It's ok son. You didn't know. You see, here in the South, we wouldn't be caught dead eating a bucket of store bought chicken at the table with the family--at a football game maybe, but not at the table, during a family meal. That's always gotta be homemade."

"Son?" Ahmed said.

Still chewing, Faisal interrupted, before Daniella had a chance to reply. "I'm sure he means it as we say it back home. When my brother calls you 'Walidee.' That means 'my boy.'"

Daniella nodded in agreement as she took another spoonful of mashed potatoes, adding, "Absolutely...Funny you bring that up. I was thinking about when I first got to the Middle East and how hard it was for me to adjust. It was then I realized the secret of adaptation, and I began to feel better."

Leila murmured, "And what's that Mom?"

Looking at Ahmed, Daniella replied, "The secret of adaptation is to see all the ways you're alike more than you see the ways in which you are different. It's only when we realize we're all human at the end of the day that we begin to feel like one big human family. There's no 'Us' and 'Them' if you look at it like that. There's only 'We'".

Faisal smiled approvingly. As everyone was munching, he felt great pride in hearing his wife speak like this to their children. He addressed her brothers and added, "Did you all know that she never taught our kids about color and races at all? I remember once when Ahmed was very small...he asked if he could go and see the brown baby. I asked him what brown baby, and he pointed out a black woman with her baby girl. It just amazed me he didn't even know to call them Black, and then I realized it's because we never taught him that people were different races."

He had never told Daniella that he'd noticed this, so she looked back at him as she took a sip of tea and gave him an approving wink. Brian was tearing into a chicken leg, so it was obvious he wasn't paying a great deal of attention. Through a mouthful of chicken, he simply murmured a muffled "Yep!"

Kelly was watching him in some degree of disgust. "Could you please *try* to eat like a gentleman? I thought all those years of living in London had taken the redneck cowboy drivel out of you."

Daniella scoffed as she said, "Ohh!"

Faisal choked on his tea and had to spit some of it out. Leo kept cool but stared harshly at her. Eventually, he couldn't help himself. Nothing stirred him up more than a "snooty falooty" attitude. He put on the deepest redneck accent he could muster, and bellowed, "Well see here Little Lady! There ain't nobody gonna take the redneck out of none of us! Ya' hear! You can take the redneck out of the woods, but you can't take the woods out of the redneck! Yeeeee Haaaaa!!!"

His rebel yell rang throughout the house, and Kelly clasped her hands over her ears. Brian really wanted to get Kelly to stop taking everything so seriously and lighten up, so he joined in the fun, aggravating her even more. He also let out a rebel yell that could resurrect the dead Confederate soldiers. She squawked, "Would you please calm down!"

Brain said, "No, not until you apologize for being too stuck up. That was a hoity-toity snotty thing you just said, and I don't wanna hear any wife of mine talking like that. God knows this family's had enough. There's no more of that around here."

"Hoity Toity? Snooty Falooty?" She blurted as she rolled her eyes at him. "What kind of language is that?"

"One you'd better get used to hearing more! That's who we are Baby." Brian said.

"Fucking A!" Leo blurted.

Daniella felt a little sorry for Kelly, being so far away from her element. She said, "Y'all settle down. Leave Kelly alone. She's only trying to set standards for her kids. We can relate to that, right?"

Kelly's eyes softened, and Daniella winked at her. Afterwards, the family enjoyed finishing their meal in peace, and over coffee, Daniella and Leo explained all about Captain Adams. Everyone agreed they'd hire a paranormal investigation team to come in and check it out, and see if they could come to a peaceful arrangement with this spirit that walked among them.

As they were about to finish up, Sadie noticed Ahmed staring at the doorway to the dining room and asked, "What are you looking at?"

"Grandma Katie is smiling at us. She's over there with Captain."

He looked at Sadie, who was obviously a little shaken by that, and said, "It's Ok Sadie. I think they made friends now."

22

RESOLUTION AND REDEMPTION

The next year went by peacefully, and the two families were very happy, mostly staying in touch via the Internet. Daniella and Faisal carried on with their normal lives, although Daniella had much more responsibility now, checking in with Leo and Luwanda now and then, to be sure Magnolia Manor was running smoothly.

They shared many pictures with her, and each time she read a positive article about how well the place was doing, a feeling of pride swelled in her chest. Daniella often thought about how nice it was to have a reason for going to the USA every year now, to stay connected with all she'd built in the home that had once rejected her. *Now I have roots and wings*, she thought.

As Thanksgiving was quickly approaching, Daniella was enjoying a beautiful November day in Dubai, and was very excited that soon they'd all be on a plane to go back and see the family and how the hotel has shaped up. Leo mentioned he'd taken care of all the renovations that she'd recommended, and some of his own. *I can't wait to see it!* She realized, smiling with pride.

As she sipped her latte, she also drank in the sight of the grand city of the future Dubai had become. Innovation was the key to success in the United Arab Emirates, her adopted home, and she felt great pride for how far they had come. The balcony off of her office was her favorite place to relax and center herself after lunch, and it gave her the energy she needed to get through the rest of her day.

She decided to check her personal emails before getting on with meeting the two new authors she had scheduled for the afternoon. When she looked down at the laptop, she was overjoyed to see an email from Leo.

```
To: Daniella Sulieman
From: Leo Pierce

Subject: New Quarter and more
Good News

Hey, Sis!

I am attaching the new quarterly
report for the Magnolia Manor Bed and
Breakfast, and I must say I'm thrilled
with the results. The hotel continues
to make money hand over fist, thanks
to your refurbishment.

The guests are in another world with
the horse-drawn carriage rides and the
delicious meals in "Katie's Kitchen".
It's all the charm of the old South,
without any of the ugliness, just like
you wanted.
```

Captain Adams has made a few appearances, but he hasn't hurt anyone, and the news coverage about our little "haunted" Southern hotel has kept the guest list at full capacity, even in a tiny town like this. You really are a wizard at media coverage.

Wanda is happier than she's ever been, which brings me to the "good news". Wanda is expecting a new edition for our family. Gosh, I sure hope it's a boy this time! I love my girls, but let's face it, teenage girls can be so dramatic! By the way, how's yours? I know Leila didn't warm up to us much when Y'all visited, but I'm hoping she'll give us another chance when you come to visit for Thanksgiving. Brian and his crew can't make it, unfortunately. Kelly isn't feeling well. It's not serious, but he needs to stay near her until she gets better. Otherwise, everything is fine with him.

We're looking forward to seeing all of you soon!

Leo

P.S. I've ordered a Halal turkey for

our Thanksgiving meal, so don't worry
about the food at all. We can't wait
to see you!

His email made her beam with love and happiness. Finally, it seemed the hotel was running smoothly, as she had always wanted it to be.

The rest of the day played out pretty normally, as she met her new authors, researched marketing strategies with her team, and authorized a new cover design. She had always loved publishing because it was what helped those amazing books get to the shelves in libraries.

Satisfied with the knowledge that she'd tied up everything, and had left the business in capable hands while her family travelled to the USA for Thanksgiving, she drove home, listening to her favorite 70's and 80's classic rock songs. Her absolute favorite, "Tom Sawyer" by Rush blared through the car speakers, and she enjoyed the sight of camels walking through the sand just off of the Bypass highway. There was something fun about that combination, she always thought. *They have their camels, and we have our horses. Arabs love horses too! They really are the same as us.* The thought made her chuckle.

When she got home, she saw Fahani darting through the house, helping each of the kids with getting their bags packed. Their flight was this evening, and everyone was very excited to go back to Magnolia Manor. Even Daniella hadn't seen the full on effect of all the changes she'd made in the house and the ambiance of the place. She was also curious to see what changes Leo had ordered. It was all she could think of that day.

Since she saw everyone was well on their way to getting ready, she thought she'd sneak in a quick workout before they left since she had packed last night. The family had recently converted one room in the house to be a gym, and everyone was happier as a result. As a family, they decided to be healthier, so daily workouts were part of the deal. As she was really working up a sweat, Faisal entered, and felt amused by what he saw. Daniella had the music up full blast, listening to "Girlfriend" by Avril Lavigne.

He stood there watching for a while, bemused until she felt someone was watching and turned around to spy the silly smile on his face.

"And just how long have you been standing there?"

"Oh, long enough to enjoy the view." He chirped.

"Don't you think it's time for you to get a shower now and finish getting ready? We need to get to the airport on time you know."

She stopped the machine and looked at her watch. He was right; they needed to get moving. Time was running short. "Ok Baby. Here I come."

The plane left on time, and the family was all tucked into their first class cocoons snugly. Everyone seemed to be able to sleep on board except Daniella and Ahmed. Daniella's mind wandered to all the events of the last year.

This year was a time of great change in the family, and everyone was better. She thought about how amazing it was to have closure with so many issues, and how this state of being brought peace and happiness. She thought she was happy during the years before, but *now* her eyes were open to what true contentment is like. Having both sides of her family together made her feel whole for the first time. She no longer felt a hole in her heart where something used to be. She looked to Ahmed, who was watching an onboard movie, and said, "You'd better try to rest. It's a long flight and you're gonna be wrecked when you get there if you haven't slept at all."

"Tell yourself that Mama." Ahmed blurted, smiling.

"You know I can't sleep on planes."

Daniella replied, "I know. Me neither."

As early morning broke in Georgia, the family finally arrived in Atlanta, and Leo was there to pick them up. Thankfully, he had purchased a big SUV lately, in spite of the high fuel costs. They all rode comfortably to Hadleyville, and finally Daniella spotted the sign for Magnolia Manor. The sign was much bigger than before and so full of color and beautiful design. Leo beamed, and said, "Wanda did it. Do you like it?"

"Yes! I love that! I get the inkling that I'm about to see a lot of great new things." She said gleefully.

"Damn right!" Leo blurted.

Doormen rushed out to help the family with their bags as they arrived, and immediately Leila noticed the horse-drawn carriage parked outside with a footman. The footman was dressed in old Southern attire, and when he saw Leila, he gave her a little wink and tipped his hat as a gentleman should. Leila was charmed, and said, "Mom, this is so lovely! Can I go for a ride in the horse-drawn carriage later?"

Daniella smiled warmly at her, and said, "Sure thing Darlin'. You're the boss's daughter. You can have anything you want, little Sweet Potato."

She beamed beautifully in response.

The entire hotel was repainted, with all the trimmings, and the lawn was spectacularly manicured. Every flower below the Mason-Dixon line was present; everything that was in season, and it was a melody of color and splendor, like a picture from a storybook about how charming the old

South used to be. The sight of the old Magnolia tree was like seeing an old friend, and it looked healthier and more flourished than ever.

As they walked into the reception area, Luwanda was waiting with Lizzie, and she was lovely, all dressed up as a Southern Belle. Luwanda kissed her on both cheeks and said, "Welcome Home Honey! We hope you're gonna love what we've done with the place."

"I'm sure that I love it already! The outside looks gorgeous! We couldn't be happier with those flowers! I hope Y'all took a lot of pictures for the brochures."

Luwanda said, "We did Girl, don't worry. Lizzie's been handling the social media campaign, and that's all she's done is plaster it with pictures she takes herself."

Daniella nodded approvingly at Lizzie, and Lizzie smiled with pride. Luwanda went on to lead them into the lobby, revealing the stunning art collection inside, not just any collection, but one that spoke volumes for what the hotel stood for. Each corner was dedicated to a different region of the world. One side was dedicated to African art and the American struggle of the African American people to achieve equality and was filled with paintings of the proud tribes of Africa, tribal masks, spears, and vintage pictures of Martin Luther King Jr. and Nelson Mandela, along with other freedom fighters for the cause.

Daniella touched some pieces with great wonder, then looked fondly at Luwanda, neither of them needing a single word to express their joy at such a wonderful display, as their eyes said it all. Leo said, "You haven't seen it all yet. Take a look over here."

He led her to the side that was dedicated to Irish heritage. She looked stunned and completely speechless to see the amazing paintings of ancient Celtic art, and those depicting images of the gorgeous green Irish country, smiling faces, and the struggles and symbols of Irish pride and independence from England, such as the picture of Kilmainham Gaol, the prison where many of Ireland's patriots were incarcerated, tortured and executed, as well as preserved newspaper headlines of Ireland's birth as a Republic in 1949.

The joy swelled in her chest, yet she wasn't finished. Lizzie let her to another side, filled with art dedicated to Middle Eastern art, complete with heritage pieces such as an early "Burka", the face cover of the early Emiratis, an early Abaya, as well as some old silver jewelry of the region. Additionally, there was pottery and a few small Persian and Turkish carpets mounted to be displayed on the wall, as well as paintings of desert scenes with strong Arabian horses riding off into the sunset, and a painting of the landscape of modern Dubai, as well as comparative pictures of early and modern Dubai.

Daniella was overwhelmed, but Luwanda led her to the last side of the room, the Southern heritage side, or as they called it, the Pierce family heritage, filled with paintings of beautiful farmlands and sunsets over the lake, Southern ladies and gentlemen in fine attire, horse-drawn carriages, and of course, Katie's chickens. Some of her finest collectible chickens were there for all the guests to see.

Leo said, "We have plans to acquire more pieces throughout the hotel, honoring other nationalities, like Chinese, Indian, Hispanic, and Russian also."

Daniella looked very pleased and said, "I'm blown away. You've outdone yourself! I'm so proud of you! My goodness gracious Leo, you are an amazing person. I love every bit of this ... How are the customers reacting?"

Luwanda chimed in, "Are you kidding Honey? Oh my

God! The customers love it! Our little hotel is booked solid for the next 6 months! People are calling it the perfect country getaway, so we've had fine big city folks around here trying to get away from all their stress...Yes, Ma'am, they love this place, and Katie's kitchen is a *huge* hit. We even had Michelin star chefs come by and rate our dishes and write reviews, and I'm proud to say they loved every little bite and told people about it. I'm surprised you didn't get word of all this!"

Leo murmured, "Well, that could be my fault. I didn't tell her because I wanted it to be a surprise."

Daniella and Faisal laughed at this, and Faisal said, "Well, can we go to Katie's kitchen now? We're all really hungry. We didn't even have breakfast yet."

Leo bellowed, "Hell Yeah Bro! You all just get yourselves on in there! We'll take care of ya!"

They were led into Katie's kitchen, which was decked out with lacy and dainty Southern décor. It looked like an old South tearoom, where people of means would meet to relax over tea and cookies, discussing the business of the day or the latest gossip. The waiters were also dressed as Southern ladies and gentlemen, and each one spoke in a most eloquent accent whilst taking the food orders. "Hi, Y'all! We have a special this morning, our Katie's Kitchen Big Boy Breakfast, consisting of 2 eggs any style, bacon, grits, and hash browns with an apple tart on the side. Of course all meals are served with coffee, tea or orange juice."

Hearing about the apple tart brought back the memory of the snake in the apple orchard, and Daniella made a mental note to ask Leo if they had taken care of ridding the property of snakes. That's all they needed ... a lawsuit or the bad publicity of having someone die at the hotel from a snakebite.

Faisal said, "We'll all have the Big Boy Breakfast, but please don't bring the bacon."

The waitress said, "Well Y'all may not know it, but we had some Halal Beef Bacon shipped here, just for you. Mr. Leo knew you can't eat the Pork."

Daniella turned to see that Leo was smiling knowingly at this, happy he'd surprised her again. She turned her attention to the waitress and said, "Well, in that case, we'll take the bacon."

Turning her attention to Leo, she said, "That was really sweet of you. Thank you."

"No problem. It's all part of the VIP treatment here. I hope you like the rest of it. You haven't seen your rooms yet."

Leo seemed very pleased with himself and went to help Luwanda with checking in other guests. The restaurant was full, as the hotel was, in fact, a bed and breakfast, so every guest there was enjoying a good and hearty country breakfast. Daniella looked around the restaurant to see the pleased looks on everyone's faces as they enjoyed the Southern tastes and relaxed in the comfort of a world that has *gone with the wind.*

After they finished, Leo took them to their rooms. He had arranged a Master suite for Daniella and Faisal, and two junior suites for the boys and Leila. He said, "Now I know what you're thinking—you're not so comfortable with Leila being on her own in a suite. That's why we're letting Lizzie and Sadie stay with her while Y'all are here."

Daniella was relieved indeed, and said, "You read my mind. It'll be so great for the kids to spend some time together."

"And for us to be alone in this room!" Faisal marveled.

The Master Suite was absolutely gorgeous and completely charming. The bed was a King size canopy with a canopy curtain swept to one side with Rose colored taffeta sachets. There were fresh daisies and sunflowers throughout, a flat screen TV, an espresso maker, and in the bathroom was a Jacuzzi. It looked like an ideal Honeymoon location, and Faisal grinned wolfishly at Daniella. Leo picked up on that and said, "Ok, slow down Cowboy! You'll get your chance. I'll be out of here soon."

Daniella put her hands on her face, feigning embarrassment, but it was to no avail. Her eyes gave it away that she was also looking forward to spending time here with her man.

There was a knock at the door. It was the Concierge delivering a bottle of champagne and two champagne flutes. Leo didn't even give Faisal a chance to react. He said, "That is non-alcoholic by the way."

Faisal smiled, relieved, and Daniella nodded her approval at Leo. He said, "I told you we've got you covered."

He winked and then excused himself, leaving Daniella and her Faisal to enjoy the rest of the morning.

After everyone had rested up from the flight, Luwanda and Leo invited them to a lovely lunch on the deck they had installed, on the West side of the property, overlooking the apple orchard and the fishing pond. This was an extension of Katie's Kitchen, and it was marvelously picturesque, with every wooden table adorned with a checkered tablecloth and a couple buckets—one full of peanuts and one for the hulls.

As soon as they sat down, a cold pitcher of Iced Tea was set on the table with chilled glasses and plenty of extra ice, along with watermelon slices to snack on. It was just as Daniella had imagined, Southern charm and hospitality with a high level of service, to make the guest feel they're very well cared for, and this is a place that they can truly relax and go back in time.

The kids ordered burgers and fries while Faisal decided on a fried fish and shrimp platter with corn on the cob. Daniella decided to try Katie's Beef Casserole with a side salad. It all sounded mouth wateringly delicious.

The family felt content, and just before desert, Leo came to join them with very special guests—it was Uncle Sheldon and Aunt Rosie. Daniella leaped up to greet them, throwing her arms around their necks and jumping up and down. She said, "I'm so happy Y'all are here! I was hoping that you're coming to Thanksgiving, but I am so glad you came early! Please! Join us."

"That's not all," Leo said.

She could not believe her eyes as the rest of the family piled into the restaurant. Brian managed to get away, along with Kelly and the girls, and Uncle Sheldon turned to lead Ricky and Linda inside with their families. What an amazing sight they were! Daniella thought, *This is it, the happiest moment of my life. I will let myself enjoy it fully.* Her many years of therapy had taught her to take a moment to appreciate it for what it is, and feel the gratitude for the happy times, because, through gratitude, the universe will send us more things to be grateful for.

This was truly a time of family togetherness and reconnecting. The children buzzed around, playing ball and blowing bubbles in the garden, each taking turns riding the horse-drawn carriage ride, and a few of them had rented fishing poles to see what they could catch from the pond, another activity the hotel offered it's guests. All in all, everyone relaxed and enjoyed the day, without a care in the world.

To everyone's surprise, Leo had asked a local

photographer to come take a family photo when everyone was together, so they all gathered in front of the property, right in front of Captain Adam's bullet hole, still left intact, and next to the house-sized Magnolia tree, and no family looked happier, as it seemed that they had come through great obstacles to achieve their rediscovered love for each other.

Daniella had promised herself she wouldn't cry, but the tears of joy have no borders. They broke through, thankfully after the picture had been shot. Leo gave her a hug and asked, "What's the matter, Big Sis?"

She pulled back to look him in the eyes and said, "I'm just so happy. I thought I was happy before, but now I know this is what happy looks like."

They both looked back at the family. The picture formation had broken up, and the kids were already getting dirty climbing in the tree that they had climbed in as children, much to the chagrin of their mothers. As the mothers squawked their disapproval, Leo and Daniella had a good laugh. They embraced once more, and Leo said, "Well, guess the Pierce family shall rise again!"

"Yep! You ain't just whistlin' Dixie!" Daniella said.

They joined their families with a sense of playfulness in the air, and everyone enjoyed a great day, as the Sun descended over the Apple Orchard. Everything was so wonderful, but then she caught sight of Ahmed staring into the window with the bullet hole. She walked up to him and asked, "What are you looking at son?"

"Mama please don't ask questions you don't want to know the answer to," Ahmed said.

"Tell me. I promise I'll try to understand." Daniella whispered in his ear.

He sighed heavily and whispered back, "Katie is over there, smiling at us, and right behind her, I see a man."

Daniella's heart felt heavy, but she tried to be reassuring as she said, "Well, isn't that a good thing? Maybe they're finally at peace?"

Ahmed said, "Well, the Captain is. Didn't you all notice he hasn't broken any lights lately?"

Daniella thought, *How does he know that?*

"I just hope Ross won't break worse than a few lights." Ahmed pondered.

Daniella gulped, then pulled him to where the rest of the family was gathered. She didn't want him to miss out on everything they'd all worked so hard to build. She took one last lingering look at the glass in the door, and couldn't see anything.

Katie's spirit looked back, smiling warmly. "We did it, Baby. We're all one now."

A dark voice whispered back, "Not everyone…"

ALSO BY DEDRA L. STEVENSON

You can also find the following books, also by Dedra Stevenson at an online source near you. These titles can also be found on the Blue Jinni Media website: https://bluejinnimedia.com

The Revenge of the Blue Jinni

The First Book of The Hakima's Tale

Phoenix Kassim and her family discover their great destiny as they prepare to defend the human world from the attack of beings from an unseen dimension, the Jinn. Benevolent, human-friendly Jinn assists the young Hakima every step of the way to keep her safe from the Blue Jinni and his loyal followers.

The Rise of the Warrior

The Second Book of The Hakima's Tale

The young Hakima trains under the direction of a mysterious old woman to learn the secrets of fighting supernatural forces. Along the journey, Phoenix Kassim acquires the tools of the Hakima, including the amber of the Enchanted Blue Whale, the Magic Carpet, the loyalty and assistance of the wolves, and the Ring and Glove of Ghalib.

The Dawn of Redemption

The Third Book of The Hakima's Tale

Humans from every corner of the Earth cower in fear as the twelve tribes of the Jinn unleash their wrath upon the world. The only hope for humanity lies in the hands of a young woman, Phoenix Kassim, otherwise known as The Hakima. The human army is joined by the benevolent tribes of Jinn, and together they strive to bring an end to the tyranny.

Desert Magnolia

Daniella Suleiman left her original home in Georgia many years ago, and made a comfortable life in the Middle East, alongside her husband, Faisal, and her children. Suddenly, her life is turned around upon hearing the news that her father has been fatally struck down due to a hate crime in her small Southern town. She finds herself compelled to go back and attempt to exonerate her cousin, who has been accused of the crime. Going back will mean digging up skeletons from the past, however, and skeletons don't like living in closets.

Breaking Bread Around the World

Breaking Bread Around the World provides easy meal plans for 30 different countries, and a bonus chapter with extra recipes for breakfast, side dishes and a few extra desserts. The book is also Vegan friendly, as there are a generous number of Vegan recipes included! There's photos of all the food available, and Dedra's personal notes on each country, thereby providing a bit of travel information as well.

More titles are coming soon!

Blue Jinni Media

ABOUT DEDRA L. STEVENSON

Dedra L. Stevenson is a multi-genre author, filmmaker, and award-winning screenwriter originally from Alabama, USA, but now residing permanently in the U.A.E. Her novels include a fantasy fiction trilogy for young adults, known as *The Hakima's Tale*, a controversial courtroom drama called *Desert Magnolia*, a horror called *The Skinwalker Resurrection*, a collection of fantasy short stories called *Tales of the Lantern*, and a children's book called *Little Loud Beatrice and the Magic Painting.*

She's currently assembling a science fiction anthology called Human Horizons and working on her new novel, The Buchanan Bastard. Both are projected to be published in 2021. She's also Co-Authoring a new young adult series, S.P.O.O.K.S. with her long time creative partner at Blue Jinni Media, Rodney Harper.

In addition to writing stories, Ms. Stevenson enjoys writing movies. She won Best Short Screenplay for Desert Magnolia, based on her novel of the same name, in Mediterranean Cannes, 2018.

She wrote the screenplay for the horror short film, Amunet, that went on to win many awards and distinctions.

She wrote several feature screenplays after that, including: The Skinwalker Resurrection (award nominated, 2018, along with many selections), C.U.P.I.D. (award nominated, 2020, along with many selections), and Earth

Angels, an original horror (semi-finalist, 2020, along with other selections)

Last, but not least, Ms. Stevenson is a playwright. Her stage play, Desert Magnolia, is currently being cast for a read at Berklee School of Performing Arts, Abu Dhabi.

Ms. Stevenson intends to keep on writing, if her genre hopping keeps her fresh and in the zone. Many more stories to come.

facebook.com/Hakimastale

twitter.com/HakimasTale

instagram.com/dedrastevenson

ABOUT BLUE JINNI MEDIA

Blue Jinni Media is a publishing imprint for books and media created by Dedra Stevenson, Rodney Harper, and various cooperative partners.

Working with other independent authors around the world, Blue Jinni Media embraces a shared ideology to help other writers get their stories out and achieve their goals as successful self-published authors.

Please join our mailing list to receive information about new releases, author news as well as opportunities for joining our Beta reader program and receive advanced copies of new books for FREE. You may join by visiting the Blue Jinni Media website - http://bluejinnimedia.com

Thank you for choosing our books and please, don't hesitate to contact us with your comments and suggestions.

Dedra L. Stevenson (Sharjah, U.A.E.)
Rodney W. Harper (Raleigh, NC, USA

facebook.com/bluejinnimedia
twitter.com/bluejinnimedia
instagram.com/bluejinnimedia